# TRACING SHADOWS

## SCOUT BOOK 1

## ALEX LIDELL

DANGER BEARING PRESS

ALSO BY ALEX LIDELL

**Young Adult Fantasy Novels**
**TIDES**
FIRST COMMAND (Prequel Novella)

AIR AND ASH

WAR AND WIND

SEA AND SAND

**SCOUT**
TRACING SHADOWS

UNRAVELING DARKNESS

**TILDOR**
THE CADET OF TILDOR

**New Adult Fantasy Romance**
**POWER OF FIVE (Reverse Harem Fantasy)**
POWER OF FIVE

MISTAKE OF MAGIC

**SIGN UP FOR NEW RELEASE NOTIFICATIONS**
at www.subscribepage.com/TIDES

Reviews are an author's lifeblood. Please consider saying a few words about this book on Amazon.

"Would you like to buy a light crystal, young master?" The girl pressing the magical pebble into my hand smiles coquettishly. She wears the drab red clothing of the Children of the Goddess disciples, and she couldn't have chosen a worse mark than me if she'd tried.

Though in truth, her taking me for a boy and a sympathizer of the hateful bigots in the Children's following is a compliment to my skill. I am a scout. A spy trained to disguise, observe, and report. I'm also under orders not to interfere.

And that's where the problem lies.

My marks this evening, four members of a terror-monger group calling themselves Viva Sylthia, have the look of violence about them. Waving the crystal-peddling girl away, I move around the inn's common room for a better view. The room is full of the king's soldiers tonight, and the stench of cheap wine and bodies ripe from long days on the road fills my nose. At least the place is warm, the fire and lanterns all burning bright to ward away the night's darkness. The heavy wooden tables and benches are plain, but sturdy enough to stand up to rough crowds. With so few inns this far out in the Dansil countryside, one can hardly be choosy about patrons.

One of the soldiers stumbles into the largest of my marks, spilling the man's drink all over his shirt. The soldier, apparently oblivious to the mishap, belches and lurches on.

My mark, a broad-shouldered man with a black mole breaking the line of his mustache, scowls but keeps himself in check. Not even a curse at the drunk idiot. Nothing to bring attention to himself.

With the soldier well away, Mustache starts for the door, his three companions closing rank behind him. And me, behind them.

My skin prickles, my heart pulsating against my chest. There is little left in the way of cover outside. Just night and shadows. This is where I should break off, head back to the estate to report what I've learned of Viva Sylthia's plans over the course of the evening. But I've learned nothing and am left with only a gut feeling that the night is heading toward a poor end.

The four men pull on hoods and masks.

My chest tightens. I'd love to have been wrong, just this once.

"That's two dozen horses," says the youngest of them as the group approaches the barn. His voice breaks slightly. "Two dozen horses and three hostlers."

Mustache puts his arm around the youngster. The gesture would be brotherly but for the boy's nervous twitches. "You backing out? Perhaps you are not ready to receive the flame."

The tattoo of a flame over the heart marks Viva Sylthia's full members. I flatten myself into the barn's shadow, my breath stilling as I listen.

"No. I'm just sayin' the barn ain't empty," says the boy.

"Those three hostlers? They are cowards calling themselves Dansil soldiers, all drunk and snoring in an empty stall." Mustache's voice shoots a chill down my back. "Tell me, was your uncle passed out drunk in Sylthia when Everett attacked? When those *soldiers* did nothing? How many thousands of our people died in the Sylthia massacre? How many more lost their homes? Dansil families have been waiting for over twenty years to return to their land, to the gravesite of their ancestors. You can be their voice. Tonight. Right now."

"By burning down a barn?" says the boy.

"By sending a message. Those are the king's soldiers drinking at the inn. Drinking instead of fighting to take back Sylthia."

*Oh, for stars' sake.* In the dozen years that I've trained under Lord Gapral, the king's distant scoutmaster, I've heard the same justifications for violence over and over: *Send the king a message—no one in Dansil is safe until Sylthia is ours again.* Never mind that it's been two decades since the kingdom of Everett invaded Dansil's Sylthia territory, the swath of land at the Dansil–Everett border that is rich with living-crystal deposits. Never mind that even if Dansil took Sylthia back, we've not the people to work the mines. Or that we've hunted down too many of our whisperers to actually make use of the living crystals.

Mustache releases the boy, who slumps in relief—or fear. "The king is a coward and a fool. He thinks negotiating with Everett will keep him safe. But tonight, you set him straight. Tonight, you make your uncle's death matter. Make all deaths in Sylthia matter."

My hands tremble at my sides. The bastards will burn the barn and kill the horses and hostlers, and I'll report back how it happened. My orders are to observe, not engage. Never engage. At best, I'm told it's because I'm too valuable to risk, that too much effort and coin have been poured into training me. At worst, Lord Gapral simply barks that weighing the value of victims against the cost of exposing his scout network is beyond my station. My shoulder burns in phantom pain where Gapral branded me the last time I dared disobey.

I'm a scout. I'm supposed to watch the terror mongers' horror show and write a rutting report.

"Viva Sylthia," says Mustache.

"Viva Sylthia," the others echo.

A horse whickers inside the barn and my gut clenches to stone. A living, faithful horse, resting after a day's work. A boy's sleepy voice soothes the animal. A child is inside that place.

Mustache drags a bar toward the barn. The bastards are barricading the doors before setting the blaze. Blood roars through my veins.

I should leave. Now.

Instead, I pick up a jagged stone and press myself against the wall. My heart pounds in my ears, sweat forming on my temples despite the chill wind. If Lord Gapral finds out . . . Swallowing, I lean around the corner and skip the stone along the side of the barn closest to Mustache's men.

The men startle. Move toward the sound. I sprint in the opposite direction, banging my fist against the barn wall. "Loose horse! Wake up in there! Loose horse!"

Curses and agitated neighs sound from inside. A moment later, the barn's back wall vibrates from the impact of kicking hooves. Good enough. Changing direction midstride, I sprint for the tree line.

"There he is," a voice calls behind me.

My legs burn as I press into a faster run. The thud of pursuing boots echoes through my bones, but I'm smaller than the men. Faster. My breaths come in short, rapid bursts. Two dozen yards will see me into the blind blackness of the forest. They have to. One dozen.

A hand slams the back of my tunic, shoving me to the ground.

I twist as I fall, landing on my back. The impact takes my breath, but my legs are up and ready to kick. Burying my boots in my attacker's hips, I lift the man into the air. The momentum of his weight rolls us, and with the next heartbeat I'm the one on top, straddling the man's chest. I slam my fist down on his jaw and scramble away.

Another man grabs me from behind, his arms wrapping around my torso.

I stomp my heel onto his foot and twist free.

Something slams into my ribs. A fist or a boot. Maybe an elbow.

I move through the shock, loosening the throwing blades strapped to my forearms. Someone grabs my arms and wrenches them behind my back. My shoulders scream. I do too. Until a blow to the gut cuts my air.

"What are you doing here, boy?" Mustache demands.

"Nothing, sir," I gasp, my voice catching. "A jest. I'm sorry. I'll . . . I'll settle the horses back for you. It was a stupid jest to wake up the hostlers. Lazy, drunken buggers. Just a bit of amusement." The pressure on my shoulders tightens and I scream again. The Viva Sylthia aren't buying my lie.

"Ahoy, there!" the slightly drunk voice of an actual guard bellows through the darkness. A lantern appears near the barn and starts moving toward us. "Identify yourselves to the king's men!"

*Thank the stars.*

Behind me, Mustache draws a sharp breath. I seize my chance, thin as it is. Slamming my head back, I smash it into

Mustache's nose. There's a cracking sound and the man's hold loosens enough for me to break for the woods.

I dive into the darkness, forcing my limbs to move fast and blind. I see nothing beyond my fingertips but each step between me and Viva Sylthia is a gift. Fifty paces later, my lucky footing ends. I swallow a gasp as I crash to the ground, shins hitting stones. My body aches and I bury my face in the soggy dirt, not daring to make a sound. It's a struggle to keep from staring into the moving shadows, but people feel when they are being watched. I close my eyes, stay deathly still, and listen.

I wait an hour before I dare move. My heart hammers against my ribs, pain shooting through me with every breath. I sit up slowly. A stick snaps beneath me, the sound deafening in the still of night. But the forest gives no sign of other intruders. Mustache and his Viva Sylthia cronies are gone.

Reaching beneath my shirt, I pull out the living crystal hanging around my neck. It is a light crystal; its magic glows. Unlike the trinkets that the Children of the Goddess peddle, which glow aimlessly for a while before dimming, my crystal is tuned to light up only when I touch it. A tool rather than a toy. I wrap my hand around the crystal, a familiar unpleasant tingle spreading through my hand and arm. Within a heartbeat, the crystal comes alight with a reddish glow that gives me a fighting chance of making it home tonight without breaking my neck.

Though tomorrow, Lord Gapral might do that for me.

## 2

---

To the outside world, Lord Gapral is a cranky hermit who takes in the occasional orphan to live on his far-off, understaffed estate. The grounds are chronically overgrown with weeds and brush; the servants are scarce, unfriendly, and silent; visitors are nonexistent. To those of us who've grown up here, the estate is our womb. Not because it's warm or kind—the estate is neither—but because our identities are safe here. On the estate, I can be Kali, the seventeen-year-old girl that I am. Outside, I'm always someone else.

Despite the late hour of my return, a scout on sentry duty appears beside me the moment I cross the invisible line marking the estate's perimeter. I freeze as the knife blade presses into my side, and I allow the sentry to examine my face. His own is hooded and stays that way, though I catch a glimpse of his features, thanks to my light crystal. A boy of fifteen who has been at Gapral's estate for seven years now. I don't know his name or his specialty. There is a lonely look in the boy's eyes, but I know better than to ask after his welfare, nor will he ask after mine. Scouts are Lord Gapral's commodities, and sharing our identities and personal details with each other is forbidden.

The boy nods and removes the blade.

"Leaf?" I ask. My sister is Lord Gapral's one exception—everyone knows both her name and her specialty. She is a whisperer, a person born with the ability to tune living crystals.

"Training room."

I nod my thanks and the sentry melts back into the shadows. For a few moments, I deliberate the merits of interrupting Leaf, but my burning ribs make the decision for me. Navigating the weeds and plants cultivated to conceal movement, I make my way to a small structure designed to look like a toolshed, where the scouts gifted with some hint of whispering can practice. Having no such gift myself, I'd usually be forbidden from coming near the training room, but with Leaf being my sister, Lord Gapral is willing to look the other way—unless I create problems.

"No, no, no." My sister's exasperated voice escapes the door. "A *light crystal* can only make *light*. It can't heal flesh or heat up or remember a song."

"Can I change a light crystal into a healing crystal?" asks a young boy.

"No." Leaf's voice turns stern. "And don't play with healing crystals; they are dangerous. Now concentrate, please. Why is the light crystal in your hands flickering and dim instead of steady and bright?"

"It's out of tune—the magic inside the crystal is scattered. I need to focus the magic to make it glow."

Opening the door a crack, I find a small hooded scout sitting on the floor, an egg-sized living crystal in his hand. My sister crouches beside her student, her hand on the novice's crystal too. I can see the faint wisps of magic swirling inside the crystal, but whisperers like Leaf and the boy can feel and manipulate them.

"Do it," says Leaf. "Feel the magic, imagine how it *should* weave together. Focused. Orderly. Now make it happen. Work *inside* the crystal. Don't try to draw the magic out. Coax the outermost strands toward the middle. That's not the middle! Yes, now that's the middle."

Inside the crystal, the strands of magic pull together into a tight ball, and the crystal's glow becomes bright and steady. The young scout jumps up and lets out a whoop before seeing me in the doorway and freezing.

The room fills with fear. It's a dangerous time for whisperers, though the child is safe enough here. Lord Gapral isn't one to give up valuable skills just because some priest cries heresy.

"It's all right," I tell the youngster. "No one is in trouble, but I need the room."

The young scout disappears in a rustle of cloak and shoes.

"Practice," Leaf calls after the boy. "Next week we'll weave *triggers* into the magic. With a trigger, a tuned crystal stays dormant until something specific—like a particular person— touches it. So you can make a light crystal stay dark until Lord Gapral picks it up."

Turning her attention to me, Leaf hobbles forward, dragging her clubfoot behind her across the stone floor. Despite being three years older, she is the smaller of us, the same birth affliction that crippled her right foot also keeping her body petite and frail. A beautiful porcelain doll with pale skin, hazel eyes, and a longer, shinier version of my golden-brown hair. Leaf is also the only person in the world with a mind to rival Lord Gapral's, and the most talented and learned whisperer since our mother—though everyone at the estate is smart enough to keep that tidbit of information very, very quiet.

"Kali. What's happened?" Leaf studies me critically.

I stumble to a bench and sit. "Stayed late watching Viva Sylthia goons and had a bad fall heading home." I pick up a vial of something bright blue left standing beside the worktable.

"Put that down, it's poisonous." Leaf snatches her latest experiment from my hand and sits beside me to help extricate me from the boy's clothing and chest bind that turn me from Kalianna into Kal. My lightly angled jawline and slender but muscled frame make me especially well suited for a male disguise, which is invaluable in a scout's world. Not only can I turn into a lady or stable boy as the situation dictates, but I can do it mid-mission.

Unwinding the last layer of cloth, Leaf sucks a breath through her teeth. "That's one bad fall."

While Leaf holds a lantern up to conduct her examination, I focus on breathing and constructing a report I can deliver without Gapral smelling a rat. The key is sticking to the truth as much as possible. That, and giving him no reason to check my injuries. He can differentiate marks from a fall and a beating as well as Leaf can. "The cuts look deep," she says.

"They aren't."

Leaf uses a corner of my chest bind to dab a cut over my lower left ribs. "This one needs stitches."

"No, it doesn't."

Leaf rises to hobble over to her toolkit.

My attention snaps free of Gapral and his inevitable interrogation, to address the more pressing matter. "I don't need stitches, Leaf."

"Are you seventeen or seven?" she calls over her shoulder. "I keep forgetting. If you don't like needles, stop getting yourself pummeled." Leaf's voice darkens. "I thought your orders were to watch and report, Kali."

My jaw tightens. "You don't know what the alternative was."

"I know that every time you step out the door, I worry whether it will be your coffin coming back." Leaf returns to sit beside me again, her small frame trembling. "It's not your bloody job to interfere. If Lord Gapral's wrath doesn't deter you, can you at least think of our future?"

"What future?" I rub my face. Viva Sylthia is my trade specialty, but it is the least of Leaf's and my personal concerns. After twenty years of two out of every three babies in Dansil being stillborn, people are desperate. And desperate people do many things, including believing Bishop Bahir's claim that whisperers are to blame for what is being called the Child Drought. Whispering isn't illegal, not yet, but that little stops people from hunting whisperers down like animals and handing them over to the bishop's Order of the Goddess to be "cured." Outside Lord Gapral's estate, there is no future for an orphan girl and her crippled, whispering sister.

"The Drought is going to end," says Leaf. "Magic has always been a vital resource, and once the Drought ends and the fear dies down, it will be vital once more. You and I—"

"I'm not a whisperer," I say, a little too forcefully. Thank the stars I have at least that going for me.

"You are *something*, Kali. What you feel when you touch living crystals is unlike what anyone else feels." She motions to the stack of books across the room, next to a large slate with the living crystals and their magic charted in hundreds of ordered squares. "Believe me, I've checked." I would ask Leaf to bloody stop checking, but I might as well ask her to stop breathing. She tells me our mother was the same way, always studying and researching something, though I little remember the woman.

I sigh, rubbing my face. "Can you just patch me up now and we can argue about the future in the morning?"

Leaf takes out her sewing kit. A needle as long as my finger flashes in the lantern light, and I promptly black out.

MORNING—DAWN, rather—brings a summons from Lord Gapral. I trudge uphill through the two fog-filled horse pastures separating my cabin from the main house, the frostbitten grass crunching underfoot. This far from Delta, Dansil's balmy capital city, it gets freezing cold at night. It isn't true winter weather—Dansil hasn't seen snow in two decades —but it is cold enough to make me suitably miserable. The main house, the only stone building on the estate, rises before me as I clear the second pasture, but I double back down the hill instead of approaching directly.

That's one of Lord Gapral's unbendable rules—always double back to ensure no one is following. Never take a direct path. Not even from your own cabin to the main house. The estate is safe from uninvited eyes, but Gapral pays his servants to report on the trainees' movements—and woe to the scout who discovers his day's activities accurately documented by Gapral's gardener. The only one excused from turning ten-minute walks into hour-long treks is Leaf, but she spends little time outdoors.

Though it doesn't look like it, the estate is waking, trainees and instructors finding their separate, convoluted ways to training halls disguised as stables, or heading out for practice into the adjacent woods. The morning air is crisp and grassy, the wind blowing freely across a vast, untended swath of hills.

By the time I approach the main house again, the early sun

bathes the courtyard, illuminating lone figures going through training. How different Leaf's and my lives would have been if the king's brother hadn't fallen in love with a whisperer scholar he could never marry. If Leaf and I weren't bastards of the king's disgraced dead brother. If the bishop's rise to power hadn't translated into magic users being treated as criminals. Leaf probably would have been in charge of some academy by now. And I . . . I might be doing normal things. Spending time with a friend. Kissing a boy. Eating a family dinner.

"He's waiting for you," the man tending hydrangeas beside the front steps murmurs without looking up from his work.

The words snap me back to reality. What I did last night. What I'm facing today. My heart speeds as I walk into the office and bow to the short, pudgy man sitting behind a polished oak desk. Lord Gapral's office is so laden with books, I must take the existence of walls on faith, though at the moment, caving walls and objects on the brink of avalanche are the least of my worries.

*You will protect you.* My mind recites Gapral's own teachings. *You are your own fortress.*

Lord Gapral keeps his gaze on a letter he's reading, stray rays of sunlight bouncing off his bald head. "Report, Scout Kalianna," he barks.

"Viva Sylthia indoctrinated a new recruit, sir," I say crisply, outlining my evening with short, clear strokes. As I approach the latter part, I choose my words carefully. "A cell of three experienced members took what appeared to be an initiate out of the inn's common room and toward the barn. I believe they intended mischief, but there was a commotion and soldiers chased the Viva men away."

"I see." He rubs his upper lip. "Any problems?"

I shrug, even as my heart pounds against bruised ribs. "None."

"You were late," Lord Gapral says with a quiet calm that I dare not underestimate. He used the same voice five years ago, upon discovering that I'd disobeyed his orders and started socializing with another trainee at the estate.

"I stayed to see whether my marks would return. They did not."

A dismissive wave of his hand floods me with relief. "Any mention of larger plans?"

"The usual rhetoric about the evilness of Everett and the need to take back the Sylthia lands, but nothing specific or actionable."

"Damn." Lord Gapral sighs. "That cell is from Delta. They keep a low profile over there in the capital and I'd hoped their tongues would loosen on this trip. I'll be damned if something isn't in the works."

"Yes, sir." Stars, but I'm luckier than I have any right to be —it would be just like Lord Gapral to have had a second scout in the area. The fact that he didn't post one, or at least not one close enough to give a contradictory report . . . I'm so dizzy with relief that it takes me a moment to realize I've not been dismissed just yet.

On the contrary, Lord Gapral is leaning back in his chair and tapping the letter he's been reading. "I've a new assignment for you," he says finally. "King Firehorn has requested a scout with a working knowledge of Viva Sylthia to attend him at the palace."

I stare at my master. "I was under the impression that King Firehorn dissolved all official ties with us when my father died, sir." A kind way of saying that after Mother's death left us orphaned, the king and his wife had been about to send Leaf and me to the Goddess's temple when Lord Gapral intervened. Had Firehorn had his way, I'd be one of Bishop

Bahir's Children of the Goddess now, selling flowers and proselytizing. Leaf would be dead.

"Things change. The queen and her babe died in childbirth several months past, which may have altered the king's thinking. Either way, the point is that King Firehorn subsidized you and Leaf, his brother's bastards, for twelve years. Now that you've both reached the age of majority and the documents forever barring you from the line of succession to the throne are irreversible, he wishes to call in the investment."

I put my hands behind my back, digging my nails into my wrist. I hate cities. I hate Firehorn. But most of all, I cannot bear the separation from my sister. "Wouldn't I be more useful to him in the shadows? I've no experience in a palace, but I do in a forest."

"You've no experience in a palace *yet*," Lord Gapral corrects. "And you've etiquette training enough to play the lady. As for the other, don't be daft about working from a shadowed outpost. I have plenty of male scouts who can do it—and can do it better than you. Your specialty lies in being simultaneously female and male, a young man skilled in weaponry and a noble lady of childbearing age and royal blood. The shadows in which you work shall be in plain sight." His face hardens. "I was informing you of your orders, scout, not requesting your opinion."

"Of course, sir." I bow quickly to distract from the shaking in my voice.

But Gapral is not done with me yet. "There is one other thing, Kalianna." He meets my eyes, and the worry there is enough to turn my bowels. "The king insists that Leaf accompany you."

"He is acknowledging a crippled whisperer as a relation?" The words are out before I can bother with diplomacy.

15

"No. The official letter claims that Firehorn little wishes to separate the family and requests that Leaf attend you as a lady's maid. But I imagine you can read between the lines as well as I?"

My mouth dries. Firehorn wants Leaf as collateral. "I understand, sir," I say, gathering myself together.

Lord Gapral nods toward the door. "Get packing then. And Kalianna—" He waits until I turn back to face him. "The king might little understand that Leaf is infinitely more valuable to our kingdom than you are, but I trust that you do. And I trust that when you are in Delta, you will not put Leaf's life in danger to save a handful of horses."

## 3

*I* have no one to say goodbye to, except the horses. And even if I did, I wouldn't dare. So I spend the week before our departure with trainers, polishing my court etiquette and debating which latest fashions would best conceal my vambrace of throwing knives. The others know I'm leaving, of course—in an estate full of scouts, we know the signs. Surges of supply orders, a change in trainers' schedules to accommodate the departing scout's needs, shifting chores. Occasionally, another scout will meet my eyes and hold them just a moment too long before we both look away. A silent "farewell and good luck." I savor those long glances, trying to wrap the memory of them in velvet and hide them inside my chest.

Leaf, on the other hand . . . I shut my eyes at the sight of little paper-wrapped parcels that line her worktable the evening before our departure. "You can't leave presents, Leaf." I pinch the bridge of my nose. "It's a giveaway that you are planning on leaving and don't expect to be back for some time."

Leaf glances over her shoulder and adds a vial of something to one of the packages. "I *am* leaving. And I *am* planning on not being back for some time. And none of this is actually a secret from anyone at the estate. People—scouts included—deserve to know that someone cares about them."

Heat tingles my cheeks and I busy myself with checking my trunk's hidden compartments. "Those aren't the rules here."

Leaf snorts. "I'm a researcher. I don't follow scouts' rules."

"And what about the scouts getting your presents?" I slam my trunk closed, refusing to let memories surface. "You realize those little packages, your tokens of friendship, come with a beating from Gapral attached?"

Leaf turns from her table and manages to look down her nose at me, despite being smaller. "Who do you think obtained these little parcels for me, Kali? So long as no one gets stupid, the trainees will be just fine. People need other people. Gapral knows that."

I don't bother arguing, or pointing out that the weakest, most deadly opening in my armor is my love for Leaf. Needing others is a vulnerability.

*You will protect you,* I remind myself over and over as our departure approaches, and again as Leaf and I settle into the carriage. *You will protect Leaf. You are your own fortress. You will be all right.*

A snap of the reins, a click of the tongue, and we're off, each bump of the wheel singeing my nerves. There will be no empty pastures and thoughtfully averted eyes in the palace. Only hordes of courtiers all staring at me, Lady Lianna, the king's distant, beloved niece. No shadows. Nowhere to hide. No reprieve.

~

BEYOND THE CURTAIN, as our first few days pass, the bouncing landscape changes slowly from countryside set against the backdrop of wild forest to small villages and farmland overflowing with unharvested corn stalks and apple trees. Raspberry bushes rise in predatory numbers, encroaching on the road and showing off sweet red berries amidst snaring thorns. The weather starts changing too as we slowly lose altitude, taking on Delta's ethereal warmth.

"You could probably plant a rock in these parts nowadays and see it grow," Leaf muses as we fight our way through the flowering bougainvillea that lines the path to what our driver assured us is the best travel inn to be found out here—a two-story, white stucco house with rooms for rent. In the past twenty years, Dansil's soil has become the most fertile on the continent, while the combination of stillborn babes and soldiers killed in the Everett war has left us with no people to actually work the land. Leaf taps my arm. "Will you gather some soil samples for me to study? I'd like to evaluate the changes as we get closer to the capital. There must be something that makes plants thrive, but not people."

I nod absently. Where Leaf sees soil samples and fertility analysis, I see graveyards. Half a day's ride after our stop at the flowering inn, we pass a decrepit building with a crescent moon on its shingle, once the Whisperer Guild's proud symbol. The words *REPENT AND PAY* are scrawled across its cracking planks in what looks like blood. As the anti-whisperer sentiment rises each day we're closer to the capital, the target on Leaf's back grows with it.

Glancing at her, I see her small hand wrapped around the blue healing stone she wears around her neck. "Stars, Leaf.

19

Take that off. Aren't you always going on about how dangerous healing crystals are?"

She blinks at me. "It is dangerous for a whisperer who is not trained as a healer to attempt tuning and using a healing crystal. A raw, out-of-tune healing crystal is inert. A talisman."

"It attracts attention. Take it off."

Leaf crosses her slender arms. "There are centuries of history and lore surrounding healing crystals. The most common stories hold that a healer is more likely to come to your aid if you have a crystal whose magic he can work with. Did you know that the magic inside a healing crystal is so highly concentrated that—"

"Stop." I blow out a slow breath. "First, the healers secluded themselves in the Monastery of Qilar, so one won't just happen to be around if you crack your skull. Second, if a healer were traveling, one would think he'd have his own crystal. And third, healers might be highly trained whisperers, but they are still whisperers. Let us not shout support for magic in a city of people who blame it for the deaths of their babies. We aren't on Lord Gapral's estate anymore, and here, few would think twice about grabbing you in the middle of the night to drop you at the doorstep of one of Bahir's temples."

Leaf tucks the stone beneath her blouse and raises her chin defiantly. "I will continue my research, Kali. It's possible that magic can fix the Drought. That alone demands exploration."

My jaw tightens, fear for her spreading through my chest. "Just do it quietly," I say, turning my face away. Temples ask few questions when concerned family members show up to hand whisperers over to the priests—to help the poor souls repent, or cure the darkness, or whatever the family members say to soothe their minds. Either way, the priests' coin soothes their pockets.

A week into our journey northeast, after we've changed

coachmen and carriages twice to better conceal our point of origin, the farmlands dissolve back into thick forest. These woods are thicker and lusher than what I grew used to near the estate, large leaves blocking out sunlight and the smell of sap and moist bark hanging heavy and wonderful in the air. Leaf, who never ventured even into the estate's woods, manages to get herself lost when she steps away to relieve herself, and we lose half a day in our coachman's attempt to find her. By the time they return, I am ready to strangle the man for his inability to read basic tracking signs, but royal Lady Lianna would have no reason to notice broken branches and bent grass.

Finally, two days later, the appearance of a large town signals our approach to Delta, the peaks of the palace and Temple of Dansil growing from the horizon. The carriage moves slowly enough that I can read bits of conversation on the lips of people we pass.

". . . humidity. The laundry will never dry."

"*Mama*! Jak called me a whisperer!"

"I will tell you right now, those Everett bastards have evil on their minds."

Leaf kicks my shin, drawing my attention from the window to the plush inside of our carriage. "Do you ever stop eavesdropping, Kali?"

I shrug. Reading lips is habit, not something I think about. But Leaf isn't really asking about tradecraft—she just wants to talk. If Delta's approach makes me tenser by the second, it hypnotizes Leaf with wonder.

"Our summons coinciding with the Everett delegation's presence at the palace is unlikely accidental," says Leaf once my full attention on her is assured. She reaches across the bench to adjust my blond wig and scrutinize the layers of makeup that leave even me hard-pressed to recognize myself in Lady Lianna's reflection. "We are in the midst of history. The first diplomatic contact in the twenty years since Everett attacked Dansil and annexed the Sylthia territory. And now, a ceasefire between Dansil and Everett. An Everett envoy in the palace. Are you not curious to watch it unfold?"

"No."

"You'll be safer living in a palace than being beaten by Viva Sylthia terror mongers in the middle of the woods."

My gut says that us living in the palace, right under the nose of Bishop Bahir and King Firehorn, is akin to mice seeking shelter beneath a cat's tongue. Leaf seems happy, however, so I keep my thoughts to myself as more and more stones pave the way northeast through Delta's outskirts, and then through the city toward the royal palace at the city's northern edge.

Stone. People. Colors. After the vast, foggy tranquility of the estate, Delta's brewing life hits me like an avalanche. Street vendors sell meat pies and raspberry tarts amidst the traffic of manure-filled carts and scurrying messenger boys. Red-clad Children of the Goddess disciples, who were lone nuisances in the countryside, are out in droves—some peddling carnations and living-crystal pebbles, others striking up conversations with anyone who looks their way too long. And the trees . . . My wonderful shadow-casting trees are reduced to nothing more than occasional decorations. As if someone carved a stone island in the midst of a forest to make room for Delta.

Which, of course, is exactly what happened.

Topped by the orange Eye of the Goddess, the Temple of Dansil shines over all the other buildings, towering even above the peaks of the royal palace. These two stone monstrosities, the palace and temple, rise like sentinels at Delta's northern border, just before the forest starts up again. The houses grow larger as we gain ground, the white stucco brighter and cleaner, the bushes manicured. By the time we're within sight of the palace walls, its surrounding gardens make their appearance with immaculate geometric fields of green grass, gray gravel walkways, and strict accents of blue and red tulips that sway in the breeze. Blue for His Royal Majesty King Firehorn. Red for the Goddess and Bishop Bahir. All is manicured to give the illusion of perfection. Just as I am.

The rattling wheels finally bump to a halt, and I find myself looking out the window at the grand archways of the palace's main entrance. A royal guardsman with the king's diamond sigil embroidered on his shoulder pulls open the heavy carriage door as if it weighs nothing. He surveys my hands, waist, and ankles with sharp eyes that look far too old for his twenty or twenty-one years.

I smile. Lady Lianna is unaware she is being checked for weapons, so she can hardly be insulted.

"My lady." The guard's voice is perfectly courteous. Holding out his hand, he helps me down the steps. "I am Trace, the captain of His Majesty's guard detail. Welcome to the Delta Royal Palace."

"A pleasure," I murmur, memorizing Trace's features while gingerly navigating the carriage's steep exit. Honed muscles, shoulder-length blond hair that shimmers like silver, dark gray eyes that track every movement. His sculpted frame has a predator's lethal grace that complements the deadly weapons strapped to his waist and back. Unlike the bejeweled strolling courtiers and stretches of blue and red flowerbeds lining the path to the palace steps, Trace is no decoration.

Wasps' soft buzzing fills my ears as my feet settle onto the gray gravel. I frown at the stinging insects circling the flowers. I hate wasps. I hate this city, so full of people and stone and flowers. I hate this palace.

Raising my chin, I meet Trace's gaze head-on. The

guardsman's cool eyes and tight jaw reveal nothing of his thoughts, but the wide, cautious berth that the other guards and courtiers give him warns me to be wary.

"King Firehorn eagerly awaits the pleasure of your company," Trace says curtly, offering me his arm.

I'm smart enough to recognize pressure when I see it. Firehorn is granting me no time to get my bearings. Annoying, but Leaf and I predicted the possibility and dressed me appropriately, in a full-skirted blue velveteen gown with lace cuffs and a high-standing collar. My eyes are lined with kohl to appear large and innocent. The kohl, together with lip paint, blush, and powder, helps me slip into Lady Lianna's skin. Still, it's all I can do not to glance back at my sister before resting my fingers on Trace's forearm.

The muscles beneath his uniform jacket are coiled with reined-in violence. No doubt the choice of my escort was likewise made with a message from my king in mind. Perhaps I should take Firehorn's abundance of caution as a compliment.

Trace's eyes cut to my face, and I force my hand to relax atop his, letting him take my arm's weight. It's fortunate that the vambrace with my throwing daggers rests high enough on my wrist that the guard feels nothing of the weapons beneath my sleeve.

Trace leads me directly to the front steps, white polished stone awash with orange light from the great living crystal topping Bahir's Temple of Dansil. Despite being the head of an order claiming magic to be the work of the Dark God, Bishop Bahir has surprisingly few qualms about using living crystals for his own grandeur.

"That is the Eye of the Goddess," Trace informs me, following my gaze from the steps to the far-off orb. There must be a mile and a half separating us from the temple grounds, yet the light bridges the space easily. "Delta never gets fully dark, thanks to it."

I smile as if finding Trace's insights both novel and fascinating, and climb the steps to the palace door, which Trace opens for me in one smooth motion to reveal gleaming marble floors. Two landings and nine corridors later, Trace leads me down a hall lined with paintings of battles and generals. A sentry standing at one of the heavy wooden doors tenses at Trace's approach and salutes with one fist pressed to his chest.

Ignoring the sentry, Trace strides to the door and knocks twice.

The door opens promptly to reveal a stocky, smiling man in his forties. His clothes are plain but tailored finely, and his dark hair has just enough gray in it to give him an air of wise dignity without the staleness of age. It takes me a moment to register the small crown.

I pull my hand away from Trace's steady arm and sink into a curtsy.

"Niece!" King Firehorn takes my hands, urging me to rise. He holds me at arm's length, his kind brown eyes studying me intently. I can't help but wonder whether my father had eyes such as his, before I remember that I should hate this man. Firehorn's smile deepens. "You are a beauty, Lianna. And a copy of your late sire. Please, come inside."

Trace takes a step forward, stopping only when Firehorn puts out his hand.

"She hasn't been searched for weapons, sir," the guard says.

"I certainly hope not!" Firehorn tells him. When this appears to little mollify Trace, the king adds, more firmly, "I shall bear the risk. Consider it a royal whim." He holds the door open for me and I step into a warm room, overstuffed brown chairs and heavy curtains creating a tasteful ambience of intimacy and comfort.

"Thank you, Your Majesty." I take the fullest breath I've taken since stepping off the carriage, allowing for the possibility that there is more to the king than I'd expected. "I am more grateful for a friendly face than you know."

"Trace is overprotective," Firehorn says flatly, his back to me as he closes the door. His voice chills. "He will not go far, even with nothing but a young girl to threaten me, so keep your voice down." Alarm bells spur my heart into a gallop as the king spins on his heels, his eyes steel. Despite myself, I retreat a step. "You are late, girl." Scowling, Firehorn examines me closely, as if I were an expensive breeding filly that didn't quite have the build he'd hoped for.

## 4

*F*irehorn's eyes stop on my bosom.

I cross my arms, my stomach churning along with my thoughts.

"Save the modesty act, Kalianna. Arms at your sides and turn around. Slowly. Now."

My face burns, but I turn slowly as instructed, tethering my mind to the throwing knives strapped to my forearm. *You will protect you,* I repeat to myself firmly. *You need no one.*

Firehorn grunts. "Well enough. Now show me Kal. Lord Gapral said you've trained as a lad." Retrieving a satchel from behind his desk, the king tosses it to me. Boy's clothes, in my size.

"Of course, my lord." I school my voice to a professional calm. "Though I will require extensive makeup to reclaim Lady Lianna's face."

The king produces a large box from beneath his desk.

Opening the lid, I find everything I need and more.

"Thank you. If I might ask you to turn around while I disrobe?"

Firehorn lets out a short, unamused laugh. "A self-conscious spy? Is that not a contradiction? Like a modest whore?"

My self-control snaps like a bowstring, sending blood boiling through my veins. My nostrils flare. I lock gazes with Firehorn, my eyes burning my fury into his.

The king meets my assault with an icy gaze. "Let me tell you one more contradiction," he says quietly. "Useful cripple."

*Leaf.* The word rings in my ears. No amount of warning or preparation is enough to hear such a threat spoken so brashly. I swallow.

Firehorn nods and lets the silence deafen me for several more moments. Somewhere beyond the window, a child squeals with delight and a playful wind rattles the shutters. With another humorless smile, the king pulls out his desk chair. "I've little trust in people, Kalianna. And less in spies." He sits, tenting his fingers. His voice is firm, matter of fact. "For you to be useful to me, you may learn more information about the kingdom's affairs than I trust you with. So I'd like the rules of our engagement to be clear up front. And I have . . . insurance. In case you find your loyalty wavering. Do you understand?"

I nod, not yet trusting my voice.

"Well then, Kali," Firehorn says, opening his palms, "I would very much like to meet Kal, if you don't mind."

I want to run, but I gather my courage and meet his eyes instead. "Kalianna," I say, quietly but firmly. "Or Lady Lianna. Or Kal. Or anything else you wish. But not Kali. Never Kali."

A hint of a smile curls one side of Firehorn's mouth. "Very

well. Now that both sides are clear with the arrangement . . ." He lifts a brow expectantly.

I strip.

The clothes fit. The fabric is of good quality but plain. The kind a son of a wealthy merchant might wear. It takes some time to clear my makeup, but once I'm done, I slouch a bit and stick my hands into my pockets. "Kal, my lord," I say, lowering my voice and bowing. "At your service."

Firehorn circles me, his face alight with pleasure. "You look a bit younger as Kal."

I nod. With hints of curves hidden, my slender body best passes for a boy of about sixteen.

"Impressive," Firehorn says finally, more to himself than to me. "I watched you change right before me, and yet I'd swear before the Goddess herself that the face has changed. You can keep this persona as long as necessary, I presume."

"Of course. And as the persona of Kal is the one more likely to engage in strenuous activity, I wear no makeup while in his skin." I open my palms. "I would be able to answer your questions better if I understood your needs. Might you enlighten me as to my mission, my lord?"

"To make yourself useful to me," King Firehorn answers, drawing a fortifying breath before proceeding. "The Drought is bringing our Kingdom of Dansil to its knees. I believe we need Everett blood to mix with ours to end this rash of stillbirths. Thus, I need the Everett alliance. And I need you to discover anything that threatens that goal."

"You want me to tell you what you don't know," I say.

Firehorn nods. "Look, listen, do what you do, and tell me what enemies I face—from within the Everett delegation, from the people in the palace, from the Viva Sylthia terror mongers running amok in my city. And you will also tell me whether anyone is so much as looking wrong at my heir. Plenty of fertile ground for your talents, I should think. Make the most of it."

"Yes, my lord," I say quietly.

"I've arranged for the appropriate placement of both your personas. Lady Lianna, my beloved niece and temporary ward —conveniently of an age with the Everett delegation's Princess Raza—will accompany me to functions with the Everett delegation in attendance. That will give you a sufficient platform to evaluate the high-society motives. As for the lower ranks, I've arranged for Kal to replace a recently deceased trainee in the Royal Guard. With both top and bottom covered, I expect that you will find yourself in an appropriate situation for whatever I might require. Do you have any questions?"

"How did the guard I am replacing die?" I ask.

"Killed in a mugging outside a local pub. Anything else?" This time, there is no mistaking the finality of the conversation.

Not being suicidal, I shake my head.

"Excellent. Then go be useful." Firehorn's smile doesn't touch his eyes. "And one other thing, Kalianna—allow your identity to be discovered, and I will personally escort you to the dungeons."

## 5

"Don't you look handsome?" Leaf adjusts the collar of my new royal guard uniform and runs her fingers over the trim marking me a trainee. Standing in the middle of Lady Lianna's plush suite a few hours after my meeting with the king, I look like a dressed-up doll. At the far corner of the room, the lit fireplace crackles companionably. It's warmer in Delta than it was at the estate, and the small flame heats the two-room suite easily, while the baskets of tulips that the servants brought in fill the air with a delicate perfume. "Kal is all grown up and off to training at the keep."

I step back and scowl. "You think this is funny?"

"You living and training with a herd of boys? Not at all." Leaf's round hazel eyes strain with the effort of holding back laughter. After the strict distance the scouts kept at the estate, the close living quarters of the keep *will* take a bit of getting used to. Leaf pulls on her lip thoughtfully. "Do you think they walk about the barracks naked? More to the point, can you be trusted to live amongst real humans without going feral and biting someone?"

I check the straps on my throwing knives and pull my jacket sleeve over them. "Not worried about it. Just focus on keeping up Lady Lianna's facade while I'm gone. She's a sickly, frail girl who must rest in her rooms, but for the occasional foray into society."

"And she studies botany," Leaf adds.

My head snaps to her. "She what?"

"Studies botany," Leaf says nonchalantly as she stuffs some fruit into Kal's sack. "That's why I am having a few things I can repurpose for my research brought to the room. I'll instruct you on what Lianna finds."

"Would this be the end-the-Drought research, the soil-fertility research, the Kali-magic-connection research, or the general furthering of study in the arena of living stones?" I ask innocently.

Leaf frowns. "All of the above. But they're not nearly as distinct as you make it sound."

"Fine. Just make sure there are no wasps taking up residence in Lianna's plants." I wave my hand and holster my sword at my waist. I prefer distance weapons, but guards all carry swords. Leaf's mouth twitches. "Stars, Leaf, what is so amusing?"

"You. Going to a training hall like a little untried boy. I'm imagining their faces when you knock the lot of them on their rears."

Rolling my eyes at her, I pull back the rug closest to the fireplace and run my fingers along the floor until I feel the latch. A trapdoor leading to the underground passages that Firehorn described clicks open silently. "I'll see you later," I tell my sister by way of farewell, and I climb down the ladder into the musky catacomb. The scents of stone, dust, and mold hit my nose, but despite their staleness, the passages are tall and wide enough for two people to walk abreast. The catacombs have the phantom feel of a space once used but long abandoned and forgotten by all but the dead.

Another trapdoor releases me into the West Wood, at the bottom of a hill overlooking the keep. Despite what I said to Leaf, my heart races as I crest the hill and survey my battlefield. On my left, tucked into the corner of the North and West Woods, the castle rises proudly toward the sky. On my right, past the keep grounds, the city of Delta begins its busy sprawl. And in the valley directly in front of me, the keep's training grounds stretch out, with their graveled yards and buildings of old white stone. On the parade field, scarlet and blue flags fly alongside each other. The Order of the Goddess has certainly climbed the power ladder in the last decade, to have its Holy Guard share the king's training space.

Compared to the misty, isolated grounds of Lord Gapral's estate, the keep is living chaos. Young men prowl around the training grounds like drunken wolves, shoving and gesturing to each other crudely. I'm surprised they aren't pissing on building corners to mark their territory. Or maybe that's an after-feeding-time kind of activity. I haven't taken a step among them yet, and I'm already feeling crowded.

*Go*, I order myself, forcing my body into motion. The din gets louder with each step, and soon I can smell the reek of sweat that clouds the keep like a blanket. Spotting a pair of boys walking in Holy Guard scarlet, I quicken my steps to come alongside them. Time to go to work. "Can you tell me where new trainees are to report?" I ask.

The holy guardsmen stop in unison. Posture rod-straight, they touch their fists to their hearts before the taller of the two looks from the blue diamond sigil on my uniform to my eyes. "To the Dark God's underworld."

"Good to know we all get along," I say under my breath, ignoring their shoves as they move past me.

Down at the main courtyard, I find a jeering crowd of trainees watching four men with practice swords square off against each other. Three shirtless men—full guardsmen, judging by their ages—stand together, sweat running down the muscled grooves of their backs. The fully clothed fourth man, I recognize from my arrival.

Wearing a pale-blue shirt that clings with sweat to shifting muscles, Trace moves with lupine grace as he herds his opponents around the ring. Behind his dark eyes, the world shimmers with violence that sends a shiver through me. I wonder whether the man *ever* relaxes.

The squat guard closest to Trace cuts his blade so fast that I cringe at the inevitable crack of Trace's collarbone.

Trace spins smoothly, his silver-blond hair streaming behind him, and parries the blow before it touches flesh. The clap of wood on wood is loud as thunder, and the guard who made the attack stumbles from the impact.

Trace seizes the moment to dip the point of his sword toward the man's sternum and lunges in.

The bare-chested guardsman gasps, bending double over his abdomen. Trace grabs the back of the man's head and shoves him face first into the sand. A heartbeat later, a second guardsman falls to Trace's foot sweep, slapping the ground with his palms to dispel the impact of the fall. Trace finds the fallen man's eyes and the two exchange quick nods before Trace steps away to square off against the last man left standing, this one with mussed red hair and a fox-like grin. They circle each other, Trace sparing a moment to brush sweat off his forehead. His movements are unlike the other guards'. Unlike anything I've seen while training with Lord Gapral. Wherever Trace trained, it wasn't in Dansil.

Tucking that thought away, I turn my back to the fray, find the guard master's door in the larger of the four buildings surrounding the central training field, and let myself inside. The man grunts in annoyance at my appearance in his dusty study.

"Your tuition buys your useless carcass a space in the keep," the guard master growls at me, shoving a key and a paper for me to sign in front of my nose. "Whether you spend your time training or scrubbing latrine troughs with your bare hands is entirely up to you. The rules are simple. One: You will train with the other diamond boys until one of the full guardsmen condescends to sponsor you, and then you will train with him. As that is as likely as you shitting flowers, you should get used to the sound of my voice. Two: Get caught fighting with any roses—the holy guardsmen—and you answer to me. Three: Bring a female into my keep, and you'll regret your own birth. Finally, the armory and black powder are off limits. I guarantee that whatever idiotic idea you have for explosives will leave you missing limbs. Any questions?"

I shake my head mutely. The guard master indulges in several wet coughs before standing up and lumbering to the door. "Luca! Get your hide in here." For a man who seemed too occupied to breathe properly a moment ago, the guard master has a voice loud enough to summon the dead.

A few moments later, the red-haired guardsman that I last saw circling the sparring ring with Trace sticks his head into the room, assesses the situation, and crooks one finger at me. By the time I'm outside, he's busy using his shirt to wipe sweat off a very clearly defined abdomen.

"Pleasant, isn't he?" Luca says, jerking his chin at the guard master's closed door.

I hesitate a heartbeat, giving Luca a chance to clothe himself—only to realize the man has no intention of doing so,

ALEX LIDELL

being fully content to walk around shirtless and glistening with sweat. About the same age as Trace, maybe twenty years old, Luca is tall and leanly muscled, with the aura of an easily amused, overgrown puppy. His auburn bangs are long enough to cover his right eye and too short to stay tucked behind an ear, despite his ongoing attempts to make them do so.

Giving up the hair battle, Luca motions for me to follow him to the barracks. "I'm Luca, as I imagine you've put together by now. One of the guards on the king's personal detail."

The king's personal detail? The puppy must have more teeth than he shows. I grunt in a manly way. "Kal Cassidy."

"Novan's replacement. I know."

*I see.* "I apologize for interrupting your training." I debate adding "sir" to the phrase, as Luca is both older than Kal and a full guardsman, but the formality so poorly matches Luca's demeanor that I can't manage the word.

Luca waves off the apology, the crumpled shirt in his hand dripping with sweat. "It's no trouble. I can get a beating from Trace anytime I wish."

With Luca walking in front of me, I let my eyes scan his torso. I saw little of the match between Trace and him, but the lack of severe bruises speaks to Luca's well-placed parries. Unlike the meticulously technical Trace, I suspect Luca's skill is rooted as much in natural athleticism as in practice.

"This is you." Luca stops by one of the doors in a long stone building and turns aside for me to work the key into a rusty lock that I could pick with my eyes closed. Luca and Trace wouldn't need to do even that, as either could take the whole door down with a good shoulder shove.

Lock conquered, I step into a stone closet that has the gall to call itself a room. The narrow cot takes up most of the space, and Luca shows me how to lift the top of the cot up to access the chest beneath. There is no space for a table, but a shelf bolted to the wall holds a pitcher of water and a washbasin. "Are all the rooms so . . .."

"Spacious?" Luca offers. "Very much so."

I run my fingers over the stone wall. Except for the size, it is not so different from the space I shared with Leaf at Lord Gapral's estate. The tougher part will be simultaneously maintaining the illusion of residence in both Lianna's and Kal's chambers. Sleep will be hard to come by. "I thought most keep trainees came from posh families."

"The keep takes some pains to remind you all that you are no longer living with those posh families. I'd be lying if I said that the cot is comfortable for a tumble, but you can manage it with the right girl." He grins and I turn my face into the shadows to conceal the hint of a blush. "Not that I *recommend* you bring one here, mind you," Luca adds, scratching the back of his head. "You'll pay with your hide if one of the guards catches you."

I lift a brow. If Leaf were here, she'd be ordering Luca to quit his nonsense and go to the baths by now. "Aren't you one of the guards, Luca?"

He shrugs and frowns at his balled-up shirt, as if unsure of what to do with it now that its service as a sweat rag has run its course and my whole room has taken on its scent. "Where you stick your prick is not one of my priorities."

"That's . . . good to know." I clear my throat and nudge my weight forward to try and crowd Luca out of the room before everything in my pack absorbs his smell too. "And what *are* your priorities?"

He cocks his head in thought but doesn't move. "The royals. Firehorn is bat crazy when it comes to William and Violet, though the princess is easy to deal with. Just smile at the lass and she'll be happy enough. The other one . . . I think

Trace might snap one day and wring the hellion's head clean off his shoulders."

I aim my shoulder at Luca's ribcage and contemplate ramming the man out of my room. Glad as I am for the diarrhea of information, having someone—anyone—between me and the door is bloody unsettling. Especially a half-naked man who is as likely to make use of my chamber pot as he is to offer unsolicited advice on handling females. I finally settle on nudging Luca over with a hand on his shoulder, the way I'd move aside a horse, and sliding past him back outside. "When does training start?"

"Easy there, cub." Luca, thank the stars, follows me out. "They'll sweat you to your heart's content at dawn tomorrow. The rest of the day varies by duties, and it will take you a while to get anything worth looking forward to. Except dinner. You will always look forward to dinner, which, I regret to inform you, we are in danger of missing right now. Do you want to go to the mess hall, or stand here wagging tongues?"

The thought of food in a crowded mess hall turns my stomach. Asking Luca to go ahead on his own, I go back into my room—locking the door behind me this time—unpack the few things I brought, check my throwing knives, and tighten my laces for an easy jog around the palace grounds. Heading north along the tree line, it's a twenty-minute run from the keep to the palace proper. The map of the underground tunnels that King Firehorn showed me rolls through my memory as I visualize the passageways running below the grassy earth. Breathing evenly, I focus on the light pattering of my feet, pushing the drowning crowd of the keep from my thoughts.

The barracks and training fields on my right yield to the manicured palace courtyards and the stone grandness of the castle itself. Unlike the main south entrance, which welcomed

Lady Lianna, the back north entrance is utilitarian, with a small courtyard for supply carriages to stop and turn easily and well-packed dirt ground instead of rich beds of tulips. In place of a sweeping staircase perfect for displaying the latest fashions, the back door is fitted with a ramp to wheel up goods and remove refuse. The palace sides are of the same gray stone here as in the front, but the harsh rock now hides behind winding grapevines.

Guardsmen patrolling the perimeter give me a passing glance, though I suspect more are stationed up high to watch the forest. They bloody have to be, since the forest is all that lies north and west. The back of the castle tapers into rough undergrowth, the North Wood rising to my left in a wall of leaves and bark. A choice: Continue east to stay along the palace perimeter and head toward the royal stables, or veer north into the wilderness I've no business exploring just now.

The woods win, the call of the trees too alluring to resist after the crowded keep. Like all plants in Delta, the foliage is lush and thick enough to block some of the sun. This close to the palace, the path is well worn—though wisely narrow, so as to prevent a wagon from passing. An enemy force might send hostiles through the forest, but it won't be moving an army through here, not without a way of hauling supplies along.

Effective against the likes of Everett. Less effective against Viva Sylthia terror mongers, who do their bidding in small isolated units. If—

My observations break off mid-thought as an explosion of breaking branches and pounding hooves echoes through the forest.

## 6

*H*ooves pound dirt in concert with a horse's frantic whinny. I spin, surveying the thicket around me. Maple, basswood, and the occasional pine stare back at me, holding the line. Finding no opening, I blow out a breath and forge my own path through the dense foliage toward the sounds of trouble. Branches slap my face and tangle in my clothes, bruising my pride—but the growing noise suggests that speed needs to trump stealth. Within minutes, I emerge onto a parallel trail, where, a short distance to my right, a bay stallion is rearing high enough to reveal the full extent of his reproductive assets, his rider clinging fiercely to the saddle.

The horse stamps his front legs back on the ground, only to get purchase and buck with his rear. The violent thump finally dislodges the rider, and I wince as the young man—a lad of about Kal's age and build—falls hard against nearby stones.

The stallion spins frantically, the whites of his eyes shining in the evening sun. His muscles bunch in preparation to bolt, which he does a heartbeat later.

Straight at me.

I throw my arms out wide, blocking the horse's path. My heart speeds but the low "whoa" I call out is steady enough. Generally speaking, horses dislike ramming into things. I hope this particular beast is aware of the generalities common to his species.

The stallion barrels forward. Five paces left. Four.

I hold my ground.

Three paces.

"Watch out," the boy calls, as if I simply might have overlooked the sprinting beast.

The stallion lays his ears flat against his head and glares. His nostrils flare and foam slips down his scar-marked flanks. Chunks of earth and debris scatter from beneath his hooves.

I hold my ground. And my breath.

An arm's length short of trampling me into the dust, the stallion skids to a sideways halt, his sides heaving and his muscles so tense, they tremble like the leaves.

Moving with more calm surety than I feel, I grab hold of the dancing animal's headstall.

His nose dips in subordination, and I finally let out a slow breath. That was more dangerous than I intended.

"Not . . . bad." The fallen boy pushes himself up, pressing his sleeve against a bleeding gash over his right eye. About sixteen and more beautiful than handsome, the boy has golden hair, a slender waist, and long, dark lashes. His breaths come in ragged gasps, which he attempts to conceal behind a cocky smile. "Maybe . . . you should . . . be wearing a horse master uniform . . . instead of a guard trainee's."

I survey the boy from head to toe. He's bloody fortunate to have survived the fall with his head and bones intact, but whether the damage he did take is superficial remains to be seen. Preferably by a healer.

"I'm all right," he says. The words come quicker and sharper than they have any right to be.

"You're a decent liar, I'll give you that."

The boy laughs. "What's your name?"

"Kal. First day."

The boy nods but offers no return introduction, and I wonder if I've overlooked one of the many unspoken rules of male etiquette. Maybe I should have cursed and questioned the boy's lineage. Too late now.

I stroke the stallion's nose, watching as his heaving chest calms under my touch. "Spirited, aren't you?" I murmur to the horse, who snorts into my shoulder and digs the ground with a hoof. A shoeless hoof. I run my hand down the horse's legs, checking all four feet. "He threw a shoe," I tell the boy over the horse's back. "That probably set him off."

"I know." The boy shrugs, wobbles precariously, and braces a hand against a tree. "Saw it fly off when we left the stable. It was a good ride until that final dismount, though." He grins as if this was all an amusing prank instead of a near bone-breaking disaster—for him and the horse, both.

I keep my silence. If getting thrown failed to enlighten him to the problem of taking a horse with a missing shoe for a gallop through stone-filled woods, my words will do nothing but waste breath. Between Firehorn and the keep, I've enough to contend with just now. For a heartbeat, I consider taking the horse back and leaving the boy to the consequences of his recklessness, but I thwart the temptation. We are too deep into the woods for my comfort—especially now, with Viva Sylthia actively demonstrating its displeasure over the Everett ceasefire. "Can you mount up?" I ask. "I'll lead you back to wherever you are going."

He cocks his head, examining me curiously, and I once more wonder what I might have said wrong. "Thank you," he says after a moment. "The palace grounds, please. The stables."

Holding the horse steady, I help the boy mount, and with a click of my tongue I start us into a walk. With an injured rider and a three-shoed horse, it's half an hour before the palace grounds shimmer between the trees.

"Hold up," the boy orders as we approach the forest line. Looking ahead from his high vantage point, he curses under his breath and speaks quickly. "If anyone asks, you saw me abusing the horse, all right? That's why he threw me."

"What?" I frown up at him.

The boy squares his shoulders, trying to appear less injured than he is. "They can put down the horse—they can't put down *me*," he says quickly, his gaze tracking someone's approach. "I'll try to talk around the fall altogether, but if I can't . . . please. He's a good horse."

Before I can reply, a girl of thirteen or fourteen, as pretty and long-lashed as my companion, steps into our path and grins like a lioness. Her golden hair is curled into a complex set of locks that cascade over the shoulders of her velvet gown, orange as the fruit. "You are in *such* trouble, Wil."

"Shut up, Violet," the boy hisses at her.

Violet's grin broadens, a dusting of freckles dancing along the bridge of her nose. "Father!" she screeches. "I've found Wil! He went out alone again!"

Wil. Violet. The names hit me like a lance in the gut. My head jerks to the boy in the saddle, who gives me a look of rueful apology before straightening his spine to face his father, King Firehorn.

## 7

*K*ing Firehorn, flanked by a team of guardsmen that includes Luca and Trace, strides into the clearing and glares at Wil and me with a mixture of relief and fury. The prince. Of all the people I could have entangled myself with, I managed to find the royal prince. No wonder Wil paused a moment too long when I didn't know his destination.

Luca's attention darts between Wil and me as he no doubt wonders how Kal could have gotten into such a mess when Luca had just left him less than two hours ago. Trace, standing behind the king, is thunder incarnate as he quietly instructs one of the other guards to call off additional search parties.

"William." Firehorn's voice is low and formal, his dark eyes a dangerous blend of parental fear and thronely power. Though shorter than the guardsmen behind him, the king stands with his feet apart and head high, the gray strands in his hair more reminiscent of hard stone than frail age. "Explain yourself."

Despite my caution, I'm utterly curious as to how the sixteen-year-old prince intends to beat back the coming storm.

Wil offers his father a confused frown, so immaculately sculpted that I'm certain the prince practiced it before a mirror. "Guardsman Kal and I are just concluding an outing." Wil's voice is all reckless innocence. "Were you led to believe something different?" He turns the frown on his sister, whose face reddens to match her painted lips. "I regret any distress the misinformation you received may have caused you, Father, but as you can see, I am with a guard as per orders."

Trace shifts his weight, crossing his arms over his chest. The light wind sweeps back a lock of blond hair to reveal a tense muscle edging his jaw. A more personal fury than I'd expect from a guard. I'd wager Trace spends a good portion of his time sweeping up after Wil's mischief, and from the look on Trace's face, his patience has come to an end.

"Liar." Violet twists to the king. "Wil wasn't with any guard when he left."

"How would you know, Violet?" Wil asks. "A princess would need to walk dangerously close to a stable to observe what company I kept when I left. I'm certain *you* would never break the rules and put your precious life in danger just to spy on me. So what is this? A chance to throw a fit?"

Violet's nostrils flare. "Take it back."

"Enough!" Firehorn snaps, and I flinch.

Trace's gaze flickers to me, noting the weakness.

I curse myself soundly. Not that a sixteen-year-old trainee is wrong to cower from a king's ire, but my reactions should be calculated, not reflexive. It was sloppy to flinch. Sloppy to let Trace see it.

"Violet, go home," says Firehorn.

"But—"

"The woods are no place for a girl," Firehorn tells her, his attention already returning to Wil. "Go . . . practice your lessons."

Violet's face falls. I'd wager gold coin that Firehorn knows nothing of the girl's studies, much less whether practice is required—and the princess knows this too. Straightening her spine, Violet opens her mouth to protest, but the king snaps his fingers and a contingent of guardsmen separate to lead the princess away, the hem of her velvet dress muddy from the forest floor.

"William." King Firehorn steps toward his son. "Are you all right? What happened? Did that horse—"

"No." Wil pats the stallion's neck, his voice a hair too loud before reining itself in. "I was dumb enough to spar with Kal, and he had me head over ass before I knew what happened."

Years of practice allow me to keep a straight face. Which is good, because the relieved look on Firehorn's face says he *wants* to believe the sack of horseshit that Wil just fed him. Wants to think his son was simply roughing around, that the spy Firehorn brought in is already proving her value by befriending the prince.

Trace's weight shifts again, this time to grace me with the scowl previously reserved for the prince. His brow lifts. "Is that so, trainee?" he asks with quiet confidence, a captain of the king's guard detail demanding a report from a fresh-faced recruit.

Which, frankly, is unjust.

A senior guardsman of one and twenty should not be forcing a sixteen-year-old novice to publicly choose between obeying his superior officer or the crown prince of Dansil. My jaw tightens and I raise my chin, refusing to shy away from Trace's stare. "Yes, sir. Just as His Highness said."

Trace's face darkens, making the contrast to his silver hair more striking. His eyes capture mine, the threat in them clear: *Don't worry about the prince, boy—worry about me.*

Heat crackles along my spine. Firehorn might have me in his fist, but the bloody Eye of the Goddess will shatter before I allow a strutting guard to cow me. Not even if he is the captain of the king's guard detail. Especially not then.

King Firehorn sighs and rubs his temples, the tension in his shoulders easing. His son is safe, the boy's story credible enough to fool himself into believing it. There are other matters demanding attention. "Get cleaned up, William." Firehorn's voice is tired. "I trust you can make it to your quarters without any more mishaps?"

Wil bows from the saddle, surreptitiously holding the stallion's mane for balance. A tiny hint of a smile tugs at the corners of the prince's lips. Even I must admit that the hellion managed his father well enough to have made Lord Gapral proud.

I start to release my own sigh of relief when Trace cuts in to the conversation.

"With your permission, Your Majesty," Trace says, bowing to the king even as he steps to block Wil's path, "I will ensure that His Highness returns to his quarters safely. Luca can see you back."

Luca frowns but Firehorn is already nodding permission and starting down the path while his detail follows. Soon it is only the three of us in the privacy of the woods. My shoulders tense, my mind trying to calculate Trace's next move, to understand why a guard is injecting himself into a disciplinary matter between the king and prince.

Wil nudges the horse forward.

Predictably, Trace blocks the animal's path. He didn't keep us back only to step away now.

"Is there a problem, *guardsman*?" Wil asks.

Trace uncrosses his arms, letting his hand rest on the hilt of his sword. "I wondered whether you two are aware that Dansil and Everett are in historic peace negotiations just now?"

"It's crossed my attention," answers Wil, sitting up taller. "And keep Kal out of this. Anything you wish to say, you may say to me directly."

Trace turns obediently to the prince. "Do you understand, *Your Highness*, that should something happen to you, the leader of the Kingdom of Dansil would become a frantic father instead of a cool-minded ruler? Do you comprehend the number of innocent lives such a disaster could cost?"

"Good Goddess, Trace," Wil throws up his hands. "Do you imagine that Viva Sylthia goons are going to set up an ambush in the woods on the off chance that I will want to take a ride?"

Of course he does. And if Wil makes these outings a habit, Trace will be correct.

Wil raises his chin. "Whatever your concerns, Trace, the fact remains that I *had* a guard with me tonight. That satisfies the protocols that you yourself put in place. I consider the matter closed and ask you to step aside and let Kal and me resume our evening."

The air between the two crackles with tension. So much so that, if I knew nothing of their identities, I'd be hard-pressed to name which of the two was royal born. I back up a step, my scout's instinct urging me to watch the rest of the spectacle from the shadows.

"Not so fast." Trace's voice jerks me short. "You've made yourself a part of this as well. Full name?"

My stomach tightens, but I step forward and touch my fist to my chest. "Kal Cassidy, sir." My voice is even, respectful but undaunted.

"Well, Kal," Trace's body fills the entirety of my vision. "I would not presume to question His Highness's word that you were, in fact, on duty as his personal protection this evening. I must thus conclude that your lack of weapons, report of activity, and basic safety considerations are a delinquency. Have you anything to say for yourself?"

A fair accusation. And a smart one. Trace cannot discipline the prince directly, but he certainly can punish Kal. Conveniently, it would send a message of consequences to the prince while discouraging a trainee from trying similar antics again. If Trace hadn't attempted to scare me into submission earlier, I'd even grant him a bow.

"It's not Kal's fault!" The thread of desperation in Wil's voice makes me swallow a groan. The prince might think he's helping, but his obvious discomfort only serves to make Kal a more valuable whipping boy.

"On the contrary," Trace says. "It appears Kal is the only one at fault." He shifts his attention back to me, lowering his voice. "Unless . . ."

My chest tightens. *Unless?* There is an "unless"?

Trace's shoulders spread, that subtle shift of weight designed to frighten me, and his voice drops even further. "Unless the trainee has a different version of events to share before I decide on his punishment?"

That hot crackling along my spine returns, any respect I've gained for Trace burning to white ash. *Throw your friend to the wolves and save your hide.* That is what he wants me to do. Not just wants—if the knowing cock of his brow is any indication —but *expects*. I wonder if Trace thinks me that intimidated or that dishonorable. Whichever it is, the guard is about to be sorely disappointed.

I meet Trace's dark eyes, my own unflinching. Frost nips my words. "I've nothing to add to His Highness's words."

Trace blinks.

I do not.

The guard stares at me for a deafening heartbeat before turning on his heels to cut a branch from the nearest tree. With brutal efficiency, he strips the rod of twigs and leaves—as if either Wil or I needed a further explanation of his intentions. "Remove your outer coat," Trace says, his attention still on his work.

Wil's mouth opens, but I touch his knee and give my head a calm shake. My heart beats too loudly in fury to leave room for fear. Shrugging free of my jacket, I fold it neatly on the ground and lower to one knee before Trace—who, for the first time, seems hesitant.

"At your convenience, sir," I say over my shoulder.

Twigs crunch beneath Trace's even steps. I brace myself, but the man steps around to face me instead, crouching to come on eye level with me. His large body blocks my view of Wil and the trees, creating a cocoon of privacy that even the sun struggles to pierce. Shifting his attention to his hands, Trace rolls the switch between his thumb and forefinger. "This will draw blood, Kal," he murmurs softly, for my ears only. "Is that what you want before your first day of training? The truth—that is all I ask of you. Tell me that the prince lies, that you were never his guard. That is all you must do, and this goes no further. What say you?"

I glance at the switch. "If you intend to draw blood, sir, you'll need a better stick. That one won't last a half dozen cuts."

8

---

## VIOLET

*P*rincess Violet Firehorn locked the door to her bedchamber and sat cross-legged on her bed, a small knife clasped in her fingers. The blade was sharp and glistened enticingly in the candlelight. A pair of maidservants cleaning up in the sitting room outside the bedchamber clamored with their buckets and trays. Violet wished they'd leave. She *should* be able to ask them to go, but had yet to find a way of making requests without being thought ill of. There was always something—a wrong word, an erroneous look, an incorrect tone—that gave servants and courtiers leave to think her a petulant little tyrant.

Violet was fourteen, but Dansil's court treated her as either a child of four or an adult of four and twenty, depending on its convenience. No one particularly cared what was convenient for Violet. She twirled a lock of golden hair around her finger, savoring the long, lush curls that cascaded down to her forming breasts. Bloody inconvenient things that made her dresses uncomfortable without a bind or corset. One of the many, *many* things that her brother didn't have to deal with.

Wil, the perfect son, the crown prince. Wil, who didn't even *try* being considerate of anyone but came out looking golden nonetheless. Even after the disappearing stunt he'd pulled today—Violet was certain Wil had gone riding with no guard, no matter what he claimed—he'd faced nothing but a scolding. If that. Violet, on the other hand, wasn't so much as permitted to step foot in the stables. One of the horses *might* get loose after all and *might* kick her by accident. It wasn't worth the risk, not with so very few girls born in Dansil. So very few future mothers.

"Is Her Royal Highness sulking again?" The words from the other side of the wall were near inaudible, but Violet minded quiet conversations by habit. It was the only way of learning the goings-on of the palace since no one bothered to brief her on anything.

"My life in the crown prince's shadow is soooo very painful," a younger woman whispered back, emphasizing each vowel. "I've been unable to eat a lemon tart in days."

*Don't listen. Don't listen. Don't listen.* Violet closed her eyes and tried to shut out the maids' words. She really did. The servants always talked. It was a fact of palace life.

"Tell me again why we are rubbing our hands raw cleaning the floor of a sitting room that no one uses?" the first woman asked.

Violet put down the little knife and slid off the bed. Padding over to the door leading to the sitting room, she cracked it open.

The two maids working there rose to their feet and sank into deep curtsies at once. One was in her mid-twenties, the other only a couple years older than Violet herself.

"Is all well, Your Highness?" the older one asked. She was

the one who'd just complained about cleaning a useless room. "You are looking a mite pale, if I may be so bold as to say so. Perhaps I might fetch you something to eat?"

"No, thank you," said Violet.

The woman frowned. "Then perhaps some fresh flowers? We were just talking about making your sitting room more jovial. I think a nice bouquet of—"

"Actually," Violet interrupted, "I was thinking of how little use this room sees. Do you think we should adopt a different cleaning schedule for it? Something that makes better use of your efforts?"

The women exchanged tight glances. "Are you displeased with our work, Your Highness?"

"No." Violet retreated a step. "I just thought you'd prefer to be elsewhere. You are welcome to stay if you'd like. Please, do what you think is best." She shut the door quickly and leaned against it. On the other side of the wall, silence reigned for several heartbeats before steps and voices resumed in barely audible whispers.

"Did she just . . .?"

"Threaten our jobs? Yes." A sigh. "When you've never wanted for something in your life, it's simple to toss others around."

Violet clicked the lock closed and returned to her bed, wrapping a scarf around her ears as she sat cross-legged again. Reclaiming her little knife, she used it to pry the lid off the wooden box beside her. With the cover off, Violet reached inside for the bits of sewn chocolate-colored velvet. The half-complete body of a stuffed puppy.

She was much too old for such useless nonsense as sewing plush animals. Especially with no children around to whom she might gift the toy when she finished it. But she couldn't help it. Sewing tiny toys was a craft she'd learned from her mother. The last craft she'd ever learned from her. And, sitting alone with needle and thread, the wonderful little animals were the one thing—other than a potential heir—that Violet *could* create. Not that a kingdom that needed anything but her womb much cared.

Violet's eyes began to sting. She wanted her mother. The one person who had loved her, who'd put her arms tightly around her and whispered kind words. Who would never, *ever* look into her eyes again. *Stop crying, you baby*, Violet ordered herself. Three months had passed since her mother had died in childbirth, together with a stillborn baby brother who was perfect. Three months, and Violet could still scarcely draw breath.

A tear slid rebelliously down her cheek. Then another. While Wil was busy scaring the living daylights out of his own guard and wrapping their father around his finger, Violet had only their mother's memory and her own impotence for company. It wasn't enough.

*STOP CRYING.* Swallowing, Violet rolled up the hem of her dress to expose her thigh. Milky white skin, crossed with thin pink scars. Her fingers tightened around the knife handle. It was the one thing that she knew worked.

Another tear fell.

With no more thought, Violet slid the blade's edge across her thigh, thick droplets of red blood trickling from the cut. She looked at the red droplets and focused on the burning pain that was so much easier to bear.

VIOLET WAS TAKING some air in the courtyard when the palace bell chimed its hour and her guard detail exchanged grateful gazes at the approaching end of their shift. Violet bored them. She was about to turn her back on the men and return to her suites when she spotted Luca taking a shift in her evening detail and halted her steps instead.

"Good evening, Highness," he said, coming up beside her. Tall, kind, and always smiling, Luca was the only one in the guard detail who bothered speaking to her more than protocol required. Like Violet herself, Luca lived in the shadow of his perfect partner, Trace, and although they never spoke of it, Violet was certain he felt the same subtle connection between them that she did. Something special. Though Luca unlikely spent his time sewing plush puppies by candlelight. The sudden thought nearly made Violet burst into giggles.

Luca grinned. "What shall you have us do this evening? Swordplay, perhaps? Or shall we go hunt boar?"

Violet did giggle then, her cheeks heating. Her mind raced for something appropriate, something feminine and delicate and dignified. "Embroidery," she blurted, realizing too late that this would logically keep her inside while Luca remained outdoors. She cleared her throat. "Outside," she amended quickly. "It's such a nice evening, don't you think?"

"I'm no embroidery expert," said Luca slowly, "but does that fine task not require light?"

Idiot. Violet was an idiot. No. She could fix this. Would fix this. "Of course it does," she said, smoothing her dress. "Which is why I'd like to walk to the Temple of Dansil. The Eye is so bright there, I can stitch by its glow."

The walk to the temple was longer than Violet had expected, and she cursed herself for not having thought of taking a carriage, as they did when attending the weekly service. But walking beside Luca was worth it, especially when he offered her his arm. Arriving at the temple courtyard, Luca led Violet to the central fountain, where little stone benches surrounded a likening of the Goddess with her hands cupped lovingly around a devout young man's cheeks.

A reminder that everything the Goddess does comes from love.

Violet sat, putting her basket beside her. When she looked up from sorting her materials, her heart sank. The area outside the temple was safe and well illuminated, so Luca and the other guards had taken up posts on the perimeter of the courtyard, while Violet remained alone on her bench. Luca wasn't even looking in her direction. She'd walked here for nothing. Worse than nothing. She was making a mockery of herself, sitting alone by a fountain like an old man. And she hated embroidery.

She lowered her face as if busy. The temple courtyard had fair foot traffic despite the late hour. Holy guardsmen striding in perfect unison, even when there were just two men walking together. Acolyte boys speaking softly. And . . . girls. Girls walking arm in arm, whispering in each other's ears, laughing softly at shared secrets.

There were so very few girls at court—almost none Violet's age. And they all kept their distance from the royal princess. Not that there was much for them to *do* together. Violet was a princess. No one ever let her forget that. No, convenient temporary ignorance of royal blood was reserved solely for her brother's antics.

"You seem lonely," a melodic voice drew Violet's attention to a pair of girls who'd stopped before her. They were probably a couple of years older than her, and both wore loose red dresses, baskets of dying carnations hanging from their elbows. Children of the Goddess.

"Would you care for a bit of company?" said the other girl, this one slightly plumper and no less pretty.

Both of the girls smiled with the warmest, friendliest smiles Violet had ever seen.

## 9

## KALI

*I* groan awake the morning after my encounter with Wil and Trace, and wince as I sit up on Kal's hard cot. Trace made good on his threat to draw blood, but after years of Lord Gapral's discipline, the welts and cuts Trace left are little more than an inconvenience. Beyond my tiny window, dawn is breaking in red and orange hues that give the Eye of the Goddess an ethereal glow. I stare out at the grounds, marking the routine of patrols, memorizing the keep's daily pulse. The distant *bum . . . bum . . .* of the temple bell calls devout women to the morning service, where Bishop Bahir and his disciples will instruct the Goddess's daughters on their duty to produce offspring at any cost to mind or body. Closer to me, trainees stumble into the courtyard with all the enthusiasm of bears waking from hibernation.

I shrug into my uniform and buckle a practice sword to my waist, hoping that Kal's second day proves less exciting than his first. I'm just starting on the jacket buttons when the door to my tiny room bangs open.

My knives are in my hands in a heartbeat.

"Hello, Trouble," says my guest, pushing a cascade of red-brown hair behind an ear, only to have the thick strands drape right back over his light-brown eyes.

"Hells, Luca." I slip the weapons back into their sheaths and make a mental note to lock my door even when I'm inside. "Have you not heard of knocking?"

"Aye. It usually makes the same sound as the whack of your head against a wall. Lounge in bed a bit longer and you'll feel that too. Have you recovered from your acquaintance with Trace?" His grin takes the sting out of the words, but my face heats regardless.

"If I never see that man again, it will be too soon." I throw frigid water on my face and attack my teeth with a brushing stick. If Luca insists on gracing me with his presence this morning, he can entertain himself.

"Yes, about that . . ." Luca helps himself to an apple I've been saving. I consider smacking him for it, but the guard gobbles it down like a starved wolf, and I decide I should be fortunate that he hasn't eaten the shelf along with the fruit. "If my information is correct, and it typically is when it comes to things that will royally annoy someone, it appears that His Royal Highness Prince William has requested that one Trainee Cassidy be assigned to his personal guard. Quite the honor."

My hand freezes mid-brush.

"But—" Luca pauses to survey my gear. Black trousers, blue shirt, a thick leather vambrace that conceals real throwing knives beneath. "But as neither the king nor the guard master, nor anyone else with any wits, believes that a trainee with four hours' experience is the optimal watchdog for a crown prince, they came to a compromise designed to make everyone unhappy in one shot."

I turn to him slowly and scowl at his spreading grin. "I *will* throttle you if you don't get to the point."

Luca pulls my newly issued practice sword free of its sheath on my hip and uses his boot knife to roughen the grip. "Trace is your new sponsor."

I choke on my tooth-cleaning powder. The man who tried to intimidate me into betraying someone's trust is my new bloody *sponsor*? The brushing stick in my hand snaps under the pressure. "No."

"Well, we both are, but mostly Trace," Luca continues as if I hadn't spoken. "He's in charge, as you may have gathered."

"Cassidy." The low bark comes from the door, now blocked with Trace's frame. Rays of sunlight curl around his hair, giving him a soft glow that's utterly at odds with the hard set of his jaw.

My quarters, lavish as they are, seem to have become a common room this morning.

"Training grounds," Trace says, the sun returning to my room as he pushes himself back into the courtyard. "Five minutes."

Luca winks and tosses my practice blade back into my hands. The grip, roughened beneath Luca's blade, is more comfortable but only half-finished. "You'll want to use one of the keep blades for now," he says, following after Trace. "See you soon, cub. And bring a waterskin."

Alone in my room, I take a moment to curse soundly before grabbing my gear and resigning myself to an unpleasant morning.

Trace and Luca are already working at the far end of the grassy training grounds when I jog out. Moving past the herd of trainees lining up before the guard master, I feel their gazes searing my back. Getting an assignment and sponsors only one day after arrival is unlikely to make me many friends—not that

I am looking for any. Not that these sponsors—one sponsor in particular—are envy worthy.

Trotting up, I find Luca in the middle of an abdominal exercise, swinging his upper body between the ground and his bent knees while Trace braces his feet. Right. Of course Trace has chosen something to irritate my back, lest I forget who holds the power in this new setup.

"Two hundred two, two hundred three," Trace counts for Luca. "Two hundred four."

I sit on the ground beside Luca, the dampness of the earth seeping through my clothes as the smell of fresh-cut grass rises around me. I wonder if Trace expects me to balk or complain, and if he'll be disappointed when I don't.

"Two hundred twenty," Trace counts to Luca's unwavering rhythm. "Two hundred twenty-one."

Maybe he doesn't care either way. Crossing my arms over my chest in imitation of Luca, I bend my knees and start lowering my shoulders to the ground. At least Trace chose grass. Lord Gapral would have had me on gravel.

"Halt." Trace's large, calloused palm braces the back of my head before my back hits the earth. "You already made your point yesterday. We meant to finish these before you came."

I pull away from Trace and rise to my feet, an unsettling shiver running down my skin.

"To be clear," Trace hefts his practice sword into his hand and motions for me to choose one off a nearby rack, brought out for morning training, "this arrangement is *not* a partnership. You will accompany Luca and me on select assignments with Prince William. I will be your trainer, your evaluator, and your commander. Understood?"

I nod mutely and move to select a wooden blade from the arsenal of offerings. I will always prefer my knives but can manage a sword without stabbing my own foot. No one would expect much more from Kal, but having seen Trace spar, I little wish to make a fool of myself. My fingers trail the wood in search of something light, easy to handle, and—

I freeze mid-motion. There is someone behind me, reaching for me, for my back. My chest tightens, my fingers grasping the nearest blade. The sun, the fresh-cut grass, the green training grounds filled with uniformed boys, they all blur into a sudden nothing. My body uncoils like a whip, the blade an extension of my hips and arm. The wooden practice sword flies free of the rack, arcing and snapping down at my assailant.

Trace's blade intercepts mine, stopping me a hair short of fracturing Luca's wrist. The crack of wood on wood echoes through the yard, turning heads.

"Holy bloody stars, Kal." Luca withdraws his hand slowly, his tawny eyes wide. "I was just going to wish you luck."

"Don't. Touch. Me." The words escape before I can stop them, my chest heaving with my racing pulse. The confusion in Luca's face demands an explanation, but the truth—that my upbringing wasn't one where people patted shoulders for luck —would raise more questions than it satisfied. Hells.

I force a rueful half smile to my face, as if nothing of significance has happened. "Forgive me, Luca. My back is bothering me this morning."

The two men exchange silent glances. Trace tilts his head.

Luca shrugs. "I've something to attend to," he says, saluting us both with his practice blade before swaggering off to provoke a nearby guard into a sparring bout. If being assaulted and dismissed bothers Luca, the man lets none of it show as his natural grace morphs into a deadly dance of blades.

"You lied to him," Trace says.

I turn, raising my palms in shameless innocence. I may owe Luca an apology, but Trace has nothing to do with this. "Not at all. My back hurts. Would you like to see the marks?"

Trace's lips press together into a line. "No."

I bring my blade to ready guard. "Then I'm at your command, sir."

Trace obligingly salutes and swings his sword at my skull. I've seen enough of his fighting skills to know he could splatter my brains across the grass anytime he wishes, so the only reason I manage to block the assault is that he allows me to do so. I've enough wits to angle the blade, letting his attack slide off my parry instead of pitting my muscle against Trace's. His next blow targets my sword arm. Then the right hip. The knees. A full circle around my body to probe my skill, which falls several measures below his and Luca's but is at least more solid than what I note of the other trainees.

Trace nods and quickens the pace, the smell of fresh grass now giving way to salt and sweat. The tip of my blade ducks down to defend my legs. Right, left, right. My wrist protests the harsh angle that low parries require but moves in reflexive obedience to the attacks. My pulse and lungs quicken and steady, fueling my body, and I savor every caress of cool wind. Right. Left. High. Low. Step. Pivot. Lunge. Within a bell's time, it's hard to be angry or annoyed or do anything but just *be*. The practice blades find a rhythm, beating like a metronome in a forever-even song of Trace's choosing.

If this is what sword practice can be like, I understand why so many prefer the weapon.

Another bell. Another hour. My muscles burn; my shirt clings to my body. My breath comes in short bursts.

And of course, this is when Trace decides to speak. "Yesterday," he feints a blow to my head, switches mid-arch, and slices at my left flank instead, "I was asking for nothing but the truth."

I snort. "You knew the truth." I block the left attack, but it's a close call. "You were asking . . . that I turn in . . . someone else . . . to save my own hide." The words come in hard-won bursts, and I'm unsure why I feel the need to justify myself to Trace at all. The hilt of my sword drops too far and Trace's next blow cuts through the weakly posed blade.

He raps my side lightly, but my flesh is sore and I wince.

Hooking the underside of my wrist with his sword tip, Trace expertly guides my hand back into proper position. His eyes are distant and he says nothing while he repeats the attack I failed to parry earlier, his movements crisp and practiced. "How old are you?"

Almost eighteen. But Trace is asking Kal, not me. "Sixteen," I pant between moves.

Trace's hand tightens on his sword, the knuckles bone white, but he doesn't speak.

"Would something be different . . . if I were fifteen . . . or seventeen?"

"No." Trace pulls his next attack mid-blow and sheathes his blade. "That's enough for today. You are free until tomorrow morning."

I blink once, then brace my hands on my thighs, my mind scurrying to catch up with what just happened, what the importance of Kal's age might be. I don't ask. The less I talk, the less opportunity I have to say something stupid.

Reaching into a satchel on the ground, Trace tosses a tin into my hands.

I open the lid and take a careful sniff. The tang of willow bark, mixed with a few leaves I vaguely recognize, tickles my nose. An analgesic salve to soothe shallow cuts and deep bruises.

"It will take the edge off," says Trace, his attention on his own gear.

It likely will, but in my world, there is no such thing as a free gift. Closing the tin, I toss it back to Trace. "I have my own." With a half bow, I store my practice weapon and walk away to spend some time in the trees, watching the palace's back entrance for anything interesting.

## 10

"You are an idiot," Leaf informs me as she hands me a foul-smelling tonic, shaking her head at the cuts, welts, and bruises covering most of my skin.

I'm back in Lady Lianna's suite, which in my two-day absence has transformed from a lady's chambers to a library crossed with an alchemy studio. Leaf even procured a giant slate somewhere and charted a hundred magical elements in a grid of neat boxes—from memory, I will wager.

"What was I supposed to do? Call the crown prince a liar?"

Leaf puts her hands on her hips and stares down her nose at me. "You were supposed to whimper and gasp and play the kind of whipping boy who'd actually deter the prince from further recklessness. Give this *Trace*"—she says his name like it's an uncouth word—"no reason to hurt you more than he had to, instead of goading him into a battle of wills."

I wince as Leaf dabs something burning onto a cut. "Kal

isn't the kind to whimper and cower," I say through clenched teeth.

"*You* aren't the kind to whimper and cower. Kal is whatever you need him to be."

I blow a slow stream of air from pursed lips. Leaf is right, of course. A new lad on his first day should have been trembling in his boots once Trace had him alone. Howling and squirming would have drawn less notice than trained stoicism while leaving me with an intact hide and Wil with a distaste for endangering others. I just . . . didn't want to.

Not before a man who's trained hard enough to face down three opponents at once. "I do have some dignity," I mutter.

"You also have *dresses* to wear and things to do besides impressing the king's warriors with your stupidity." Leaf's voice softens. "Is it very hard for you, Kali? To work and train *with* people instead of beside or against them?"

I get up and head to the closet, looking for something very concealing that Lady Lianna might make an appearance in this evening. "No," I call over my shoulder. "They are all still marks. Just ones I'll be spending months with instead of hours."

The silence from Leaf is laden with unspoken thoughts, but when I turn to lift a brow at her, my sister is back in her books. "What do you make of the Eye of the Goddess?" she asks.

I pull out a pair of gowns, their fabric oddly soft and colorful after Kal's rough wear. The pale-green one, topped with a woolen cloak, will do fine for a short walk this evening, but the other—a rich blue velvet with a flattering waist—needs to be altered to cover my back for the formal dinner Lady Lianna is attending tomorrow. "It makes lots of light."

"Magic can't make or destroy light, or anything else. It manipulates what already exists," Leaf responds on reflex. She runs a hand over her face. "Sorry. I can't help myself. What I don't understand is how such a monumental glow stays steady. Living stones don't tune themselves."

I shrug. "What I don't understand is why everyone is all right with Bishop Bahir setting the biggest living crystal in the world atop his temple, and simultaneously claiming magic is the Dark God's work. Hells, to hear the Holy Guard talk among themselves—and that's from both Kal's and Lianna's vantage points—Bahir is the oracle of all truth, no matter what nonsense he utters."

Leaf lifts her book to pull out a folded sheet of parchment, which she extends toward me. "You can ask him all about it yourself tomorrow night. This is the guest list for the dinner, and His Holy Grace is at the top of your esteemed company."

I take a deep breath and bury my face in my hands. My body is dead heavy and my head aches, pulsing with merciless jolts. It's only been two days and I'm already barely able to stay awake. An evening of strolling around in Lianna's disguise —followed by a night of cataloging my observations, only to be back in Kal's bed before dawn's wakeup bell—looms over me like an insurmountable boulder. And this is my easy day.

Leaf frowns at me. "Do you need something?"

I shake my head. Leaf's *something* would wake me like a jackrabbit but I'd be paying for the borrowed energy for days. "I'll manage." By way of proof, I force myself to my feet and start hiding Kal behind a dress, jewels, and enough makeup that my head is heavier for wearing it.

The walk about the palace, at least, is uneventful. A guard I've not met before escorts Lady Lianna politely around the grounds, pointing out flowers and similar nonsense that— thanks to Leaf—Lianna is supposed to find fascinating. I only jump away from the wasps once, spending the rest of the walk reading courtiers' lips and counting the number of holy guardsmen gracing the palace grounds. Once enough servants and courtiers note my walking about to solidify the impression that Lady Lianna is in residence, I claim a headache and return to my rooms.

THE FOLLOWING DAY at the keep proves no easier than I expected. Trace is busy somewhere but Luca decides I need to work on parries and spends two hours launching his practice blade at my skull, knees, and elbows. Again. And again. And again, until my muscles tremble and sweat drips down my hair and arms, stinging my eyes and making the blade in my hand slippery. Just when I'm about to drop my guard altogether and my gaze starts wandering to what other guards and roses might be doing, Trace strolls up wearing a pair of loose black trousers and a billowing shirt. His hair, usually hanging loose to his shoulders, is captured in a bun at the back of his head.

"There you are," Trace says, plucking the practice blade from my hand. "We're going for a run before strength training. If you are going to be of use, you'll need more muscle on you."

Oh, bloody hells. Bracing my hands against my thighs, I force salty air into my lungs. Three deep, calming breaths, and then I push off to catch up with Trace, who is already loping across the courtyard.

By the time I'm back in Lianna's suites getting ready for my debut family dinner, I'm ready to scarf down rats raw.

"How is this?" I ask Leaf, adjusting my throwing knives beneath my dress sleeves. The velvet is a rich, confident blue, made only slightly less fashionable by the shawl covering what should have been a bare back. My breasts, for once unbound and supported by a gentle corset, fill out the embroidered bodice better than I expected. The lines of the dress are made to accentuate my subtle curves, just as my makeup highlights my lashes, making my eyes and lips seem large. Pretty.

I run my hands over the wonderfully soft fabric one last time before pulling away to twirl before Leaf for inspection. Lady Lianna is beautiful and feminine and soft—I can't afford to be. Just as I can't forget that Lady Lianna exists for King Firehorn's pleasure, not my own. "Can you see anything of Kal?" I ask Leaf.

She adjusts the shawl covering my back and adds a few quick stitches to hold the cloth in place. That done, Leaf holds a tuned light crystal beside my face to scrutinize the wig and makeup I spent the last hour applying. "Not a trace," she says finally. "Your eyes even look a different color, though I know it's just the play of a brush."

I have time for a single relieved smile before someone knocks on the door. Leaf and I exchange final glances.

"Your escort is here," she says unnecessarily.

I draw a calming breath and open the door—and nearly slam it shut again when I see Trace standing in the corridor. Firehorn could have warned me that the same man I've been trading blows with the past two days will be the one gallantly escorting Lady Lianna all over the palace grounds. Bloody Firehorn and his bloody stupid games.

"Are you all right, my lady?" Trace's eyes narrow in concern as he offers me his arm. He looks as easy in his dress uniform as he did in his training garb this morning. "I did not intend to startle you."

I give him a demure smile and carefully suppress my instinctive hesitation, then lay my fingers atop his forearm. As before, the coiled muscles are alive with leashed violence, though now I'm quite familiar with what those muscles can do. A wave of heat rushes through my blood. *He doesn't know. He*

*can't tell. You are nothing to him but a royal brat to be escorted about.*
"Not at all. I'm simply nervous about meeting everyone."

Lady Lianna sounds like a simpering idiot. Brilliant.

Trace's eyes soften. "It's only dinner, my lady. Everyone chews and swallows the same way, no matter what station they hold."

I give him a tightlipped smile and allow him to guide me down the gilded corridors to the second part of my mission.

The dining room is heavy with velvet curtains, deep wood, and cushioned chairs. A long table, already full, extends the length of the room, candle-filled chandeliers reflecting in its polished surface. At the far end of the room, a trio of violinists sets an intimate ambiance. When Trace releases me to take up his place among other guards standing against the wall, I immediately miss the solid platform of his arm. My heart speeds, longing for the shadows. But there is no place to hide.

Standing alone before a table of finely dressed strangers, I feel naked.

A girl in Everett colors, who can only be Princess Raza, looks up at me. She is breathtakingly beautiful, with a thick, shining blond braid and emerald eyes. Her earrings, chosen to offset her irises' deep green hues, reflect the candlelight in imitation of living crystals—a subtle insult to Dansil. A diplomat, Raza is not.

The princess's eyes stay on me long enough that I've the odd sensation of being measured. An echo of the manner in which boys' gazes weigh Kal. Competition. I just wish the princess would bother to inform me of what we are competing for. Or how.

"Ah, Lady Lianna," says the king, following the girl's gaze. He waves me forward and directs the attention of the diners seated beside him. "Allow me to introduce my niece, Lady Lianna, who's just arrived at court." In royal families, "niece" is a loose term that carries little genealogical meaning, but it does signal me as some sort of royal relation. Which is how Firehorn can use the term without anyone suspecting my true closely twined bloodline. "Lianna, please meet Prince William and Princess Violet, Envoy Jajack and Princess Raza from Everett, and the leader of the Order of the Goddess, His Grace Bishop Bahir. I imagine the others will introduce themselves to you in short order as well, but for now, I thought you and Raza might enjoy spending the evening together."

The other dinner guests nod their welcome while a servant pulls a chair out for me.

I smile at the princess.

"I never realized such modest dress and flat color was a fashion in Dansil," says Raza. She cuts a quick glance at Trace before returning her attention to me. "Is that what intrigues Dansil men?"

My cheeks heat beneath my makeup as I feel Trace's gaze join Raza's. I've faith that whatever Firehorn placed in my closet is appropriate for Lady Lianna's social standing, but tonight I was more concerned with hiding welts and bruises than bringing out beauty. Have I done such a poor job that my unattractiveness calls attention to itself? Enough that Raza and Trace have both noticed? Certainly, Raza's gown accentuates her perfect body in a way that no clothing could manage on me. "I can hardly say, Your Highness," I tell the girl. "I've always thought it was my poisonous personality that scared away admirers. But perhaps it's just my clothing choice."

The corner of Trace's mouth twitches in a suppressed smile.

Raza's jaw tightens, her gorgeous green eyes darkening to a storm. "One hardly excludes the other."

Besides Raza and myself, Violet is the only other female in

the room. Fourteen, and finely framed like her brother, the girl has plainly gone to some trouble to make herself seem full grown this evening. Her golden curls are perfectly arranged, her posture pristine, her lips painted. She is attempting to look like a queen but comes off a doll.

"How do you find life at court, Lady Lianna?" Violet asks, leaning forward.

"Don't bother your cousin, Violet," Firehorn tells her quietly. "Children are to be seen, not heard."

"I'm not a child," Violet hisses, but she sinks back into her chair at her father's stern glare.

I smooth the shawl that covers my shoulders despite the heat and smile at Violet. "To be honest, I'm so newly arrived that I find it all a bit overwhelming."

"Quite understandable," interjects the man sitting on the other side of me—Bishop Bahir, the second most powerful man in Dansil. With a full goatee cut to a point and coal-black hair brushing his rich blood-red robes, Bahir resembles a wealthy merchant more than a pious guide. His eyes, a dark brown with speckles of yellow and green, are uncomfortably intense despite an otherwise kindly smile. A heavy golden ring inlaid with a stone I fail to recognize adorns one of his fingers, which are manicured but calloused. "Do let me know how I might help you adjust. The Goddess embraces her returned children, for fresh young minds pave the way to our future."

Wil grins, his eyes filled with mischief that sets the hairs on the back of my neck standing at attention. "So then, Cousin Lianna, have you a thought on how Dansil and Everett might resolve their differences in the mortal world? Speak now, for by the end of dinner you will be so fatigued of everyone's opinions that you will agree with anything just to get dessert!"

I wait a breath for Firehorn to shut Wil down as he did Violet, but discover my hope to be in vain. When it's clear that

Wil's trap-filled question stands, I check my voice to the light, breathless timbre of an awe-stricken girl. "I would not presume to offer an opinion on so complex a matter, Your Highness. But I am grateful for the current ceasefire and hold hope that one day both our nations might peacefully prosper."

Raza folds her delicate hands in her lap. "Yes. Well, unfortunately, trusting Dansil is like shorting a whore—you never know how the night might end. The last time Everett agreed to pull back our troops, Dansil destroyed two of our mines in Sylthia."

The envoy's face flushes in shame. "Princess Raza," he says pointedly. "Perhaps you might take some water?"

She flips a hand at the man. "Really, Jajack, do you imagine that the king of Dansil can't speak for himself?"

The corners of Wil's mouth twitch in a suppressed smile. The brat knew exactly what he was baiting.

"Unless there is something I am misunderstanding?" Raza adds, batting her curled lashes. "Dansil loses Sylthia to Everett. Dansil fights a losing war for twenty years." Raza ticks the items off on her fingers as she speaks. "Dansil begs for a ceasefire. As soon as Everett agrees, Dansil attacks Everett's mines in Sylthia. Have I misunderstood something?"

"Dansil didn't attack Everett's mines. Viva Sylthia did," Firehorn tells Raza. "They are a rebel group, and we denounce their violence as much as you do."

"How . . . convenient." Raza empties her water glass and holds it over her shoulder. "Get me another one," she snaps at one of the servants.

I avert my eyes. With the Dansil heir a rebellious adolescent and the Everett crown princess a spoiled, entitled damsel, my fear for the future of both our kingdoms goes beyond military conflict. Lord Gapral used a heavy hand in raising me and the other scouts, but I'm willing to bet my life that even the youngest of his trainees is a more responsible human being than either of the royal heirs.

King Firehorn clears his throat. "Perhaps you might bless the meal, Your Grace. A full belly does wonders for both spirit and mind, and I admit that I have been admiring those meat pies for some time."

Bahir waits until everyone at the table bows their head, then raises his powerful voice across the room. "In the spirit of the Goddess, our mother, blessed be the food before us," Bahir intones with an orator's presence that hints at how this man of barely forty years has singlehandedly grown the Order from a scattering of small temples into Dansil's dominant spiritual force. Before Bahir, religious followings were as numerous and varied as the kingdom's towns. "May it strengthen our bodies against disease. And may it strengthen our spirit against unholy temptation and corruption of your grace. So say we all."

I cut my gaze to our Everett guests, gauging their emotions, while the others murmur the prescribed "so say we all." None of the Everett delegation look the bishop's way, their dislike of him palpable. Everett's late Prince Rune, who died five years ago at Viva Sylthia's hands, was a strong whisperer and the love of his people. Bahir's views on whisperers earn little goodwill from our intended allies.

*And given the delight that is Raza, it's little wonder they wish Rune still lived.*

Picking up a basket of rolls, I offer one to Raza. "How were you ever able to travel here, Princess Raza?" I ask in Lianna's butterfly-light voice. "I hear no child drought plagues Everett, but did the journey not pose a great risk to the crown princess?"

Raza lifts her wine glass and offers a smile that falls short of her eyes. "Some journeys are worth the risk. It's crown business—I would hardly expect you to understand."

I force myself to smile politely. "Indeed."

"Plus, I think Rune would have been happy to see me here," Raza continues.

I think Rune would have been appalled at the pretty monster his sister has grown into. Seizing the bread basket again, I turn away from Raza and offer the rolls to Bishop Bahir.

Engaged in conversation with the Everett envoy, the bishop reaches blindly for a roll. His hand glances against mine as I hold the basket steady, and then slides forward toward the bread.

Blinding pain explodes behind my eyes as the bishop's ring touches my skin.

## 11

*I* gasp, dropping the basket to the table. Bahir's eyes lock on mine, the specks of yellow and green in them flashing for a heartbeat with identical shock and agony—and then fury—before narrowing to a placid concern that mirrors the others'.

Servants rush toward me with water and cool towels that pose a grave threat to my makeup.

"What's happened?" the king asks, the concern in his voice genuine.

"Will you take some water, Lady Lianna," Bahir says, his goatee shifting with his worried frown as he leans closer to offer me his own goblet.

I raise my hands defensively. "A migraine hit me with an arrow's force. I am so sorry."

"Your handmaiden warned the staff that you suffer headaches," Firehorn says smoothly. "Is the excitement of the evening too much for you today?"

"Not at all," I manage to say, though my head is still

buzzing with phantom jolts. "I'm sure a bit of food in my stomach will set me to rights in no time." I sway in my seat, staying upright only thanks to Trace's steady hand suddenly cupping my elbow. I hadn't seen him move to my side. As my mind recoils in a toxic mix of humiliation and confusion, I catch the furious flash of Raza's eyes and Bishop Bahir's emotionless glare. My stomach churns.

Before I can draw a breath, Trace shifts his weight subtly to put himself between me and the other guests. "Shall I escort you to your rooms?" the guardsman asks, already braced to pull my chair out for me.

As much as I want to decline, my body's threat to fail me in the middle of this viper's nest calling itself dinner is too great to ignore. I accept the offered arm.

Once in the corridor, however, I snatch my hand away from Trace's forearm to conceal my trembling fingers.

Trace frowns at me from above, but only for a moment. His eyes are busy surveying the corridor's shadows, the face of each person passing by us. I've seen him do as much while on duty for the king, but it's different now that he is protecting me. Stars, he is good.

Unlike Kal, who is a sham.

We walk in silence. Trace's familiar presence beside me is steadying, even if I'm the only one aware of the familiarity. In my memory, Bahir's mirroring shock plays itself over and over. I swallow.

"What happened, my lady?" Trace asks quietly.

I rub the bridge of my nose. "I don't know. The bishop's ring brushed my skin and . . ." I make a vague motion with my hand. "I felt a jolt that seared through my whole body."

Trace's gaze shifts, his dark eyes weighing me. "Have you experienced such a jolt before?"

"Never." I shake the hand that touched Bahir's skin. The

pain is gone but the flesh still tingles as if asleep. "Do you know what it might be?"

A muscle twitches on the side of Trace's jaw, his fingers brushing the pommel of his sword. "No."

He's lying. I stop, forcing the guardsman to stop with me. My hand clamps on to his forearm. "What aren't you telling me?"

Trace looks down at my hold, which is too strong for a lady's touch.

I yank my hand back. His eyes narrow. Slowly, as if touching an injured animal, he takes the hand I just pulled away and brushes his finger over my exposed wrist.

"What—" I cut off my question, seeing the shadow of a bruise that has crept out from beneath my cuff. Bloody stars, I should have taken better care. An unforgivable slip, no matter how occupied my mind. There seem to be a lot of unforgivable slips when Trace is around.

"Who did that to you?" Trace's voice is dangerously low.

*You, yesterday. Or was it Luca this morning? I'm not keeping track.* "I tripped over my embroidery." I pull away, hugging my arms across my chest. "You didn't answer my question. Do you know what happened in there?"

Trace straightens, his face a mask. "Most likely a coincidence, my lady. Your headache struck while you spoke with His Grace, but the two are unrelated. I recommend you get some rest." He pauses, his voice dropping. "And if that embroidery trips you again, come tell me."

*What happened at dinner? – FH*

*The touch of Bahir's ring sent a jolt of pain through me. Has it happened to anyone else? – K*

*Don't be ridiculous. Next dinner in seven days. Be useful. – FH*

"KAL! THERE YOU ARE." Wil's head, followed by the rest of his body, rises from the top of the royal stables' hayloft ladder. He sneezes, grins, and looks around. Dust peppers the beam of early evening sunlight coming from the little window, illuminating similar flecks on the prince's shoes. "Though I'm not quite sure why you are here."

Because I needed an hour's refuge from the keep's crowd, an hour that Wil is now expertly spoiling. I was up late last night writing my report on the events of dinner, and my eyes feel like they're filled with sand. Stifling a groan, I wrap up the remnants of the bread and cheese I took from the mess hall and rise from the bale of hay that served as my chair and dinner table a few moments ago.

"It's quiet and I like the company," I say. In the main barn below us, horses whicker and knock their feed buckets against wooden stalls. The occasional hostler—one of whom is no doubt responsible for directing the prince to my whereabouts

—shuffles tack that forever needs mending. I tilt my head, the energy coming from the boy setting my caution on edge. "What can I do for you, Highness?"

"It's just Wil." He cracks his knuckles. "Wanted to see how you were. And how you are liking your new assignment."

I cross my arms. "I've yet to fulfill it, but I imagine I'm more pleased with the idea than Trace is."

"*That* part wasn't my idea. Plus, have you ever seen Trace pleased with anything?" Wil knocks the toe of his boot against the floor and grins like a cat with cream. "Anyway, he's off duty for the evening, and you and I have plans."

I tense. "We do?"

Wil jerks his head and starts back down the ladder. "Come along or not, guardsman," he calls back up to me. "Entirely your choice."

I curse and scramble after my prince.

"WHAT ARE WE DOING HERE, WIL?" I turn about the alley, wrinkling my nose at the stench of piss and rotting garbage. There is little here. A few back doors, trash, mud-splattered walls. My eyes flash between shadows, my fingers aching to stroke the hilt of my sword. There is no way in the realm of light or darkness that Firehorn would approve of this outing, but I'm certain Wil would have come here whether I was along or not. In fact, I'm certain he's been here before.

Wil pulls the hood of his cloak to further cover his face. "I'm seeing what someone might possibly want here. It's where the City Guard found Novan's body."

"Novan?" I tense, recalling my conversation with Firehorn. "The guardsman trainee who was mugged?"

"Murdered. Not mugged." Wil runs a gloved hand over a brick wall. "He was my friend."

I grab the prince's wrist. "Let me get this straight, you just brought the two of us to a murder scene? Are you out of your bloody mind?"

Wil jerks his hand free and stares me in the eye, his chest puffing up like a rooster's. "Scared, Kal?"

"Of course I'm scared. You know what your father will do to me if you get hurt?"

"I won't get hurt." Wil shakes his head. "I thought you were different, Kal. I thought you were like Novan. But maybe I was wrong. You can go back to the palace, all right? If someone finds out you were here, I'll say I ordered you."

"Wil."

"Forget it. Go home." Turning on his heels, the prince walks out the mouth of the alley. Groaning, I follow a few steps behind as he skirts the building and ducks into a pub.

"Weapons, lad?" the man at the door asks Wil, motioning to the rack of tagged swords behind him. "You get them back when you leave." Wil raises his arms in emphasis of his sword-free waistline. I unstrap my blade and hand it over, my throwing knives safely hidden under my shirtsleeves. "All right, go on in," the door guard tells us both.

I nod my thanks and stick my hands in my pockets as I step forward. The familiar rumble of merriment rolls over me like a blanket. Kal's spent a good deal of time in pubs—though, being in the countryside surrounding the estate, most were a step below this one.

Unlike the alley behind it, the Wandering Dog is as upscale as pubs come. The floor is swept clean, the serving girls are courteous, and the pair of strong-arms—one at the door and another standing watch near the back of the room—try to seem inconspicuous instead of flexing muscles in preemptive warning. The evening is in full humor, with many blue and scarlet uniforms in sight. I even see a trio of green-clad Everett guards sitting at the bar.

Wil freezes. I follow the prince's gaze to the south end of the room where, just visible in the shifting mass of patrons, Luca and Trace share a side table with mugs of ale. It seems the possibility of finding his own off-duty guardsmen at a pub that caters to off-duty guardsmen failed to enter His Highness's mind. My first instinct—to use this fortune as an excuse to go the hells home—dies after a moment of thought. If the prince fails to get his fill tonight, we'll just be doing this again tomorrow.

Luca rises, ignoring Trace's emphatic headshake, and starts toward the dagger-throwing targets that are attracting a small crowd in the pub's corner.

Gripping Wil's elbow, I steer him to a table at the opposite end of the room from Trace. "The hood covers your face, so stop fidgeting. What did you want here?"

He shrugs. "I don't know yet."

Brilliant. I signal the serving girl to fetch us drinks and drape my arm over the back of my chair as I survey the place. Conversations rise and fall in a familiar harmony, the topics as common to me as the rhythm of the words. It is instinct to listen to the chatter of the patrons closest, to read the lips of those farther off.

". . . so perfect. But so still. Not one breath," sobs a man trying to drink away the Drought.

"See how the brunette winked?" says another, who will go home tonight with a lighter purse.

"Would you buy a flower to support the Children, young masters?" Two young women stop at our table and hold out a basket of wilting carnations. I'm about to shake my head, but Wil is already reaching for his coin purse. Fine. Letting the Children of the Goddess have their way with Wil's charity, I continue reading the room—and the dagger-throwing game by the pub's west wall.

Luca is still there and losing terribly, but my attention skips past him to a mustached man with a mole at the corner of his mouth and a rose's scarlet uniform on his shoulders. Standing behind Luca's opponent, the man directs the round with the efficiency of one used to the task. A regular.

Except . . . I think I've seen him before. My gut tightens, though I'm uncertain what exactly is triggering the recognition or where the holy guardsman and I have crossed paths.

"Wait, wait, wait!" Wil leans closer to the two young women, who've now pulled chairs up to our table. "The Drought is a punishment from the Goddess?"

I want to roll my eyes. The rhetoric is well known; Wil is feigning ignorance for the sake of female attention.

Not that the girls seem to mind. The prettier of the two leans closer to Wil, nodding enthusiastically. "She punishes Dansil for consorting with the Dark God's disciples. Once we cleanse our lands and minds of their evil, the Drought shall be lifted." Her eyes open wide, shining with excitement. "We live at the very edge of a great battle, and it is up to us sitting here to ensure that the light prevails. What did you say your name was?"

I cock my head in curiosity, dividing my attention between Wil's answer and the mustached man's steady presiding over the dagger throwing.

"Liam," says Wil. "It's Liam. And who are these Dark God disciples?"

"The whisperers, of course," says the girl. "They helped Everett invade Sylthia and butcher our people. The Drought is because of them. What do you think, my lord?" That last is addressed to me.

Pulling my eyes away from the rose, I flicker my gaze into

the girls' baskets. A nest of glow charms—the most basic of living stones, with only a spark of magic—flicker inside. More trinket than charm. "I think the Children of the Goddess are hypocrites for simultaneously proclaiming the Drought to be the Goddess's punishment for tolerating whisperers *and* selling the crystals that whisperers tune."

Wil kicks my shin beneath the table.

The second girl smiles. "These crystals are made by whisperers who've given themselves to the Goddess's will, my lord. They use their craft to support her mission and balance the darkness within them. Shall you buy one and carry a piece of the Goddess with you? It will guide your way." Her eyes dance to Wil. "I might help you choose one if you'd like. So you always remember what happened in Sylthia . . . and our meeting."

*Sylthia.* I swallow, looking back at the holy guardsman, my memories churning and ordering themselves into the improbable. Yes. A mustache and a mole and that face . . . except my mark from the inn near Lord Gapral's estate was a violent Viva Sylthia terror monger, while this man wears the uniform of a rose and works to keep the heated game civil and fair.

I tap Wil's hand, interrupting his conversation. "I'd like to take a trick at the throwing knives. Are you all right here, *Liam*?" Wil nods absently, plainly more interested in the girls' bodices than their words. Judging the prince to be in danger of no more than a broken heart and a lightened purse, I stride the several paces to the west wall.

"Bad turn of luck, man," Luca's opponent is telling him as I approach, and Luca empties his purse.

I grab the opponent's wrist before he can hide away the silver. "Rematch. Double odds."

87

## 12

"Kal?" Luca shakes his head, shifting his bangs for a moment before they fall right back over his eyes. "What are you doing?"

Mustache stops clearing the target and looks over his shoulder at me. His face shows no sign of recognition, but that means little. If I'm right, our last meeting was in the dark and far from here. "Invitation only. Sorry, lad," says Mustache.

Digging into my pocket, I toss two silver coins on the table and wink at the rose who just lightened Luca's purse. "Good thing I'm invited."

"Then let us dance, little bird." The rose grins, and though his words slur, his hand is steady as he places his coin beside my own. "Three throws."

Mustache shifts his weight, putting himself between us. "Come back when you start shaving, lad. And you, Cameron, let the new boy be. We are all here for a good evening."

Up close, Mustache's familiar voice is quickly erasing any doubt of his identity. This man *is* my old mark. Yet . . . his words, his behavior, they little match the terror monger who wanted to burn a stable-full of horses and hostlers alive just weeks ago.

"Aye, and I'm having a good evening, Samuels." Cameron lifts his beer mug in salute to me. "Well, lad?"

"Don't be an idiot, Kal," a voice I know says quietly behind me. I turn my head to find Trace at my back, his muscled arms crossed over his chest. Luca, now flanking Trace's left side, nods along with his partner. "How do you imagine this will end?" Trace asks.

"Your concern over my purse is noted," I tell Trace, throwing him a stony glare before grinning at Cameron. "At your leisure, my lord."

Cameron makes an elaborate bow and takes the knives. The patrons gathered around us murmur, small bets being offered and accepted between them. Across Dansil, pubs are all the same. Sticking my hands in my pockets, I watch Cameron embed his first knife in the third ring from the middle.

"Five points," calls Mustache—*Samuels*.

Cameron takes a breath and hefts his second knife in his palm. A quick aim and step. He is either not as drunk as he seems or good enough that the drink little impacts his aim.

"Seven points," says Samuels. Luca groans.

The thwack of Cameron's last knife earns full applause. "Dead center. Ten points. Twenty-two is the number to beat." Samuels clears the target and nods to me encouragingly. "All right, boy, first time is always the hardest. Choose your blades."

"I'll use Cameron's." I step forward to the chalked line and, accepting the offered blades, rest the first one in my palm. As decently balanced as one can hope at a pub. I'm not about to show my real knives over a few silver.

"Were you planning on gracing us with a throw this evening?" Cameron croons.

Glancing at the target once, I sink the knife into the center of the silly painted circle on the wall. Whoops and murmurs spring to life around the game. Cameron's sudden anger ignites so hot, I'm half-surprised it doesn't boil his beer.

Pausing only long enough to palm my next blade, I sink it beside my first knife. The two handles stick out beside each other like butterfly wings. I reach for the third.

And pause.

Something is wrong. I feel it in the sudden silence, the watching eyes, the shifting of feet for better purchase. My jaw tightens as the word *cheater* whispers off someone's lips.

It wasn't the fate of my purse that had Trace and the rest worried; it was the no-win reality of a stranger challenging Cameron. If I lose, I'm out money. If I win, I cheated.

Beside the door, the strong-arm locks the weapons case. The barman puts his good liquor into the safety of lower cabinets.

Trace and Luca take a casual step toward me.

"Twenty points," Samuels says quietly. "Last throw."

Right. Taking a deep breath, I let my heartbeat return to a quiet steadiness. I need no help from Trace or anyone else. Resisting the urge to watch his face as I throw, I let my knife slip smoothly from my hand and don't bother to look at the target.

"Two," Samuels says quietly, then clears his throat and repeats with more force. "Twenty-two. Tied match."

The exhales of many breaths at once is palpable.

"Looks like everyone is back where they started," I tell Cameron, sliding Luca's coins into my pocket to return later. Cameron grunts, but I'm done with games for the evening.

"Not bad, cub." Luca goes to clap my back and then thinks better of it. "Will you join us? You've earned yourself a drink."

Trace's jaw tightens. He might tolerate—even teach—Kal at morning training, but plainly, spending his liberty hours with me is low on his list. Not that I blame him. Spending liberty time with Trace is low on my list as well.

"No, but thank you." Separating from Luca, I sit myself at the bar, angling a stool to watch Wil, who is still talking with the girls, and Samuels, whose day and night jobs still rub me oddly. Is a rose moonlighting as a terror monger, or is a terror monger feigning a Holy Guard allegiance? More to the point, how many Viva Sylthia members are hiding in plain sight, leading public lives?

"Might I welcome you to the Wandering Dog, guardsman?" A pretty blonde with a melodic voice perches on a stool beside me.

I push my own stool away. "I'm quite all right, thank you." The girl follows.

Luca, back at a table with Trace, salutes me with his mug. "Enjoy," Luca mouths, and I swallow a groan. Bloody stars. The girl is hired and paid for.

"I'm Sonia." Her fingers slide toward mine. Clearly, she has no intention of risking her business or reputation by failing to properly seduce a young lad. "You have a name?"

"Luca-killer," I mutter, shooting my benefactor a dagger-filled glare.

"Killer, I like that." The girl traces the curve of my ear. "Very strong."

"It is actually Kal." I push my chair back another foot. "And I'd prefer to spend the evening alone. No offense intended, Sonia. You are very lovely."

"Kal." Sonia plays with the name on her lips. Her smile is kind and inviting. She's about my age—my real age—but at the moment, I feel as young as Kal looks. Sonia's gaze brushes my hair and continues behind me, an eyebrow cocked in question. When the gaze returns to me, no doubt after visiting Luca, it's more determined than ever. Sonia reaches toward my thigh and the appliances that I am very much missing.

I block her hand.

Sonia studies me with the air of a cook determined to pluck an evasive chicken. "Will you take a walk with me, Kal? I could do with a bit of air." She grabs my collar and pulls me none too gently toward the back until the sounds of rutting applause from the onlookers make it impossible to do anything but follow. Bloody Wil, my last line of defense, gives me a thumbs-up.

In a moment, the cool evening wind is kissing my skin and the sounds of the Wandering Dog dampen behind the shut door. At least now I know what might have brought Novan into the back alley.

"I like the bit of quiet, don't you?" Sonia asks, all but pinning me against the wall. She places a gentle finger on my face, tracing my cheekbone. "You've not done this before?" she says kindly.

I grasp both her wrists and hold them a safe distance from me. "Whatever Luca paid you, I'll double it if you say we did it and . . . and . . . that I was good. All right?" I clear my throat, changing tack. "Wasn't someone killed here not long ago?" I ask before Sonia can return to her original mission of corrupting Kal. "A guardsman trainee, like me?"

Sonia nods reluctantly. "It happens."

"Got drunk and got dead?"

"It wasn't like that." Sonia pulls her arms from my grip and wraps them around herself, a flash of grief sparking in her eyes. "Novan . . . Novan was kind and not usually one for excess. I don't want him remembered as a drunk just because of one bad night."

"He picked the wrong night to change his habits," I mutter.

"He had a bad night," she says again, gazing down at her feet. "He told me that a girl he cared deeply for had fallen in with the wrong type of people. The day he was killed, he had tried to get her to come back and . . . well, rejection will put anyone in his cups for a night." Her eyes return to me, professional once again. "Enough about such things." She ruffles my hair. "You are downright adorable, Kal. If you've no wish to do *it*, perhaps you've some questions about *it* that I might help with?"

The questions I have are more to do with Samuels's trade than Sonia's, but I little want to raise her suspicions. Plus, I've had both Samuels and Wil out of my sight for longer than I'd like already. Taking off my cloak, I wrap it around Sonia's shoulders and place my hand on the small of her back, the way men do. "We should head back inside," I say, slipping the promised coin into her pocket as I steer her toward the door.

The greeting applause—unabashedly led by Luca—is enough to turn my face the appropriate shade of burgundy to support their theories.

"A strong buck, this one," Sonia says, winking in my direction as she returns my cloak.

Except I'm not paying attention to Sonia anymore because the table where I left Wil not five minutes ago is empty.

## 13

# VIOLET

"*A* valiant effort, Lady Violet, but I fear your answers slightly missed the mark." The tutor's words were perfectly polite, but Violet saw the disdain lurking in his eyes. They sat beside each other at a large, polished table in the palace library, the glass covering some of the most valuable tomes on the shelf in front of them reflecting the expressions Master Tril thought safely hidden from Violet's sight. The tutor had never liked her, not since it became apparent at an early age that none of Wil's cleverness had bothered to visit her. Even at fourteen, Violet's head ached from trying to read. The letters and numbers turned and jumped about the page like ants, and she'd grown sick of fighting this losing battle years ago.

Master Tril sighed, writing a new set of sums on the slate. "If I might ask you to concentrate, my lady."

Violet looked. The numbers wouldn't stay still, as difficult to interpret as the pages of the books surrounding them. She hated this place. The dusty smell of paper, the shelves of stories she could not read, the pressure of knowledge that hung in the air and mocked Violet's every mistake.

"*My lady*—"

"Why?" Slamming the chalk down on the table, Violet forced Tril to meet her eyes. "Why does this matter? Give me one reason why you and I are here, wasting each other's time."

Tril flinched, for once losing the veil of patient suffering he wore like a second skin. The stunned look on his face was satisfying, if only for its honesty. He *was* wasting his time, as well as hers. "You are a princess, my lady." He cleared his throat. "One day, you will—"

"I'll be a valuable bride and a fruitful mother?" Violet finished for him, wiping her chalky hands on her skirt. "And will my value increase by virtue of knowing these sums? Dansil is at war with Everett. People are dying. Crops wither for lack of hands to work the fields. Infants are stillborn. And you think my knowing *sums* is going to change that?"

The bell tolled a late evening hour and Violet rose from her seat without waiting for Tril's answer. She had no more time to waste with him, not when there were people waiting for her in the one place where she mattered for more than her *value* as fertile royalty.

"What would your mother say?" Master Tril said to Violet's back.

She spun on the plush carpet to glare at him and buried the pain behind a growl. "As you well know, my mother has been dead for three months. When the spirits decide to speak to me from the underworld, I shall be sure to enquire."

AFTER THE GRANDNESS of the library, with its thick rugs and delicate books, the temple courtyard was wonderfully uncluttered. Gray cobble, circular benches, a statue spurting water, all bathed in the Eye's orange light. A flock of pigeons took flight from Violet's path as she approached the fountain where Dasha and Zalia waited for her, their unshapely red skirts billowing in the wind. A knot in Violet's chest loosened. Despite their promise to meet her, Violet had half expected to find the courtyard empty.

But it wasn't. The temple girls rushed forward, crushing Violet in a group hug. Dasha, the plumper one, bounced on her toes. "I'm so glad you came," she chirped.

"We've missed you, sister," said Zalia with more dignity but no less sincerity. Pulling a crown of wilting carnations from her basket, she held it out to Violet, as if presenting the rarest of roses. "I made this for you. So you'd know you are thought of even when away."

Violet bit her lip, weighing the distaste of laying the dying things on her hair against the offense a refusal might give. Plainly, Zalia was proud of the gift, and Violet felt obligated to reciprocate the kind gesture. Especially after Zalia had called her sister—not Princess or Highness, but *sister*.

"It's perfect. Just perfect!" Dasha squealed as Violet settled the monstrosity onto her head and inclined it in gratitude.

"I apologize for my lateness—"

Zalia placed a finger against Violet's lips. "That was the Dark God's fault, not yours," she said, linking her arm through Violet's elbow. "He felt the Goddess's pull on you and tried to impede your coming. I'm pleased to see you fought him off."

Violet blushed. She'd meant to leave directly after Tril's lesson but had started working on the stuffed pup's nose to calm herself and lost track of time. In the end, she'd missed the candle mark by a whole finger's width. "I don't think I can lay blame too far from my own feet this time," she confessed sheepishly. "I was in the middle of something and forgot myself."

Zalia patted her arm. "That's how the Dark God acts, sister. Interfering with us through things and thoughts and, worst of all," her voice dropped, "through the people we love. The Dark God is cunning, you see, but the Goddess is stronger. And so are you."

Violet thought of the puppy, now securely hidden in a wooden box beneath the loose floorboard in her bedchamber. Whatever schemes the Dark God meddled in, they could not possibly involve tiny plush puppies with happy eyes. Not that she was about to argue the point.

"Come on, you two," Zalia tugged on Violet's arm. "Brother Joshua is waiting for us and we should not keep him longer than we must."

Violet stopped, her brows knitting together. "Who is Brother Joshua? I . . . I thought it would be just us three. That you wished to talk together again."

Zalia pulled her arm free of Violet's elbow and frowned. "Of course we wish to talk with you. You are open minded and smart, and you catch on fast as a hawk. But do you not wish to hear our thoughts as well?" Hurt flickered in Zalia's eyes.

Violet held up her palms. "Of course I do, Zalia. We are friends. But who is Joshua?"

"Just someone who leads evening discussions." Zalia smiled, putting her arm back through Violet's. "We listen and we talk. And we want you to be a part of it too. Please?"

"It will be interesting." Dasha's voice was a warm, husky alto to Zalia's soprano. "Plus, the other sisters and brothers have been begging to meet our new friend for days. Won't you indulge them for a bit?"

Shrugging with resignation, Violet followed the girls to the wooden temple doors. Zalia *had* made her a crown, hideous as it was, and the need to do something nice in return chafed uncomfortably. If her joining them for an evening talk would make Zalia and Dasha happy, Violet was willing to try. For her friends.

The temple being the roses' domain, Violet's royal guard detail unhappily peeled away to remain outside.

"The Goddess's love and soldiers will protect us all," Zalia said to the guards as they walked past. "Fear not."

The door shut behind them with a windy thud that made Violet jump. One moment she was in the open air with her guards and the pigeons and the sun, and the next she was here, in this quiet sacred place that cocooned her in its damp, dark womb. Violet traced her fingers along the cool stone wall as she followed the girls down flight after flight of stairs that she'd never imagined existed in the temple. Living stones the size of ripe grapefruits bathed the passage in rich, colorful lights of orange and red and green. Stopping on a landing for breath, Violet frowned at the still-descending stairway. "Where are we going?"

"To the Order's sacred rooms," Zalia said, offering Violet her hand. "They are below ground, and only those invited may go inside. It's only a bit farther." A single door waited for them at the bottom of the steps. Zalia opened it with a key, revealing a long hallway with doors and corridors bending from it like branches. A temple beneath a temple. "This way," Zalia said, herding Violet into a room beside the entrance. "We call it the Revelations Room."

Barren but for a thin rug covering the stone floor, the Revelations Room hosted a small group of young people, ranging from Violet to Wil in age, who sat cross-legged in a rough circle. They smiled warmly at Violet, as did the man sitting in the room's sole chair. Twin paintings of the Goddess and Bishop Bahir hung above a crackling fireplace, which bathed the room in both light and warmth.

"You must be Violet." The man, who was handsome despite his baggy scarlet robes, rose and took both of Violet's hands in his. "I am Brother Joshua. Zalia and Dasha told me what a smart, conscientious young woman you are. We are all most pleased you are joining our study."

Heat rose to Violet's cheeks. "Thank you, but I'm not so much joining as keeping Zalia and Dasha company for the evening."

"Of course." Joshua smiled. "Please, sit with us. We have been discussing the ways in which the Goddess has changed our lives and are just about to recount the story of the Messenger's coming." Settling beside Dasha and Zalia, Violet gave the girls a questioning look. *Is this really how you wish to spend the evening?* Both girls smiled eagerly and Violet schooled her face to polite interest.

Once. She would join them for this silliness once.

"For eternity, the Goddess and the Dark God have battled," Joshua began in a voice honed with practice. "And when humans came, birthed from the Goddess's love, the Dark God crafted a plan to turn them away from their mother. He sowed corruption and hate and disease amidst the Goddess's people. The Goddess cried, promising to one day send a Messenger to her children. A Messenger who would come when the time was most dire, who would pull the Goddess's children from the brink of the darkness's abyss and prepare them for battle." Joshua paused, letting everyone in the room ready themselves for his next words.

The energy of the silence crackled against Violet's skin.

"The Goddess made good on her promise," Joshua declared triumphantly. "Two decades ago, when the darkness of Everett invaded Dansil, when so many fell to the Dark God's temptation, when we truly stood on the abyss's edge, she sent the Messenger to us. And so today, when Dansil's resolve wavers before the vileness that Everett wants to bring inside our borders, we look to him for guidance. A prophet of truth. A general battling whisperers' attempts to corrupt our souls. A sentinel against the heresy of Everett."

Smiles spread around the room as everyone bowed to the paintings of the Goddess and the bishop.

"Is it true that you know him?" a younger boy whispered to Violet. "Zalia claimed that you had *dinner* with him last week." A few chuckled at the boy, who blushed, swiveling to face them. "It could be true," he insisted.

Violet shrugged one shoulder, the reverence in the boy's eyes difficult to dismiss. "I have dinner with Bishop Bahir every week."

The boy beamed triumphantly as if it were *he* who had shared stew with the holy man. Several others, Violet noted, subtly scooted closer to her. Faces pregnant with more questions turned her way. She shied back, her hands hugging her arms.

Joshua's eyes flickered to Violet. "Leave our guest be, you vultures," he ordered, his voice gentle but firm. "Perhaps someone has a personal story to share today?"

Zalia adjusted her skirts. "I do," she said softly. The group turned, all eyes giving Zalia their full attention and empathy. The girl took a fortifying breath, as if whatever she was about to say had the power to flay her bare. "Five years ago, I lived in darkness, spending my days tending a whisperer's booth, squandring my coppers on ribbons. I stood helpless as my mother birthed three stillborn babes. After the last, she refused to rise from her bed. And still, I did nothing."

Violet's gaze shot to Zalia's. She'd known nothing of this, and now, hearing the words . . . The image of Violet's own mother brushed her mind and stung her eyes. She reached out to pat Zalia's knee, as others were already doing.

Zalia caught Violet's hand and squeezed it before continuing. "One day, I came home to find that my mother had spilled her own blood. I was so lost, so alone. I would have done the same had the Messenger not found me and brought me here, to my True Family." Her voice rose, strength and pride slowly replacing despair. "The hope and love you all gave me pulled together my broken pieces. You empowered me to stand against the Dark God, to be a soldier in the fight to stop the Drought, heralding the Goddess's victory in the coming dual. I want to thank you."

Applause came from everyone in the group. Several of the girls rose to give Zalia hugs while the boys nodded in approval.

It was an odd kind of thing, the way they cared for one another like a family would. Or at least, how Violet imagined a family would, since neither her father nor her brother much concerned themselves with her thoughts and words. Not like this. "What's a True Family?" Violet heard herself ask.

"Us." Zalia smiled at her before looking at Joshua to explain.

"When the Goddess sent her Messenger," Joshua said, "she told him to assemble the True Family together, the children whose hearts are pure enough to channel her love and whose spirits are brave enough to fight for a better world."

"That's us," Zalia whispered into Violet's ear.

"The Children of the Goddess are born to different birth parents," Joshua continued, looking into Violet's eyes, "but they all feel the pull to their True Family. Like you did."

Joshua's words hit Violet's chest, taking her breath with their surety. "Me?" She shook her head quickly. "No, I—"

"Is your heart tainted with the Dark God's evil?" Joshua asked gently.

"No," said Violet. That much she was certain of.

He smiled. "I thought as much. And we know your spirit is

brave, for you came here today. Is that not so?" She nodded shyly, blushing at the compliment. "Now tell me this, Violet," said Joshua, leaning in toward her, their gazes once more locked as if there was nothing more important in the world than this moment. Than her. "And think deep down before you answer. Do you want to *really* understand what's happening? Is one of your goals to find a way to truly help the world?"

Violet's whisper rustled on her tongue. "Yes," she said, and meant it. "Yes."

## 14

## KALI

*M*y heart lurches, blood pounding hard against my temples as I survey the Wandering Dog. Wil is gone, as are the two girls, the Children of the Goddess. The knife-throwing targets are clean and cleared, with neither Samuels nor Cameron in sight. Stars.

Ignoring Sonia's farewells and praises, I shove a path toward the door and sprint outside without pausing to retrieve my weapon from the doorman. My mind roars, my eyes roving the dim streets for any sign of the prince. Even here in the city, many of the shops stand abandoned, like monuments to a dying people. Soldiers defending the border from Everett, women in childbed, babies who never drew breath. Firehorn is right, we need peace with Everett, peace and so much more. A trio of shadowy figures disappears around a corner two blocks up. I sprint after them, only to run into three men who are none too pleased at my intrusion.

I stomp away, catching my jagged breath. If the prince gets hurt tonight, Leaf is dead. I'm sure of it.

The back of my neck tightens in warning a moment before a rock-hard hand clamps on to my shoulder. I duck away and spin, my knives out and ready.

The man spins with me, as if he knew exactly what I'd do. His hands capture my wrists like shackles as he spins me toward him. "Kal, it's me." Trace's dark eyes grip mine, calm and steady. "What's wrong?"

I struggle against his hold. There is no time. Wil couldn't have gotten far yet, but "not far" is a quickly moving target and, unlike a forest, the cobblestone streets leave few signs to track by.

"Kal." Trace shakes me, though his voice remains even. "What's happened?"

My blood sprints in my veins, my words coming in a sputter. "I believe Viva Sylthia kidnapped the prince."

"Take a breath." An order. When my body obeys, Trace nods in approval. "Now, report what we have."

Trace is so certain of himself that I open my mouth to respond before my mind finally catches up. What *we* have? There is no *we*. Like Lady Lianna's family dinner parties, Kal's presence in the Royal Guard is just a cover. Trace, Luca, the other guards, they are but chess pieces on my scouting board. They aren't allies; scouts have no allies. I'm on assignment from Lord Gapral and the king, and I work alone.

I'm also neck-deep in trouble and sinking fast.

"I won't punish you for telling me the truth," Trace says quietly.

I stare at him incredulously. "The prince's bloody life is in danger and you seriously think I'm worried about you punishing me?" The words are out before I can catch them.

Trace's brow cocks in surprise, but then he offers a small, apologetic bow. "Point well taken." He sighs. "I know the measure of the man you are, Kal. Tell me what you have before you and we will work through it."

Mostly what I have is a lack of options. I've lost the crown prince, and every moment I waste trying to discover what Trace already knows about this city is a moment Wil could be dying. As I meet Trace's gaze to explain, I feel as though I'm stepping into a carnival looking glass, a reality that grinds against every fiber of my being and my training.

"The young man I brought to the Wandering Dog was Wil," I say quickly, before I can change my mind. "He was at a table when I stepped outside with Sonia and he was gone when I returned. Samuels—that's the mustached dagger-game rules master—disappeared at the same time. I know Samuels to be a Viva Sylthia terror monger, and I suspect the two disappearances are connected."

Trace tilts his head to the side, studying me carefully. "Sergeant Samuels, your mustached holy guardsman, left with the other roses at the top of the hour. They had a shift change, like every other evening. As for the rest, come with me."

I follow Trace in a daze, back down the street, back to the Wandering Dog. Luca meets us by the door and Trace shoots me a *stay put* glance before outlining the problem to him. "We need to find the wee idiot before Kal tears his own heart out," Trace finishes, strapping on the weapons Luca retrieved from the doorman while I was sprinting through the streets.

"The hooded boy sitting with Kal left with a girl on each arm," says Luca. "And more than willingly. I'll check in with the mistress out back to see if they perchance paid for a room."

"Don't get lost in a room yourself," Trace calls to Luca's retreating back. He turns to me. "Kal, you and I take the streets."

Nodding, I step up beside Trace in tense silence, his

presence oddly reassuring. But reassurance isn't the same as a living prince. Within three blocks, sweat soaks my tunic and the pommel of my sword cuts into my palm, where I'm gripping it like a lifeline. Each skip of broken cobblestone jerks me about, the strange linear shadows of rooftops unfamiliar after years of studying the forest. Smells change with every passing door, from the stench of vomit in an abandoned alcove to a cheap brothel's reek of perfume.

"Get used to it, Kal," Trace says, peering into the door of another pub to exchange a few words with a guard, who shakes his head. "The royal disappearing trick is not a one-act kind of show." If Wil lives that long. My heart threatens to crack my ribs. I force my breath to slow before Trace sees just how close to shaking I am.

But it's too late.

Trace steps in front of me, and with deliberate slowness, as if careful not to startle a deer, he lays a heavy hand on my shoulder. My muscles coil, but his arm stays steady. "Young William is more likely in a bed than a dungeon. But yes, I know the danger is there. And real." Trace holds my eyes. My body feels torn between wanting to jerk free of Trace's grip and savoring the oddly curious sensation of his body heat caressing my neck. Trace's jaw tightens. "But whipping yourself over that spoiled little whelp's stupidity will change neither the facts nor him. Just as my whipping you for it did not."

An apology. I shake my head, finally jerking free. "Like I said, I little care about that."

Trace's hand lowers, his fingers gripping the pommel of his sword. "I know," he says quietly. "And I hope one day you will shred to bits whoever made it so."

Lord Gapral? I snort despite myself and start us back into a walk. Yes, us. Despite my best efforts, Kal seems to have found himself a partner. "What do you know about Samuels?"

"Only his name and reputation for keeping the games civilized. Appears decent enough for a rose." Trace turns to square the block, his voice back to its usual stoicism. "An unlikely candidate for a terror-monger group."

"I didn't say it was likely, I said it was true," I mutter, but decide against pressing the issue. There is no reason for Trace to take Kal's word and no reason why Trace's trust should matter to me. Samuels is my first solid lead into what may be happening in Delta, and the fewer people who get underfoot while I track it down, the better.

"Trace!" Luca calls, strolling toward us from the other end of the street.

I sprint forward to meet him, slowing at the sight of Luca's self-satisfied smirk. "You found him?" I ask.

"He's still in the rental room now." Luca's smirk morphs into a full grin. "And none too happy. Apparently, the ladies only took him up there to discuss the work of the Goddess and her Messenger. Serves him right."

Relief rushes over me like a wave, and I start back toward the Wandering Dog, only to realize that Trace is keeping stride with me. "It might be better if I retrieved the prince without you, sir," I say quietly.

"The hellion is all yours," Trace says, his own voice low. "But a word of caution before I depart—you go around slandering holy guardsmen, much less accusing them of associating with Viva Sylthia, and you won't live long in this city."

I tighten my jaw and glance over my shoulder at Trace. There are a lot of things in Delta that can shorten one's lifespan, it seems. "Do you know how Novan really died?"

Trace's lips press together but he nods. "Yes. A fight with a holy guardsman over a girl," he says with a resigned exhale. "I found a note in the training hall the following morning, warning the Royal Guard to stay away from anyone under the roses' 'protection.'"

The Holy Guard killed a man and morphed the murder into a message? Perhaps Samuels's dual loyalties are not as distant as I thought. "That isn't what Wil thinks happened," I say instead. "Did you not tell anyone?"

"And start a bloody riot? Are you insane?" Trace snorts. "Speaking of which, the details of Novan's death are not for the prince's consumption. We've enough trouble without that idiot deciding to go looking for either the wench or her friends."

Fair point. Except . . . "Why do you hate Wil so much?" I ask. "I understand the frustration, but it seems personal for you—as if Wil poisoned your dog. Why?"

"I've no notion of what you speak," says Trace, veering away from me. "Just keep your mouth shut and your piece in your breeches."

# 15

For being a murderous terror monger, Sergeant Samuels leads a rather routine life. After six days of watching him patrol the temple grounds with other roses, keep the peace at the Wandering Dog's games, and return home to a small house with a portly wife, I'm hard-pressed to say when exactly he schemes up plots to burn people alive in the name of Sylthia.

"Maybe he does his evil while Kal is shadowing Trace on guard duty or Lady Lianna is having evening tea with courtiers," Leaf says as I kick off my shoes and throw myself on the bed beside her.

The divine softness of the feather mattress envelops me soothingly. "I checked on him at different times and spent two nights just watching his bloody house from a nearby rooftop. Samuels isn't slithering to a secret meeting in the dead of night, and unless he is scheming violent plots with the Holy Guard in broad daylight, I haven't seen him talk to anyone suspicious during the day either. He has a routine and he is around other people all the time." I rub my face. I sent a note with my suspicions to Firehorn but have received no response. "Maybe Samuels gets his instructions through written correspondence—I haven't breached that yet. What are you doing?"

Still sitting on the bed beside me, Leaf has her legs crossed and takes slow, rhythmic breaths. Her hands clasp a crystal rod that swarms with yellow tufts of magic. Bit by bit, the tufts weave themselves together like slivers of coiled yarn. I touch Leaf's arm and the magical tufts scatter like the wind throughout the crystal. Leaf scowls. "Tuning a memory crystal. If woven correctly, the magic will remember the sounds it hears. A conversation, a song, anything. The base weave itself is difficult enough, but the trigger is worse." She shakes her head. "The bloody thing is only useful if it starts imprinting on command."

"Mmm." I close my eyes, fatigue making my limbs lead. "Where are you getting all these crystals?" The answering silence is too long for comfort and I pop open an eyelid. Bowing to Bishop Bahir's pressure, Firehorn officially ended all crown-sponsored magic study over a decade ago. The occasional servants or courtiers with the gift are not stupid enough to advertise it.

Leaf jerks her head toward the same catacomb passages I've been using to move between Kal's and Lianna's lives. "There is a small trove of crystals and knowledge beneath Delta. I'm not the first living-crystal scholar to set foot in the palace, Kali. Just the only one currently alive." Pulling a journal out from beneath a pile of books, she tosses it to me. I sit up and open it carefully. Neat lines of meaningless words stare at me from the pages. "It's written in code," Leaf explains over my shoulder. "I'm still working out what it says, but I think it's magical theory."

I fall back onto the bed. "If Firehorn finds out—"

"Firehorn all but gave me a map," says Leaf. "You think he just happened to put us into these rooms, beside a hoard of living stones and years of notes? He could have held me anywhere for collateral, but he wanted me here. The Drought is killing Dansil and the king is desperate for any ideas—even if they come from magic."

"Then why didn't he just—" I stop midsentence, the answer to my own question suddenly obvious. If anything goes against his interest, the king needs complete deniability. He can let Leaf work, keep me in line, claim moral superiority, *and* ensure both Leaf's and my silence without lifting a finger. Lord Gapral told me that Leaf is the more valuable of us. He wasn't wrong. "And have you any ideas?"

"Maybe. I'm not sure yet. On a different matter, however . . ." She takes the journal away and pulls out a handful of unfamiliar crystals. The magical tufts inside are woven into tiny intricate patterns that mean nothing to me. "Pick these up one by one."

I make a face, bracing myself for the horrid mix of tingling numbness and sharp prickles that crystals spread over my skin. The first stone doesn't disappoint.

Leaf counts to ten, then lets me put it down and pick up the next.

The third one hits me like a swarm of angry bees. I yelp, dropping the rutting crystal onto the bed. "What in the Dark God's name?" I say through clenched teeth as I rub my hand.

"Was that anything like what you felt when Bahir's ring touched you?" she asks.

I frown. "No. I mean, they both hurt, but it was nothing alike. What was that crystal?"

Leaf picks up the small orb. "Just a heat crystal, nothing special. But I tuned it to your blood. That is, I wove a trigger into the magic, telling it to stay dormant until it feels your blood. The fascinating part is that it felt your blood through your skin. Not only that, but it's glowing hotter than it ever has before."

A chill runs through me. "I'm not a whisperer."

"No, you're not. But you are something."

"What I am is a step away from being late for dinner," I say with forced lightness. There is enough complication in my life without Leaf researching more. "Do you imagine Princess Raza will be as delightful this week as she was the last?" I say, pulling a black satin dress out of the closet. This one is cleverly designed to let the slippery material slide against itself instead of entangling my legs if I run, while still underscoring Lady Lianna's soft curves and grace.

Standing in front of a mirror, I practice moving my arms so as to conceal the extra weight of the throwing knives strapped to them. Coming up behind me, Leaf adds a few stitches to the cape covering the gown's originally open back. The extra fabric feels soft and cool, while hiding the scars and lingering pattern of striped bruises that Leaf assures me still look spectacular. Short of the dress being ripped from me, I'm safe from inconveniently roving gazes.

"What do you think?" I twirl, the skirts floating obediently into the air.

"Stunning." Leaf smiles. "You look like liquid night."

"*Lady Lianna* looks like liquid night." I collect my body into a feminine posture—long neck, shoulders down and spread, my hip swayed slightly from a taut stomach. Each body part isolated and shaped. I check my sleeves one last time when Trace knocks, then stride forward to face the evening.

Trace bows when the door opens, his dress uniform hugging his muscled frame, and his gray eyes survey me efficiently, lingering a second too long on the extended sleeves. As if he knows I'm concealing abused flesh.

Which, of course, I am. An absurd part of me wonders whether Trace might also notice the rest of me, whether he knows that his own dress uniform makes him look every inch the formidable warrior. My insides shift uncomfortably at the thought. First I break the scout's rules of solitude, and now I'm looking at Trace like . . . I don't know what like. But I know that no good can come from it.

Trace flips his cloak aside and offers me his arm, his voice quiet and confident. "My lady."

I lay my hand on his sleeve, the hard muscles underneath shifting in a pattern I recognize from Kal's morning training. The scent of Trace's soap still lingers on his hair, tickling my nose. *Stars.* Soap and hard muscle. That is what I'm thinking about.

Tonight's dinner is being held in the family residence, which sits apart from the castle in the far northeast corner of the palace grounds, past the royal stables. Trace leads me out the back entrance before turning right to walk along the North Wood. The sticky scent of pine and the majesty of towering oaks form a backdrop of intoxicating wilderness. I draw a lungful of air, savoring it for as long as I can until Trace herds me inside.

Heads stare at me from the wall. Boar, deer, a buck with antlers that weave up like trees. "Wil and I fancy ourselves hunters," says Firehorn, coming over to kiss me on both cheeks. "I'm so glad you could make it." The king's mouth lingers by my ear and his voice lowers to a whisper. "First the bishop jolts you with mystic agony, and now a holy guardsman from the capital is secretly a countryside Viva Sylthia rebel? I'm surprised you managed to conjure up all that between

Kal's gambling and whoring. Have you gone mad?" He pulls away from me, his gracious smile disguising venomous eyes.

"If you distrust my judgment, why did you bring me?" I murmur.

"Not for this nonsense," Firehorn answers just as quietly, his smile as welcoming as ever. I curtsy and force a smile of my own as I glide to the dining table, finding myself once again seated between Princess Raza and Bishop Bahir. She gives me a subtly condescending nod, and he smiles at me, sickly-sweet and insincere. The man is wearing his red velvet robes again, the ring on his finger reflecting the candlelight. A rich ensemble that overshadows King Firehorn's more demure blue tunic. As he moves his arms, Bahir's wide sleeves flow and pool so artfully on the table that I'm certain he's rehearsed the motions before a looking glass. Godly, gaudy, and carefully presented—whatever else Bahir is, the bishop is a performer, and I'm hard-pressed to say where the man ends and the role begins.

"You are quite the student, Cousin Lianna," says Wil, digging into the meat course with an appetite to match most of the keep's trainees. "Both times I've tried to call on you, your maid has informed me you were in lessons."

I know as much. Moreover, as Kal has been on the crown prince's guard duty both days, I know *why* Wil called on his cousin. Some days, I'm unsure whether Wil is sixteen or six. "The customs of the palace are so complex that I find studies taking up a great deal of the day," I say politely. "For instance, I'm still puzzled as to the purpose of water buckets balanced atop certain partially ajar doorways. Might you enlighten me?"

Wil's eyes widen while the corners of Trace's mouth twitch in a suppressed smile.

Raza's eyes flash at the guardsman before returning to the

guests. "I hear Dansil attacked our heat-crystal mines in Sylthia."

"Viva Sylthia attacked the mines," Firehorn corrects. "Not Dansil."

Raza shrugs. "Many in Everett rely on those crystals for warmth. Quite a toll for a time of ceasefire, don't you think?"

"Abhorrent," agrees Bishop Bahir. "I will pray to the Goddess for their souls."

"What a comfort," says Raza, her fingers wrapping around the belly of her wineglass like vipers.

Firehorn inclines his head. "I've received the report as well, Princess Raza, and have already discussed it with Envoy Jajack." He rubs his face and looks wearily at his daughter. "Violet, you've not touched your food. Are you unwell?"

"On the contrary, Father." The girl raises her chin. "I'm fasting. It is my tribute to the Goddess." She casts a shy glance at Bahir, who smiles approvingly. Violet blushes.

Wil snorts. "The Goddess must be exceptionally bored to care whether or not you eat dinner, Violet."

"If we might return our attention to—ah!" Raza gasps as her wineglass shatters inside her grip. Eyes wide, she clutches a bloodied hand to her bosom.

Guests rise to their feet. Wil vaults over the table. "Are you all right, Princess Raza?" he asks, the concern in his voice surprisingly genuine. "Let me escort you to the infirmary, or shall I summon a medic to attend you here? It's a bit of a walk, I'm afraid."

Raza blinks, as if having just registered Wil's presence, and then draws composure around herself like a cloak. "A well-thought idea, Prince William, but please, don't disturb your dinner on my behalf. I believe I'm more startled and embarrassed than injured. Certainly, one of the king's guardsmen might escort me to a medic?"

"Of course," Firehorn says, but before he can make a selection, Raza beckons to Trace.

"Come along," the princess commands.

I don't need to see Firehorn's meaningful look to know that I am to follow. I give the princess to the count of fifteen before excusing myself to check on my injured companion.

My gut, or perhaps simply occupational conditioning, keeps me sliding silently along in the shadows instead of approaching the princess directly. Hugging the wall of the hallway, I watch and listen from the darkness.

"Where are we heading?" asks Raza, pulling up the hood of her cloak.

"The infirmary," snaps Trace, holding the door open for her. The fury rolling off him is as palpable as a hurricane, and the pace he sets appears more suitable for professional soldiers than an injured princess. "Where did you think?"

Raza's answer dissolves into the distance of the outdoors. Slipping out after them, I feel the cool night air whispering against my cheek. Fortunately for me, Trace and Raza are keeping to the path along the North Wood, allowing me to melt easily into the trees while we head west from the residence toward the palace. With the calm familiarity of the woods embracing me like an old friend, I stalk closer to Raza. I wish I were wearing pants and a tunic, but if I must find myself in a dress, the liquid night is a fortunate choice.

The princess's voice drips with disgust. "How does being Firehorn's dog suit you, Trace?" My gut tightens. Raza's tone is too familiar, her word choice too sharp, even for her. I wait for Trace's signature formality, but he says nothing. Not at first.

Then, a soft growl. "Your display at the dinner table is befitting a spoiled child. Firehorn is what's keeping us from war. Do you know what the world would look like with Bahir in charge?"

My arms crawl. Not a foreign princess toying with a handsome guardsman, but rather a conversation between two people who know each other. Perhaps well.

"The welfare of Everett—" Trace starts again.

"Don't talk to me about the welfare of Everett," snaps Raza.

"You are the heir to the throne. We can't not talk about it."

"I don't want the bloody throne," says Raza. "I want you."

I hear more than see Trace grab Raza's shoulders and haul her into the trees. My breath catches. I flatten against the oak beside me and, after a moment's thought, haul myself into the branches. Sprawling like a cat on a tree limb, I focus on the words being exchanged mere paces from me.

"What under the stars are you doing in Dansil, Raza?" Trace demands.

Raza takes a breath. When she speaks, the haughtiness in her voice is gone. "Begging you to come away with me. I thought that if you saw me, if I asked in person . . . that for me, you'd come."

Trace's hand cups the princess's chin and my heart stops. "I can't," he whispers.

"You can." She buries her face in his shoulder, wrapping her slender arms tightly around his middle. After a moment, Trace's own large arms envelop Raza. He rests his cheek atop her head as Raza's desperate, pleading whisper rushes into the wind. "Please. For me. Choose *me*. Please."

"Shhh." Trace smooths his palm over Raza's head in a way that says he's done it so many, many times before.

# 16

My fingers dig into the bark, my chest squeezing, crushing my ribs, as I watch the betrayal laid open before me and listen to the distant movements of patrols. *No, no, this is good,* a dark part of my mind whispers. The knowledge that the captain of Firehorn's personal guard is bedding the daughter of his enemy is a powerful weapon. One that might one day keep Leaf safe. My jaw tightens.

On the ground below, Trace's body suddenly stiffens, his head rising like a hawk's. "Quiet," he orders, pushing the princess behind him. His hand goes to his sword.

My heart stops.

But Trace steps away from where I'm hiding.

I focus my gaze on the ground beyond and listen, trying to discern which of the many unfamiliar sounds has unsettled the guard. Only the footsteps of the patrol I heard earlier disturb the silence.

Or maybe not a patrol. Trace's lethal stance gives credence

to my thought. That, and the arrow that embeds itself in a tree inches from Raza's head.

*Stars.*

Raza opens her mouth to scream as four men pounce on her and Trace. My throwing knives are in my hand in an instant. Trace cuts down one of the attackers as my knife lodges itself in the throat of another. In the moonlight, the blood gurgling down his shirt looks like oil. The third and fourth men have long daggers and circle Trace like enraged coyotes.

"Run," Trace orders Raza as he lunges at the remaining assailants.

The Everett princess scrambles back, tripping over the bloodied corpse of my victim. She screams and the attackers' heads snap toward her.

My fingers close around my second blade, but I don't have a clear line for a throw. Cursing, I slide to the ground—my dress floating to my ears in the process—and sprint the dozen paces to the melee. I grab Raza around the waist. "Move," I hiss to the princess.

"Trace," she breathes.

"Trace can take care of himself," I snap, half supporting, half dragging the shaking Raza away from the fight. Depositing the girl behind a large tree trunk surrounded by leafy foliage, I leave her to the relative safety of the concealment while I check for more visitors.

"Who are they?" Raza asks between sobs.

"Do I look like I collected calling cards? Stay down."

I circle back to the initial ambush point in time to see Trace take down his final foe with a vicious cut across the man's chest. My eyes race over the fallen bodies, trying to put words to something that feels wrong. "No bow," I breathe. "Where is the bloody bow?"

Trace freezes, his eyes burning into me in the darkness. "Lady Lianna?"

"Yes, pay attention," I snap at him. "Someone shot an arrow but none of the bodies have a bow."

Trace brings his bloodied sword to ready guard, sweeping me protectively behind him with his arm. "What are you doing here?"

"Saving your hide, apparently." I step away to snatch a sword from one of the fallen attackers, wrinkling my nose as I wipe the blade on my satin dress. Part of me is as bewildered by Lady Lianna's appearance in the middle of this mess as Trace is. I try to imagine myself as Kal, only to find the air flowing too freely beneath my skirts and the weight of Lianna's wig distracting. I shove both identities aside and return to stand back to back with Trace, feeling his motions and complementing them with my own. Stars, the man moves like water. He's been holding back in Kal's training sessions. A lot.

"What . . . No. Later." Trace draws a breath before steadying his voice to a stoic briskness. "Are you injured?"

"I'd call it shocked." I cut my gaze between tree branches. "I hadn't taken you for the princess type."

A growl vibrates through his body. "That is not what I meant."

"Down!" It's all I have time to shout before the nocked arrow I spotted in the foliage explodes from its string. I roll to the side, coming up on one knee and nearly tripping on the hem of Lianna's dress as I launch a dagger into the archer's nest.

He must little appreciate the gesture, because his next arrow cuts across my neck. Gritting my teeth, I loose my final dagger into the leaves and the archer topples to the ground.

Trace strides forward and presses the tip of his blade against the man's throat. "Who are you?"

"The voice of salvation," the man hisses. I take the five steps toward them and rip the shirt from his shoulder. He grunts. "What, not even a drink first?"

Using his own shirt, I wipe the man's blood off his chest until I can see his skin. And the flame tattooed over his heart. "Viva Sylthia," I tell Trace. *Stars take me.*

A distant thumping of boots has me reaching for my sword, but Trace bellows our location into the night. "Guard patrol," he says to me quickly. "Where is the princess?"

"In a bush." Twisting, I stride back to where I left Raza and pull her from the foliage. Keeping the giant tree between Trace and us, I lean my face close to hers. "Who knew you planned to lead your lover here today?"

"What?" Raza's eyes are wide.

Grabbing the front of her dress, I shake her like a doll. "You broke the glass on purpose, to leave dinner alone with Trace." I swallow bubbling anger. "Who knew of your plan?"

"No one! Let go of me." She digs her nails into the webbing of my hand.

I hold on. "Your lover has a prisoner. I'd recommend not rushing into Trace's arms unless you want said prisoner selling that detail to anyone who will listen. Understand?" She scowls at me but nods, comprehension blooming in her eyes. When I release her, she walks toward Trace at a dignified pace, stopping well short of the guard.

"Are you all right, Princess?" he asks formally, though his eyes scan her for hints of injury. "A patrol will be here any moment to escort you where you wish."

"You summoned?" Luca's voice breaks the tree line, another four guards trailing behind him. Striding onto our makeshift battlefield, Luca takes in the carnage and whistles. "Stars, Trace. Have you no other way to impress the ladies but to take down five men by yourself? What happened?"

"Take the prisoner, Luca," Trace orders. "And have one of your men see to Princess Raza. Lady Lianna—"

"I'll have someone escort me home," I say, backing away from the mess with my palms raised in the air while I scan the other guards' faces to pick out the least attentive man. Lianna's eye makeup runs down my face in streams of black kohl, and the wig is close to toppling from my head altogether. At least my desire for a hood and shadow will be a simple sell. "Perhaps—"

"I'll escort you, my lady." Trace stalks up to me before I can finish my thought.

My heart pounds against my chest, my soul stinging. "I would prefer someone else. Better yet," I lower my voice, "I'll escort myself." I turn my back to Trace and stride with purpose deeper into the shaded woods, ignoring his call to wait. It's all I can do not to bolt at a full run.

I'm ten paces away from the assault point, just out of sight of Luca and his patrol, when familiar footsteps crunch the earth behind me. A hand reaches for my shoulder.

I yank away violently.

Instead of flesh, Trace's fingers close around the cape of my ruined gown, and the sudden ripping sound makes us both jump.

My feet stutter and I stumble over a branch, the air nipping my exposed back as I fall to my knees. I'm up with the next heartbeat, my stomach in knots as I twist about to find Trace holding a fistful of black satin, his moonlit face frozen in shock. I swallow, summoning indignation. "How dare you, sir?"

Trace stares at the cloth in his hand. At my face. At my shoulders, as though he can see right through me to the skin of my back and the telltale switch marks he left on Kal not long enough ago. His intelligent face shifts with calculation and memory, his body stiffening.

I wait, every muscle in my body tensed.

"Who are you?" Trace whispers, his eyes wide. "Who the bloody hells are you?"

# 17

My chest is tight, my heart beating so hard that my body shutters with each pump. Never. I have never been compromised. Never been caught between personas. Even when Samuels and his Viva Sylthia bastards caught me near that barn, they never suspected I was anyone but the boy I pretended to be. This moment was never supposed to happen.

Except it did. With Trace.

"Who are you?" Trace repeats, his voice growing harder. Interrogation, not curiosity. "Why are you in Delta?"

I swallow. "Might I borrow your cloak?"

Trace's gaze remains on me even as he tugs loose the knots at his neck. Swinging the cloth off his shoulders, Trace holds the cloak open, ready to lay it over my shoulders, the way one does for a lady.

I snatch the cloak from his hands and wrap it tightly around me. The blue wool still smells of Trace, his lavender soap mixed with a male musk of sweat and leather. Who am I?

Who should I be? I try for the truth first. "I am exactly who I was an hour ago. Lady Lianna."

"Aye." Trace crosses his arms. "That's who you were an hour ago. How about this morning, when I crossed swords with a trainee named *Kal*?"

I pull the cloak tighter still, stepping away from Trace without knowing where the hells I think I'm going. Lady Lianna won't be outrunning a troupe of guardsmen, and Trace need only raise his voice to summon help. My hands tremble and the shadows call with their sweet illusion of safety, even as the wound at the base of my neck trickles blood. The blood is nothing compared to the damage a few words from Trace would cause. If he exposes me, I'll be useless to Firehorn. And Leaf will die.

My pulse flutters. "Can we talk somewhere else," I whisper. "Please."

Trace's jaw tightens, but after a moment's hesitation, he offers me his arm. I pause, my fingers hovering a heartbeat too long above the curve of his wrist, where the muscles curl around the forearm. It feels odd to touch him now that I've seen him hold Raza. Now that he holds Leaf's life in his hands.

Raza. Yes. I should be grateful for Raza, whose existence in Trace's life gives me leverage. Yet I find little comfort in the thought.

Starting us toward the palace, Trace lowers his voice. "How did you know about the ambush?"

My face jerks toward him, anger shoving away the shock. "I didn't know about the ambush. Raza's exit from dinner was suspicious and I followed."

"With weapons?" Trace counters. "How convenient."

I bare my teeth. "First, there is *nothing* convenient about this evening. And second, I'm always armed."

"Does the king know?"

I stop, pulling my hand from his arm. My heart pounds, each beat deafening. No more dancing. No more defense. Raising my face, I meet Trace's gaze. "King Firehorn is the one who summoned me here," I say with a flat coolness that I don't feel. "Royal scout, at your service." I sketch a bow, smiling without humor. "What of you, Trace?" I step forward, making him retreat to keep our bodies from colliding. "Does the king know of you?"

It's Trace's turn to swallow, the apple of his neck bobbing. "Of course not."

"And why are you with her?"

"I love her," Trace whispers, meeting my eyes, letting me see the plain truth in his dark gaze.

*I love her.* Such simple, short words. I've nothing to say to that.

Silence and the forest's shadows wrap us in their cocoon as Trace and I face each other, neither uttering a sound. One heartbeat. Five. Ten. Finally, Trace clears his throat and reaches up to touch the side of my neck, his fingers coming away slick with blood. "You are hurt," he says, "and we . . . Have you a place we could go?"


TRACE PUSHES after me into Lianna's suite and closes the door behind him, having the decency to color lightly at Leaf's gasp. He raises his palms toward her. "Lady Lianna is injured. I thought she might prefer to come here before the infirmary, given . . ." he trails off, frowning. "You *are* female, right? Not a boy dressed—"

"Of course I'm female, you bastard." The first words I've spoken to Trace since directing him to Lianna's suite. I pull off my wig—the bloody thing is uncomfortable and useless at present—and ruffle my own short hair in relief. As for Leaf, my sister needs no explanation for why going to the infirmary with my marks and bruises isn't an option. She does need one for why Trace is currently in our suite and I'm covered in blood. "There was a Viva Sylthia attack in the woods," I say briskly. "Followed by some inopportune disrobing and piecing of two and two together in the process."

Leaf freezes, the color draining from her face. As if the compromise of my identity weren't trouble enough, Trace and I appear to have barged in on my sister in the middle of research. Living crystals, books, and that rutting board with the charted magical elements leave little to the imagination as to Leaf's field of study. Stars take me.

My blood heats, my fingers curling into fists as I step between my sister and Trace. "In case I was unclear before, you will tell no one that Kal and Lady Lianna are one and the same. Compromise my identity, and we will discover just how kindly the king takes to his captain of the guard sleeping with an Everett princess."

Trace crosses his arms, composed except for a vein that pulses along his temple. "Threat little becomes you, my lady. Why don't you try a civil tongue and see where that gets you."

"Why don't you spare me your notion of manners."

"Why don't you both shut up and sit down before you bleed on the rug." Leaf turns her back on the battle raging between Trace and me and retrieves her medicine chest. She pops open the lid, her upper body disappearing inside the box. "Worktable, not the good chairs. Both of you."

Trace stares at my sister's back, a flicker of amusement touching his face.

I grip the cloak more tightly around my shoulders before remembering that it's Trace's. My fingers release the cloth at once and I cross my arms over my chest instead. The wound where the arrow nicked me throbs in dull waves, but I'll wait until Trace is gone to attend to it. "I'm fine, Leaf."

"As am I," Trace says, but Leaf spins around on us, her arms full of bandages.

"No. No, neither of you is *fine* in any sense of that word. And neither am I." Her thin voice trembles once, and she draws a breath before continuing with borrowed strength. Her eyes glisten. "There was an attack on the palace grounds, my sister is bleeding, and words that will shatter the lives of everyone in this room are being tossed about like confetti. So you two will let me do the one thing that is actually in my power, and you will sit on that table. Now."

My breath catches. Trace weighs Leaf's words for only a heartbeat. "Yes, ma'am." Touching his fist to his chest, he crisply takes the half dozen steps to Leaf's worktable and hoists himself onto it. His hand hesitates at the hem of his shirt.

Leaf glowers at him.

Trace pulls the linen off in one smooth motion.

It's all I can do to keep from sucking in a breath. The skin stretching taut over Trace's muscles is covered in scars. Scars from knives, from whips, from brands, from worse. In that company, the bloody gash that crosses his pectoral and disappears around his flank seems trivial. A blue healing crystal, like Leaf's, dangles against his sternum on a leather thong.

Seeing my stare, Trace's eyes pierce into me, daring me to say one word, ask a single question. I don't.

"You too, Kali," Leaf snaps at me. "And take that damn cloak off so I can see what happened."

I pull myself up onto the table beside Trace. Without a shirt, the man gives off more heat than a furnace and is impossible to ignore. I shoot a glare at my sister but let Trace's cloak fall from my shoulders, leaving my back and shoulders bare. The front of my once-beautiful dress is a mess of rips and stains, the sleeves little better than baggy satin rags.

Trace leans over and nudges one of my shoulder straps down a bit. I open my mouth to snap at the man, but something in his tight gaze makes me stop.

"When I asked who left bruises on Lady Lianna," he says softly, "the answer was *me*, wasn't it?"

I shrug, tilting my head obediently as Leaf steps behind me to examine my wound. "Might have been Luca. It little matters."

"It matters," says Trace.

Leaf snorts, shifting her attention from me over to Trace. The room is quiet for a few heartbeats while Trace watches Leaf's too-experienced fingers wipe away the blood and inspect his wound. "I see you've a bit of practice tending trauma," he says gently to my sister. "You have good hands."

She flashes him a scolding look. "I see you've a bit of practice getting skewered, which puts you in good company with this one." Leaf jerks her head in my direction. "Don't move, either of you. I need to get a few things."

Trace raises a brow. "Not easily cowed, is she?" he murmurs, watching Leaf pile sutures and sharp needles into a small metal basin with more force than necessary.

*My chest squeezes. "Leaf—"*

"If you don't want needles, don't get sliced," Leaf snaps over her shoulder before striding back to us. "Simple logic."

Trace's eyes narrow on me, his mouth breaking into a small grin. "Are you . . . Don't tell me you are afraid of needles."

My face heats.

Trace throws back his head and laughs. A deep, rich sound that fills the room with sudden, unlikely warmth.

"Are you through?" I demand when he stops for breath.

"Yes." Trace's lips press together, though his shoulders still shake even as Leaf begins to stitch his wound. Trace's fingers tighten around the table's edge, the only indication that he feels anything at all. "Given everything else that's happened, you must concede the absurdity of it."

I shudder and turn away, watching the fire until I hear Leaf's voice.

"You wear a healing crystal." Leaf cuts the thread and lays a clean linen bandage across Trace's muscled chest, her eyes fully consumed with her task. "Why?"

"A superstition. Though I hear healing crystals are unkind."

"An interesting way of putting it," says Leaf. "When a whisperer properly tunes a healing crystal, the magic transcends the crystal's shell," she explains. "That focused magic entering the body is what generates the healing. It is terribly painful for both patient and healer alike. The connection between healer and patient is what classifies healing crystals into the melding family."

I exhale quietly. If Leaf is rambling about magical theory and classifications, she must be feeling better. And if she is feeling better, I might be able to escape this table and keep from becoming Trace's entertainment.

"So you've no plans of using my own crystal against me?" says Trace with a tinge of sarcasm.

Now it's my turn to grin. If I know Leaf, that small jest is about to earn Trace an earful.

True to form, Leaf's face snaps to the guard's. "Using potent magic without proper training is not a jesting matter. You think living crystals are benign, pretty gems, all safe as light pebbles? That healing crystal around your neck? If tuned, it will produce magic potent enough to kill a patient

133

and break an untrained whisperer's mind. Stars be thanked that healing hurts, or else fools would be paying with life and limb for their recklessness."

Though Trace dwarfs Leaf three times over, he has the good sense to lean away from my sister's wrath. "Yes, ma'am," he mumbles, this time with no hint of mockery, though a plain sense of relief.

Seeing Leaf nearly finished tending to Trace, I slip off the table and scout my escape route.

Trace's arm blocks my path. "No you don't," he murmurs before raising his voice. "Leaf, your sister is attempting to make a run for it."

"I will kill you," I say through my teeth.

Sliding off the table to stand behind me, Trace gently tips my head to the side. His calloused fingers are warm against my skin, which suddenly feels naked. No one but Leaf has been this close to me before outside of combat. My pulse races, my body unsure whether to make a dash for the door or elbow Trace's gut.

"You are lucky that arrow missed your artery." His fingers trail from the back of my neck forward, stopping at the top of my collarbone. His quiet voice tickles my ear. "Leaf is right, though—the wound would do better closed."

"Go away."

He chuckles, his hands sliding to my shoulders and growing heavy. The bastard is holding me down, and my bloody sister is letting him do it. I grit my teeth. *If I die of mortification, I am killing them both,* I promise myself as I close my eyes to keep from watching what happens next. As the stinging pain of the needle comes, I feel Trace's finger tracing a small, soothing circle across my skin.

## 18

The following morning, my muscles vibrate with tension as I slip back into Kal's body and face the training yard. I've never worked beside someone who has knowledge of my mission, and I can see exactly why Lord Gapral ensured it so. I feel naked, my identity and secrets hidden only behind Trace's promise of silence. What will that promise do when it's time to cross practice blades, when one of the men makes a raunchy jest unsuitable for Lady Lianna's ears? Will Trace prove capable of carrying the act smoothly? Is he my ally now, or my adversary? Trace. My skin prickles at the memory of his touch along my shoulders, his warm breath tickling my hair, the scent of his lavender soap filling my nose. Maybe it's me and not Trace I'm worried about.

Stars take me.

The lush green training yard bristles with trainees lining up before the guard master and older guardsmen bringing out racks of practice swords. The air is fresh and sweet with cut grass. Squinting into the sun, I brace myself to find Trace in our usual spot on the northwest side of the yard.

I find only Luca.

"Trace is busy," Luca says with a shrug when I ask. "Viva Sylthia assaulted Lady Raza and Lady Lianna while you were farting in bed last night, so there is a massive sweep of the grounds planned." He settles into a fighting stance. "Let's hurry up and fight before real work interferes with sparring."

True to Luca's prediction, within an hour we are both swept up into a mass search of the palace grounds for lingering threats. To add insult to injury, the bishop's holy guardsmen supplement the king's forces, making the woods and corridors bleed scarlet. With Samuels amidst the search parties, it's like sending foxes to guard the chicken coop.

It's midday before I finally catch sight of Trace by the front steps of the palace, leaning over a map with other senior guards while wasps buzz above the nearby flowers.

"Might I be of service?" I ask, stepping up to the group on the wasp-free side, my heart speeding.

Trace's face turns toward me, and I freeze at the cold, dark gaze. There is nothing of the man from yesterday behind those eyes, and I wonder if I only imagined that moment of gentleness last night. "No," Trace says curtly. "Stay inside the palace grounds with the other trainees. It's too dangerous to roam the woods just now."

Heat rises to my face and I turn quickly before the others see the flush in Kal's cheeks. When I glance back, I find that Trace has shifted his body to efficiently block me from approaching the gathering, as if keeping a child from interfering with the adults' discussion. Or keeping a woman from joining the men's.

There is nothing left for Kal but to go, as ordered, to join the amateur trainees making a mockery of a search through the palace rooms. By dinnertime, my most useful—and only—accomplishment lies in having read the lips of a few stray roses passing through the palace corridors. The most I glean from them, however, is that the Holy Guard is giving the search their surprisingly full effort and attention. That, and something about prisoners, which I've no context for interpreting.

With the setting sun, I'm finally able to disengage from Kal's duties long enough for Lady Lianna to answer Firehorn's summons. Beyond the palace windows, the courtyard is slowly clearing off, the flowers somewhat worse for wear after the herds of guards who came through today. I am striding up the marble staircase that will lead me to the king's private study when the click of heels reaches me from behind.

"Lady Lianna." Raza's trot slows to a dignified pace as she nears me, her dress flowing around her like liquid flowers. The princess's delicate hand grips the railing, her perfect eyes studying me from their perfect face, and she joins me on my step. "I've been looking for you for some time, Lady Lianna. You seem to be quite the accomplished hermit."

"Do I? How odd," I say blandly, giving the princess a shallow curtsy. Trace's lover. This hateful little thorn is Trace's lover.

Raza grabs my sleeve. "The unfortunate events of last night's dinner engagement weigh on my mind. With Prince Rune's tragic experience in Sylthia, you can understand my worry."

I force what I hope is a sympathetic look onto my face, but if the distressed princess is looking for a shoulder to cry on, she already has one. I, on the other hand, seem to have become a rodent that the man intends to keep clear of. "No doubt the palace security—"

"—would have little to say about why you decided to

follow me," Raza snaps. "Or why you've failed to apologize for the intrusion as of yet."

I turn to face the girl and blink, trying to clear my shock. "Is this a jest, Your Highness?" I ask carefully, as if speaking to one slow of thought. "I saved your life."

Raza's sharp chin darts forward. "My life was never in danger. I had a guardsman with me to see to my safety."

"Yes, I noticed." My jaw tenses and I climb the next step. "Excuse me."

Raza follows, her hand clamping around my elbow and her voice lowering to a hiss. "I hear your uncle wishes to see you. Say anything that would hurt Trace, and I'll make you wish that arrow had pierced your heart. Understood?"

I shake myself loose from the girl's grip and stalk away, my skin hot with rage. I'm so very tired of being threatened, of being made to parade before crowds of people, of twisting like a worm on a hook before royalty. I'll keep Trace's secret for the same reason he'll keep mine—mutually assured destruction. Nothing else.

Firehorn motions for me to sit before I even finish curtsying. His face is drawn, with circles under his eyes that speak of deep fatigue.

"Do you think it was a setup?" He asks by way of greeting from behind his desk, his elbows braced on the wood. "The Everett princess creates a ruse, walks into a band of hired attackers, and uses the incident to pressure Dansil into concessions?"

No cutting words for me. No threats to Leaf's life.

I pull my brows together, choosing my own words with care. "For Princess Raza to orchestrate such a ruse, she would require a means of negotiating with Viva Sylthia. I know nothing to suggest she has any such contacts."

A corner of the king's mouth twitches, a flicker of

amusement lighting his tired face. "That was a very diplomatic way of calling me an idiot, Kalianna."

*"I didn't—"*

Firehorn shakes his head. "At ease, girl. I think the time for establishing our relationship is behind us. By now, you either understand my power over you or you do not. Either way, we've more pressing matters." He sighs. "Then perhaps the attackers were not Viva Sylthia after all?"

I frown, tasting his words for a trap. I find none, but my chest still clenches, this new Firehorn making me as nervous as the tyrant one had. Perhaps more. "May I speak freely, sir?"

Firehorn waves me on with his hand.

I draw a breath. "The attack *was* from Viva. At least one of the men bore the tattoo—I saw it myself. Is the prisoner denying his affiliation?"

"The prisoner is unconscious. My questioner expects it to be a few days before he can begin interrogation." Firehorn sighs again, leaning back in his chair and drumming a finger on the desk's edge. "But let us suppose you are right and that Viva Sylthia is behind the attack. Let's even suppose the absurd notion from your report is correct—that the Holy Guard's Sergeant Samuels is a Viva terror monger. Isn't it still possible that Raza hired the ruffians without knowing of their Viva roots?"

"To what end, sir? Why would an Everett princess hire thugs to attack her?"

"To force Dansil into apologies and concessions," Firehorn says without hesitation. "Why else would she orchestrate the ruse to leave last night's dinner?"

Stars take me. Our first open, respectful discussion, and I'm about to bloody lie. And not a small lie on a matter of little consequence, but a true misdirection. "I cannot think of a reason, sir. But I will look into it." Disgust coats my tongue but

I swallow the bile and try to steer the discussion back on course. "Might . . . it be possible that you are going out of your way to convince yourself that Viva Sylthia has not infiltrated your court, my lord? Why do you feel so strongly that Everett, and not anyone else, was behind the ambush?"

Firehorn's jaw tenses. "Because this morning, Envoy Jajack demanded reparations for the distress and now insists that Dansil is not negotiating in good faith. He threatens to end the ceasefire immediately and resume an active offensive."

"Ah." I lean back in my chair and pinch the bridge of my nose. "That . . . that is a very good reason."

THE PALACE SEARCH is long done by the following morning, but Trace does not return to training. Luca and I practice alone. As we do the next day. And the day after that. With my needing the evenings to watch Samuels in the wake of the Viva Sylthia attack, there is no occasion for Lady Lianna to see Trace either.

Three days pass until Trace finally walks onto the green grass, his hair pulled back and his face blank of emotion. Trace refuses to meet my eyes when I ask Luca to let me take the first sparring round, and when Luca nods, Trace returns my salute with only a disinterested flick of his sword.

Fine. It's fine. It's better than fine. I'm supposed to be working alone.

Adjusting my grip on the practice blade, I square off against Trace while the rest of the training yard clatters on through morning routine. The guard master's wet cough and rhythmic orders, directing trainees through parries and lunges, rumble across the open space. Beneath my feet, the lush grass is starting to get too tall for comfort.

"ANY YEAR NOW," Luca drawls.

Trace does nothing.

*Fine.* I send my sword sailing at the man's skull.

Trace blocks.

I spin with the impact, reclaiming my footing in a fluid motion that Luca drilled into me. My feet grip the overgrown grass, my knees bending as my sword tip aims at Trace's heart. My breath slows, in and out, as I hunt for the right moment. The right shift in the man's weight. A tiny opening.

*There.*

Blade extended, I throw my whole body into the lunge. Fast. Deep. Hard.

Trace steps out of my reach. Just *steps.* No parry, no answering attack. Nothing.

My heart pounds. Heat rises to my face, setting my skin ablaze. I swing for Trace's knees, his head, his shins.

The same response greets me always. A passive move, a calm shift of weight, a mocking nothingness.

My teeth grind together and I let my practice blade fly wild, leaving my right side open wide enough for a blind man to land a blow. I'd rather have pain than this silence. When nothing comes again, the thin tether keeping me civil finally shatters.

"Enough." I plunge my practice blade into the dirt between us. "This isn't training—it's a child's cat-and-mouse game."

Trace shrugs, the even cadence of his breath showing his lack of exertion. "I'm defending."

"Why in stars' name would I ever fight an opponent who isn't bloody fighting back?" I demand.

Luca clears his throat. "I'm going to go check on His

Highness's plans for the day," he says, backing away from where Trace and I glare at each other over a stretch of grass. "Send someone with word when my standing beside you no longer poses a danger to my life and limb."

Neither Trace nor I answer, our eyes still locked while Luca strides away. After a night of divulged secrets and three days of avoidance, we are down to glares across practice grass. Wooden blade still in hand, Trace stands tall, blocking most of the training yard from view. Not that anyone is watching. Despite the pairs working drills, the *clank clank clank* of practice swords, and the occasional dull thuds and pained grunts, the keep feels as empty as Lord Gapral's estate.

"What is this, Trace?" I ask, finally breaking the silence. "Since when do you dance around a sparring ring like a child playing keep-away?"

His face is unapologetic stone. "I will not strike a woman."

"I'm the same trainee I was a week ago. Nothing has changed."

"Everything has changed." Trace sheathes his practice blade with more force than required. "You can't honestly believe it hasn't. I will keep your secrets, but do not ask me to compromise my decency."

My chest clenches even as a small voice inside me laughs bitterly. *What did you expect, Kali? You think scouts work alone by accident?* The budding camaraderie between Trace and Kal was an illusion based on a lie of my own making. Stars, just over two weeks away from Lord Gapral's estate and I am already making the very mistakes he trained me to avoid. "It's your choice, of course, *sir.* Have you anything against my joining in with the other trainees in the morning? I'm keeping up enough farces without adding the illusion of sword practice to morning routines."

Trace's jaw tightens. "Denied. I don't want other men assaulting you either."

"Very well, then." I swallow and cross my arms over my chest, my heart pounding against my ribs so hard, I hear the rush of blood. "Just one question, if I may. Since you refuse to actually train with me, or let me train with others, what do you imagine will happen when Kal needs to defend the prince? Or is compromising Wil's safety for the sake of your decency an acceptable tradeoff?"

"If there is an attack, I will protect you both." Trace's nostrils flare. "Enough. I refuse to strike you, in training or otherwise—and if you classify that as a *bad* thing, I recommend you find the common sense you appear to have misplaced."

"I'll start the search at once." I give Trace a mocking bow. My whole body strains to stalk away from him now, but responsibility tugs at my conscience. My mission has never been about sword training—it's been about protecting the throne. I'm not yet so spiteful as to keep information from the man charged with guarding the king. "I listened to the roses' chatter during the post-attack premises sweep," I tell Trace with quiet coolness. Read their lips actually, but I'm not in the mood for specifics. "I've also followed Samuels these past few nights, and his conversations corroborate the roses' earlier remarks: The Holy Guard is planning for some sort of imminent prisoner influx. I thought you'd wish to know."

Trace cocks a brow.

"No," I add in response to the silent question, "I've no additional proof that Samuels is with Viva Sylthia. But I do find it irregular that the Holy Guard is transporting prisoners in secret. Especially when the roses' duties are supposed to entail guarding temples. Don't you?"

Trace's jaw tightens, his gaze flickering east toward the

Temple of Dansil and the Eye on its peak. "Do you know when these prisoners are expected?" he asks finally. Reluctantly. As if it pains him to share in my information.

"No."

"And the prisoners' identities? Origins? Numbers?"

"No." My pride winces, but my face remains steady as I wait. When Trace fails to comment, I prod the ground with the toe of my boot. "Well?"

Trace shakes his head, his silver-blond hair shimmering in the sun. "Stay away from Samuels. And the roses. If your suspicions are correct, your being in the Holy Guard's proximity is too dangerous. If they are incorrect, your being there is irrelevant."

The fire simmering in my blood turns to molten lead. I step forward, coming close enough to ram my index finger into Trace's chest. Coiled muscle beneath a blue tunic presses back, the subtle earthy scent of male sweat touching my nose. "The king brought me here—"

Trace catches my arm, his large hand encircling my wrist like a shackle. "I don't give a damn why Firehorn brought you here," Trace hisses into my face. "I am the captain of the king's guard. If something needs to be done, *I* will do it. Not a young woman. Not on my watch." Trace's nostrils flare and he lowers his head, his lips a breath away from my ear. "If you want to put yourself in harm's way, I suggest you shout both our secrets off the rooftops—because having me executed is the only way you'll get past me."

19

# VIOLET

The warmth of the Revelations Room wrapped Violet like a blanket. The hollow loneliness that had plagued her for as long as she could remember, the one that had exploded into a black abyss when her mother died, was slowly starting to fill with something besides shallow cuts and droplets of blood.

Friendship. Love. Hope. Purpose. Mission.

Kernel upon kernel, each gifted by her True Family, fell into place. Violet found it hard to imagine how she had survived as long as she had without the Goddess and her warriors.

"How has the Goddess helped us recently? How did she speak to us through her actions?" Brother Joshua looked around the room and leaned in, as if sharing a secret. His encouraging gaze stopped on Violet and his eyes smiled. "You know, don't you?"

She didn't. Worse, her sisters and brothers were all looking at her in eager expectation. Her chest tightened at the thought of letting them down.

"Relax, Violet. Let the Goddess guide your mind." Joshua's quiet voice was like a calming trance. "This is a search, not a test. Let the Goddess help you find the answer. What very important event happened at the palace five days ago?"

Violet bit her lip. "Princess Raza was attacked." The sisters clapped. Happy, giddy clapping, as if Violet had shared news of a healthy birth, not a near death.

The confusion must have shown on her face, because Dasha put a hand on Violet's shoulder. "It was a codex, and you recognized it for what it was. That is very impressive for one so newly come home."

"Will you decipher the codex for us, Dasha?" said Joshua.

Dasha nodded, laying a hand on her belly. "The Goddess was sending a message, reminding us that Everett is our enemy."

"Excellent." Joshua looked back out across the room. "But we must look further. What makes us *certain* that the attack was a codex and not a random trick of fate?" Taking out a large slate and chalk, Joshua wrote "PROOF" in big letters across the top.

A few moments of contemplative silence settled over the room before a brother called out, "The princess lived despite terrible odds. Only the hand of the Goddess could have kept her safe."

"Quite right," said Joshua, writing "impossible odds" on the slate, reading the words aloud as he chalked them. The Children close to the boy who'd spoken clapped him on the shoulders, the brothers using more force than the sisters, but all with grins on their faces. "What else?" Joshua prodded.

"Certainly, we should have more proof before we accept the attack as a codex."

The Children fidgeted, some girls closing their eyes in thought, others biting their lips. Dasha put her tongue between her teeth and stared at the ceiling. The desire to get the answer was infectious, pulling Violet into its sacred current.

"With Prince Rune dead, Princess Raza is the next in line for the Everett throne—the future ruler of the Dark God's disciples," said Zalia, speaking slowly at first but gaining confidence with each word. "Without the Goddess's guiding hand, the attackers would have chosen easier prey than Everett royalty. In fact, how could the attackers have penetrated the palace grounds at all but for the Goddess's help? Whether they knew it or not, the attackers became the Goddess's soldiers that night. Their souls will be rewarded."

Joshua smiled, writing "chose Dark God disciple as target" and "breached territory guarded to keep out mortals" on the slate. Cheers erupted again, this time surrounding Zalia, who basked in the praise like a sunbathing cat.

"Wait," Violet said, though she doubted her voice would carry amidst the din. To her surprise, the Children turned their attention to her at once, as if nothing was more important than hearing Violet's next words. She sat up straighter. "Aren't these signs—er, codices—contradictory? Why would the Goddess both send attackers *and* protect the target of their attack?"

Silence. The sisters shifted uncomfortably and the brothers avoided Violet's eyes, as if she'd suddenly lost her clothes and was ignorant of the accident. Violet swallowed.

"Sister Violet is newly returned," Joshua reminded the Children. "That she learns quickly is not a reason to expect her to know everything at once." He turned to her, his voice gentle. "What you call a *contradiction* is in itself a codex, Child.

One perhaps meant for you specifically. A sign that the Goddess wants you to think harder on her message, to really understand what her actions teach you."

Violet shifted, readjusting her skirts. Her thoughts itched, wanting to push back. "But—"

"You do *want* to understand what's happening in the world, don't you?" Joshua interrupted, his voice now stern, certain.

Violet nodded.

"And do you think someone who wants to understand the world should think things through, or argue on reflex?" Violet's face heated, but Joshua did not break his gaze. Warm. Firm. Certain. "Do you still *want* to stand beside your brothers and sisters, fighting for that better world, Violet? Or is the Dark God's path more alluring than the Messenger's? The darkness is admittedly easier to follow, demanding no analysis, no effort of thought."

"I want to stand with my True Family," Violet said quickly, that dark, lonely void threatening to return for her. "I don't wish to be the Dark God's pawn."

Joshua nodded gravely. "Then I ask you again, should you channel your energy into understanding the Goddess's message or arguing against it?"

"Understanding it," Violet whispered, lowering her head. As soon as the words left Violet's mouth, she felt Dasha's hand close over hers.

"It's all right, sister," said Dasha as others nodded in agreement, reaching out with sympathetic touches and encouraging smiles. "We all were confused once. But now we've come to understand. As will you."

Violet swallowed.

"Can you answer your own question, Violet?" Joshua asked gently.

Violet searched her mind, struggling like a drowning man

looking for shore. She had to come up with something. Anything. "Maybe . . . maybe the Goddess wanted to remind us of the truth as kindly as she could? And to encourage the Everett delegation to return to their own borders without provoking an all-out assault before we are ready?"

Joshua's triumphant smile loosened a knot in Violet's heart. "So you can see the truth, if you try," he said with a nod. "Keep at it."

"We do this together, sister," added Zalia. "Your True Family will stay with you every step of the way."

"Tell us what the world will be like when the Goddess triumphs," Dasha begged of Joshua.

The man smiled. "We will live in peace, as will our children, who shall be born healthy and strong with the Goddess's love in their hearts. There will be neither pain nor sorrow. Instead of war and hate, those who quarrel shall ask the Goddess for guidance and justice, which she will give with compassion through her disciples. Through you." Joshua paused to shift into a more comfortable position. "Now close your eyes and listen to how it shall be."

20

## KALI

*I* have little more to say to Trace, not after his training-yard declarations. From the sulky silence with which Trace now tolerates Kal's presence on Prince Wil's guard duty, it seems Trace is of a similar mind. Since we aren't speaking, I feel no need to ask Trace why he goes out to sweep the wilderness every evening. Nor do I feel obligated to tell him that Princess Raza waits for him every night on the opposite side of the palace grounds.

"If I didn't know better," Luca drawls three days into our new wordless routine, "I'd say you two are quarreling over a girl. And that she probably isn't worth the headache." The man divides a sardonic look between Trace and me.

Trace snorts, following quietly in Wil's wake as the prince strides past the stables, the mess hall, and the rest of his usual haunts for the third time since we started the outing an hour ago. A wind that's chilly for Delta ruffles the grass, the blades bending beneath its force. It's unusual for Wil to meander about, but today he seems in no more mood for conversation than Trace is.

I glance at Luca. "How do you know we aren't?"

Luca tips his head back and laughs. "Because the only girl who would be interested in both of you is a whore, and she'd have found a way to make coin long ago." He nudges Wil's shoulder. "Wouldn't you agree, Your Highness?"

Wil nods absently, his eyes on the ground as he turns our procession to skirt around the palace.

Luca frowns. "Where are we going exactly?"

Wil's eyes trail the ground. "It's just around the corner now," he says, his face pale and his fingers gripping the sides of his long, formal coat in a white-knuckle hold.

"Around *that* corner?" Luca's brows climb. "But those are . . ."

"The dungeons," Wil mutters in affirmation.

"Why under the bloody stars do you want to go to the dungeons?" I ask. After the evening at the Wandering Dog, I'm little worried about propriety, and Wil seems to be taking the directness in stride. Unlike Trace, who tightens his jaw at the familiarity. Because pawing a foreign princess is exponentially better than speaking plainly to your own prince.

"'Want' isn't the word I'd choose," Wil says with a sigh. "The prisoner who attacked Princess Raza is awake. My father has charged me with his . . ." He fumbles, shaking his head like a dog. "Interview."

I exchange a glance with Luca. I'm all for a bit of responsibility, but this?

"In that case, feel free to take another turn around the palace," Luca mutters. "Or five more."

Wil gives Luca a ghost of a smile and, squaring his shoulders, heads for a heavy door at the base of the round tower. A row of lanterns thoughtfully hangs on hooks outside the entrance and we each take a light before going inside. It takes Trace two tries to light his.

Many of the scars I've seen on his flesh are the kind you get in a place like this, not a field of battle. I wonder how many nightmares this walk down the stairs will cost him.

The yellow light cocoons our small group in imagined warmth as we make our way down the spiraling steps into the belly of the underground. The stench greets us before the sight, a putrid mix of shit and vomit, urine and blood, terror and agony. A pleading scream rips through the air and Wil stumbles, bracing his hand against the wall for balance.

"We should have left a guard outside," I say, catching Trace's eye. The first words I've uttered to him directly in days. "The bloody staircase is too cramped as it is."

A bead of sweat creeps down the guardsman's temple despite the underground chill. "You can go up," he says evenly.

"I'm not the one who takes up all the space," I say, adding the lifeline he just threw back in my face to the list of reasons I hate Trace.

At the end of the passage, Wil raises his chin and strides to the guard on duty. "Good afternoon," he says with a gracious nod of his head. Apparently the boy can be princely when he needs to. "Might I speak with Questioner Calvin?"

The guard touches a fist to his chest, little surprised at Wil's appearance in his lair. "Of course, Your Highness. This way, please."

We follow the guard to a dusty room, where mismatched wooden benches surround a low table. A shelf on the wall holds ledgers, ink, jugs of water and wine, and, of all things, a teapot. With a set of painted porcelain cups beside it.

"I will tell Questioner Calvin you are here," the guard says, touching his fist to his chest again before disappearing.

Wil, Luca, and I sit. Trace chooses to stand. Ten minutes pass. Fifteen. Half an hour. I'm beginning to wonder if Firehorn has specifically ordered Calvin to keep Wil waiting all day when the door to our room opens and a middle-aged man glides inside.

"I'm Calvin, Your Highness," the man says with a half bow. Loosely tied-back graying hair and manicured fingers complement the soft, confident timbre of his voice. "Chief questioner."

Wil rises to his feet. "Thank you." He pauses as if searching for words and, upon finding none, points to us. "My guards. Kal, Trace, and Luca."

Calvin greets each of us in turn. My gaze brushes past his thoughtful eyes and clean clothes to his blood-spattered shoes. He smiles wryly. "Ah, well. I imagine you're quite familiar with what happens here, no matter how benignly I dress. Tea?" Without waiting for a reply, the questioner takes the teapot and fills five delicate cups with steaming liquid.

"Were we waiting for the tea to steep?" I hear myself ask.

Calvin smiles and places a cup in my hands. At once, the strong aroma of the brew overpowers the other smells assaulting my senses. A veil of pretense that we are somewhere other than a torture chamber, speaking with its master-in-chief.

"Well then, Prince William," says Calvin, inclining his head respectfully. "I understand that His Majesty has placed you in charge of obtaining intelligence from a certain prisoner. Do you wish to question the man yourself, or shall I tell you what I've learned thus far?"

Wil places his untouched teacup back on the table. "I'm to do it myself," he says quietly.

"Of course." Calvin sets his own cup down and holds open

the corridor door, sending a shiver of dread through me. "This way."

We follow Calvin past cells of misery to an isolated corridor. An alcove with a bench and some water jugs opens unexpectedly and quickly disappears behind a sharp corner as we reach our target.

My stomach turns as I behold the man in the cell. Despite the bars, the man is also chained to the back wall, with manacles on his wrists and ankles. He snarls at us.

The hate and rage are the only recognizable remains of the rebel Trace and I brought down a week ago. Bile rises in my throat as I see slivers of abused flesh peeking out from beneath the rags passing for clothing. Even with everything Lord Gapral put me through under his tutelage, he never made me question a prisoner. I don't know whether the other scouts' training was similarly shaped, but it's a kindness the depths of which I'm only now appreciating. A wave of dizziness slams into me and I jam my hands into my pockets, focusing on the nails digging into my palms. Feeling a solid warmth beside me, I realize Trace has stepped forward. Our shoulders touch.

The prisoner's eyes focus on Wil's pale face, like a predator scenting blood. "Princeling."

"Hello," says Wil. The man growls and struggles against his chains, stopping abruptly when Calvin steps from the shadows.

Calvin nods to Wil. "Your guards and I will wait for you around the corner there, Your Highness. The man's chain will stop him short of the bars. Please call if you require anything."

I glance at Luca. *Are we really leaving him alone?*

"The king's orders," says Calvin quietly. "This particular corridor ends in a stone wall. I assure you that the prince's safety will be little compromised by you taking the twenty-five steps to the alcove."

I turn my face. A preplanned game, that's what this was. Following silently in Calvin's wake, I claim a space on the stone bench and search for some place free of the questioner's tools to look at. The crack on the far side of the floor is the winner until I realize it comes equipped with three fat cockroaches. Crossing his arms, Luca leans against the wall beside me. Trace stands statue straight, his fingers gripping his sword tightly when a moan ripples through the air.

Calvin's eyes dart to him lazily. "If you are going to be sick, there is a bucket in the corner."

"Tell me, questioner," Trace says with deathly quiet. "Which part of your job do you enjoy the most? The screams or the blood?"

Calvin purses his lips in thought, taking the question seriously. "Understanding how people work is most enjoyable. Finding each person's strengths and vulnerabilities. Learning how to exploit each to its full benefit." A thin smile. "No two people are alike, you know."

Trace's teeth flash. "We all bleed the same."

"Do we?" Calvin cocks his head. "You, guardsman, I could break without touching a lash."

Faster than I can blink, Trace grabs the front of Calvin's tunic and slams the man hard against the stone wall. Luca and I are on him in an instant, our combined strength doing nothing to shift Trace's hands. His lip curls, white teeth snapping in the dim light.

Calvin winces and, despite his feet dangling in the air, takes a moment to probe the back of his head. He clicks his tongue at the smidge of blood that comes away on his finger. "Ah, here you are, proving me right." Trace drops the questioner like a poisonous snake. Calvin smiles.

I'm unsure which of them I want to strangle more.

Trace's chest heaves. Once, twice. On the third inhale, he turns on his heels and storms toward the exit. The echo of his footsteps still sounding in my chest, I glance at Luca and nod at the question I knew was in his eyes before I even looked. *Yes, I'll be all right alone. Go on after him.* Peeling away from the wall, Luca leaves too. With the two guards gone, Calvin picks himself up off the floor. After expertly regrouping his mussed hair, the questioner straightens his tunic, running his fingers over the edge of the collar until it lies flat against his shirt.

I give him a stare. "Why?"

"That boy had no business being down here," says Calvin, turning his attention to his cufflinks. I've never imagined someone daring to call Trace a boy, but Calvin is comfortable with the word. He pulls his sleeves down straight. "Not with— excuse me, Kal," he cuts off as Wil stalks around the corner, his face flushed with fury.

"You'll talk to me," the prince hollers over his shoulder, ignoring Calvin and me. "You hear me?" Laughter answers him from the cell. Wil slams his palm against the stone and grabs a long-tailed whip from its bracket. With a snap of his wrist, the leather cracks the air.

Blood drains from my face as Wil turns on his heels to return to the cell. Before he makes it two steps, Calvin's hand clamps over the boy's wrist. "What seems to be the problem, Your Highness?"

Wil whirls on him, his chest heaving. "That bloody bastard thinks this is a jest."

"I see." Still holding Wil's wrist with one hand, Calvin taps the fingers of his free hand against his thigh. "And you believe this tool will convince him otherwise?"

"That's what it's here for, isn't it?" Wil bites back, his breaking voice a sharp contrast to Calvin's eerie calm.

"Sometimes." Calvin gently plucks the lash from Wil's fingers. "But I've some doubt that it will serve your goals just now. Let me fetch you something more effective." Returning the whip to its rack, the questioner picks up a water bucket and fills two wooden mugs. He drinks one, refills it, and hands both to the prince, handle first.

"What do I do with this?" Wil asks. "Throw it at him?"

"Share it with him," suggests Calvin, motioning the prince back toward the cell. I wait until the prince has disappeared around the corner before raising an eyebrow at the questioner.

Calvin raises one shoulder. "Did you truly believe it would be wise to leave the questioning of a vital prisoner to an untried boy, whatever his bloodlines? The prisoner was ready to talk before you lot stepped foot down here. A bit of kindness and dignity is what's needed now to loosen his tongue." He smiles without humor. "The games we play here can shatter a man's soul. I believe the king's intent was to teach young Wil, not break him into pieces."

I'm still mulling over Calvin's words when Wil returns to the alcove, his face a mix of satisfied triumph and utter bewilderment. "Princess Raza was never the intended target," he says by way of greeting. "The rebels mistook her initially, with the age and the escort, and it being dark and all. The girl they meant to kill was Lady Lianna."

## 21

*W*il's words echo in my head as we ascend the stairs. Lady Lianna is a fictional hermit, a bloody decoration. She has neither power nor enemies, much less secret homicidal nemeses. Why under all the stars would Viva go to the trouble of killing *her*? If my identity has been compromised, certainly Kal would have been a simpler target.

The confusion on Wil's and my faces finds its match in Trace's and Luca's expressions once we sketch out the details of the discovery to them.

"How do I tell Lianna?" Wil whispers, his forearm shielding his eyes from the sun. "How do I tell my cousin that the attack she barely survived targeted *her*? That she might be a target still?"

It's all I can do to keep my eyes from rolling. "Just tell her, Wil," I say, running a hand through my hair as my mind returns to the matter at hand. Perhaps Lianna was intended as a sacrificial pawn, a message from Viva Sylthia to Firehorn that his family is fair game in their wrath? Seeing Wil's dubious look, I add, "How to break the news to Lianna is the least of our worries."

He shakes his head. "Girls aren't like you, Kal. I have a sister, and trust me, I know. Lianna will be frightened but able to influence nothing. Perhaps the wise choice is to increase security but say nothing to Lady Lianna herself."

Good stars, why are we even discussing this? "I think the lady would value the truth."

Wil frowns, looking to Trace and Luca for support. "Might not the stress harm her health? With the Drought . . ."

"If Viva Sylthia wants her dead, they pose the greater risk to her health," I snap, finally bringing my full attention to the men around me. My gaze stops on Trace, who I realize hasn't bothered to speak up on Lady Lianna's behalf. "A person needs to have all the tools available to defend herself, even if doing so leaves a few bruises."

Trace's face darkens, his voice clipped when he speaks. "Perhaps Kal would have us invite women into the guard."

I smile, showing all my teeth. "Perhaps one might save your hide."

"Perhaps I need to work harder to ensure that never need happen."

"Perhaps you are an arrogant ass," I tell him.

"Perhaps you should remember your place," says Trace.

"Perhaps you two need a drink," drawls Luca, exchanging gazes with Wil. "Or several. And perhaps well apart from each other. At least, that would be most beneficial to *my* health."

THAT EVENING, I find myself back in Firehorn's study, examining the king on the other side of the desk. My dress, a silk number in pale blue, is a beautiful mockery of my thoughts. Watching Trace's cheeks color when he escorted me here was downright entertaining, especially when the silver chain along the curve of my hip drew several lingering glances from the male courtiers.

The mirth of that short stroll is long gone now.

"I don't know, Your Majesty," I say more forcefully than I mean to. "Perhaps the intended outcome was the one that happened: Injure our negotiations with Everett. Or else convince you that the cost of a continued negotiation with Everett is too high. Viva Sylthia has attacked the crown's assets before. This may be a natural escalation."

"First my niece, with the next stage being one of my children?" says Firehorn, his voice deathly calm.

*I don't know, I don't know, I don't know.* My chest tightens. It's my bloody job to know. I was supposed to be Firehorn's defense against Viva Sylthia, and I'm damn bait instead. "Are you considering calling off the negotiations?" I ask.

"If I do, Dansil will fall within five years." I freeze, staring at the king. Firehorn sighs. "Such is the grimness of mathematics, Kalianna. Dansil lacks the people to sustain itself. With the Drought, most of the generation of children who'd be of age now to farm and build and bear their own offspring never came to be. And the precious few that survive do so only to die on battlefields or birth beds. We need more than peace—we need Everett blood to mix with ours, and we need Everett's goodwill to aid us in discovering the Drought's end."

Fear coats my tongue. "Stars take me."

Firehorn nods. "Why do you imagine Bishop Bahir has a seat at my dinner table? I've little love for the man myself, but Dansil's survival thus far is in large part thanks to Bahir's preaching. The promise of a bright future and a goddess's love gives hope and purpose to those who have nothing left. Still, hope goes only so far."

Hope served with a side of hate. "Bishop Bahir blames whisperers for the Drought. Yet Everett has whisperers and the babes there are born healthy."

Firehorn waves my words away. "Desperate people need someone to blame. The suffering of a few to give hope and strength to the many is acceptable." Except it isn't. Not to me. But I'm smart enough to shut my mouth before the king's candor turns to choler. "With regard to the assault on Lianna," Firehorn says, and I brace myself for the reprimand. What the king says instead stops my heart. "Perhaps she should depart. Kal too."

"Sir?" The word comes in a whisper.

"We are no closer to safety than we were prior to your arrival." He holds up his hand. "Not for any lack of effort on your part, I believe. But simply for the fact that imagining one person might make a difference was too great a folly. I do not see the need to risk your life further, not when your skills might be needed another time." He smiles with exhausted eyes. "I'm releasing you and Leaf back to the estate."

My fingers curl around the edge of Firehorn's desk. The king is granting me everything I want—a return to the shadows, an end to the farce with Trace and Wil and Luca, an old master who takes me at my word even when the news I bring is difficult to believe. All I must do is nod. Thank him and accept the fact that I failed. Go hide behind others' backs like Trace thinks a woman should.

"Give me one more chance," I hear myself say, my voice thin. "Discovering Viva Sylthia's intentions falls squarely in my line of expertise. I will find what we need."

Firehorn shakes his head. "I've seen you work, Kalianna. If you tried any harder, you'd turn night into day. Sometimes . . . sometimes the wisdom lies not in driving someone harder, but in knowing when to stop pushing, when protecting a resource is better than using it. Sometimes we must know when it's time to yield."

"One week." I'm on my feet. My heart pounds, my hands opening and closing at my sides. "I've tried fitting myself into someone else, but now let me try it my way, sir. Give me one week and enough reins to use my own tactics. If at the end of that I fail to deliver, do as you must."

Firehorn weighs me with his gaze. "What would you need?"

I swallow. "I presume the prisoner knew nothing about the source of his orders?" I ask, waiting until the king confirms the assumption before continuing. "Then all I need, sir, is for Kal to be granted a bit of liberty without raising suspicions."

## 2 2

# VIOLET

*V*iolet strode across the palace grounds to a True Family meeting with her face raised high in the bright afternoon sun. It was a good day. Everywhere her eyes fell, she saw scarlet uniforms of the Holy Guard, Dansil's true protectors. Brother Joshua had been right—last week's attack was a codex. More importantly, the attack had been necessary to enable the Goddess's soldiers to take their posts. And the Goddess managed it all without actually harming the princess.

Witnessing the results of the Goddess's work firsthand, Violet had trouble understanding her own previous confusion. But looking forward was more important than looking back, and now Violet was on her guard. Her sisters had warned her that the Dark God would fight hard now to get Violet's soul back, and she was prepared to defend it.

"Vi!" Violet halted as her brother jogged to her from across the courtyard. Only one guard, Luca, trailed behind the prince, making Violet wonder what Wil had done this time to lose the other two. Or to drain away Luca's usual happiness.

Wil stopped beside her, panting lightly. He was pale, a haunted look in his eyes that Violet hadn't seen since their mother's funeral. Something was wrong.

*The Dark God works through the ones we love*, said Zalia's voice in Violet's memory. *Be careful, sister.*

Violet checked the sun's position. If she lingered too long, she'd be late.

"Where have you been hiding the last week?" Wil asked, looking Violet up and down. He made a face. "And what in stars' name happened to your hair?"

Violet ran a hand over her short tufts. She still missed the shining golden locks she'd given up to show her devotion to the Goddess, but the self-imposed *condition* fortified Violet's internal core. She knew better than to tell Wil as much though.

*The Dark God twists the truth into his own weapon. Keep it to yourself, lest you give him ammunition.* It was another of the Order's teachings.

Violet bit her lip. Wil was not ready to welcome the Goddess into his heart, but the thought of her brother falling to the Dark God's clutches filled Violet with horrid grief. For all his mischief and self-importance, Wil was made for carrying light, not darkness.

The challenge was to get past the Dark God's wiles.

"I've taken up embroidering handkerchiefs with the Children of the Goddess girls. We sell them and use the money to help war orphans. Since Father refuses to allow any additional donation to the cause, I am doing what I can myself." She tilted her head, smiling at her brother. "Perhaps you would buy a batch?"

"Eh, sure." Wil scratched the back of his neck.

"That's wonderful, Wil," Violet exclaimed, throwing her arms around her brother, though she knew he little understood the importance of what had just happened. Wil's money would support the Messenger's work, and when the Goddess's forces triumphed, Wil would get full credit for his contribution. The sisters called the method "divine deception" and promised it worked wonders to keep the Dark God from interfering in the Children's work.

And they were right. One day, all too soon, Wil would look back on this afternoon and feel the joy of having been a part of the Goddess's victory. Violet squeezed her brother's hand and resumed her path to the temple.

"Vi! Wait!"

She hesitated. "I need to go, Wil. I'll send someone with the embroidery batch to you soon."

He grabbed her wrist. "Are you all right, Vi?" He blurted, his eyes narrowing on hers. "You've been acting odd, and with the attack on Raza and patrols of every color roving around like cockroaches . . . Master Tril said you've not attended one lesson the whole week."

Violet winced at Wil's ignorance, his focus on all the wrong things. There was a war brewing, climbing to its inevitable apex. Not the silly squabble of Dansil and Everett, but one with truly high stakes.

Wil drew a breath and spoke again. "What I'm trying to say, Vi, is that with Mother keeping the Goddess company now, I thought you might want to talk."

Violet's chest tightened. What Wil meant was that *he* wanted to talk. For all the grandness of being the crown prince, there were sides of her brother that only Violet had ever gotten to see. The Wil who'd sobbed beside her the night of their mother's death, the one who stole Violet's favorite sweets from the kitchen and brought them to her, the one who'd confessed to breaking a vase that Violet had shattered, and taken her punishment without complaint.

Violet's heart broke for that Wil. Truly and deeply. But

things were different now. Violet was a soldier in the Goddess's army, not a silly little girl. And she was a target. The Dark God worked through the people one loved, and Violet could not let his evil pour into her through her brother's voice.

"Let's go to the kitchens," said Wil, his slender fingers still on her wrist. "We'll take some sweetcakes. Tea." His eyes turned with that familiar mischief. "Or ale."

Sadness spilled from every chamber of Violet's heart, but her eyes saw through the deception that the Dark God was spreading. She pulled her arm free. "I'm busy, Wil," she said briskly, and hurried away.

"Violet!" Wil called after her. "Vi, wait!"

She kept going. For both their sakes.

## 2 3

## KALI

"You are going out alone? When you could be not going out at all?" Leaf draws her knees into her arms. "I thought you were done with this lone huntress act."

"I'm a scout, Leaf. And I'm bloody close to something, whether or not Firehorn or Trace or anyone else believes me. I can't just tuck my tail between my legs." I pull on a foliage-painted tunic and breeches and review my gear. Calvin's prisoner might know nothing about the origin of his orders, but he sure as hells knows where he met up with his cadre prior to the attack. It's a start. "Viva Sylthia targeted Lady Lianna, which might mean I saw or know something that I don't yet realize is important. Following up on the prisoner's information through woods and shadows, that's what I'm good at—not this dress-up-doll routine." I force a smile to my face. "Stop worrying, this is hardly my first track."

With a resigned sigh, Leaf slides off the bed and pulls a hand-sized pouch from her trunk. She tosses the pouch to me.

It's heavier than it looked from afar, with clever straps to attach it to my belt and thigh. "What is it?"

"It's what *I* do," says Leaf. "Your new survival kit."

My fingers prickle as I pull open the laces. I yelp and pull back for a moment before gritting my teeth and pulling the cloth flap all the way open. Three polished crystals sparkle at me from their holsters.

Leaf points into the pouch. "These first two, you've used before: light and heat. Should stay in tune for up to twenty hours of use once triggered. They are tuned to your blood, so just wrap your fingers around the crystal and the proximity of your blood to the crystal will activate the magic."

My eyes widen. Three times longer than any Leaf has managed before. "And the last one?" I brush my finger down a crystal with a complicated red weave that pulses slightly.

"That is a love stone."

"In case I meet a soulmate I think I'll die without?"

"Love stones—which you would know about if you paid attention—are mated pairs of crystals." She shows me a similar crystal hanging on a thong around her neck, beside the blue healing one. "Hold yours in your hand and close your eyes." I obey, feeling a tiny heartbeat-like vibration on the right side of the crystal. "Move in the direction of the beat," Leaf instructs.

I step right.

"Open your eyes."

I obey, to discover that I've moved toward Leaf, who changed position while my eyes were closed.

"If something happens, I can use my half of the love stone to guide me to its mate. I've not tested the range fully, but it worked well on the palace grounds."

My throat dries. "We won't need the love stones, Leaf," I promise, wrapping my arms around her. "Not this time."

She sets her jaw. "But you will take it anyway."

"I will take it anyway," I agree. "But for research purposes. All right?" I wait until she nods before strapping the pouch to my thigh and undoing the latch on the concealed passage leading from Lady Lianna's rooms. My hand stills. "Leaf . . . if something *does* happen—it won't, but if it does—go to Everett, all right? Blackmail Trace if he won't help outright, but make sure Raza takes you with her."

As BEFORE, the dungeon's stench greets me well before I finish descending the dark spiral staircase. This time, however, Calvin appears promptly after I ask for him. Taking off a leather apron, he hangs it on a hook before leading me into the dusty room.

"Tea?" he asks.

"No. Thank you."

"You'll forgive me if I indulge in a cup while we speak?" I nod and Calvin pours tea for himself and settles into a chair. "How can I be of service?"

Taking a deep breath—and regretting it immediately—I sit across from the questioner. Once I outline the basics of my plan and the information I seek, Calvin nods with understanding.

"The prisoner claims to have met with the others to receive orders about a day's trek into the North Wood." He sips his tea. "He claims he could lead someone to the spot."

"Would you trust him to do so?"

Calvin smiles. "Absolutely not. His only hope for survival would be to lead the man he guided to his death."

I tap a finger against my knee. "Could he provide a description of key landmarks?"

Another sip of tea. "I expect so. Perhaps you wish to ask him yourself?"

I try and fail to read the thoughts behind Calvin's deceptively open face, but the words feel like a test. "Do you believe my doing so would elicit more accurate answers?"

He shrugs. "Unlikely."

"Then why under the bloody stars did you suggest it?"

"Some people come to me for information. Others enjoy the process we use to obtain it. I wished to know which you were after." He puts down his cup and rises. "I will get the landmarks as well as they can be described for you." I nod my thanks, my stomach twisting as I realize how bad a day someone is about to have because of my inquiry. Calvin's gaze seems to penetrate through me. "Perhaps some good can come from this mess yet."

I nod my head. As the questioner shifts his weight to leave, I gather breath for my final question. "Calvin," I say quietly, my eyes on his discarded tea as the sight of Trace's marked torso shimmers through my memory. Those marks didn't come from battle—they came from a place like this. "Do people recover from what's done to them here? The ones who are not executed—do they recover?"

"They can," Calvin says gently. "With help. Who are you concerned about, Kal?"

I shake my head quickly. "Just the prisoner you're questioning because of me."

"He'll be executed soon," says Calvin. "But you already knew that."

I LEAVE the palace a half hour later, slipping into the North Wood just as the trainees back at the keep are finishing up the morning training and wistfully fantasizing about the too-far-off midday meal. The king's arranged note of Kal's temporary departure will have already reached the guard master, the message being spread to Trace and Luca, as Kal's sponsors. I wonder what the men make of it, how relieved Trace is to be rid of me for a spell.

Each step farther from the palace centers me in the forest's splendor. The smell of sticky sap and moist bark is a welcome change from the reek of manicured flowers and courtiers' perfumes, to say nothing of chattering squirrels and the occasional woodpecker providing a calmer backdrop than the bloody stinging wasps that the palace seems to breed.

My feet fall silently on the forgiving earth as I navigate the forest, marking the land features. The prisoner told Calvin that he'd followed a stream to a man-sized mossy boulder, where he met his cohorts. The description, together with signs of disturbed branches and moss's preference to grow on the north side of its host, offers a solid start to my search. I just wish I knew what I was looking for.

I find the prisoner's stream and boulder five hours into my hike, just as the joy of the wilderness begins surrendering to fatigue. I stop with my hand on the stone, listening to the gurgling water. Someone was here before, recently enough that the boot prints they left in the mud are still clear. But there is little else at this rendezvous point but more bushwhacked trails, leading in different directions.

*What did you expect, a flag and a manifesto?*

Stifling a sigh, I retreat from the boulder, careful not to add my own boot prints to the mix as I pick a trail at random and follow it west. I've two and a half, maybe three hours of sunlight left before I need to settle in for the night.

It's the sudden silence of the forest that stops me in my tracks an hour later. Not total silence—the wind still rustles the trees and the burbling stream still sings in the distance—but the animals and birds, those I hear none of now. As if they've scattered from something or know better than to approach. My pulse thumps hard, casing off all fatigue.

Stepping silently toward a sturdy tree, I scamper into the branches for a better view. And freeze.

There is a *road* here. A trampled path wide enough to let horses pass and so long that I cannot see its end. My body tenses. The well-worn ground cleared of trees and foliage has as much legitimate business being in the middle of the woods as I do in the Royal Guard. Someone put it here for transport. Of what?

I shimmy back on my branch, concealing myself in the tree while I think. My heart and mind race, weighing and discarding the possibilities like gowns. Not wide enough for a wagon, but worn well. People pass here. In large numbers. And from this point, they are less than a day's travel to Delta.

A wail, long and pleading, cuts through the forest, followed at once by a crack and a scream of pain.

My limbs tighten around the branch that I lie on. The animals are steering clear not just because the path is here, but because there is someone on it. Someone who isn't here willingly by the sound of it.

*Prisoners.* The memory tickles my throat. The prisoners I told Trace about. My jaw tightens. The same bushy foliage that keeps me well concealed is also blocking whatever is happening from my view. Climbing back to the ground, I swim between the trees toward the origin of that wail, each step a careful, silent shuffle along the earth. Speed, stealth, proximity to the mark—a scout can have only two of the three at once, and with the coming darkness, time is not on my side.

Not that I will be sleeping tonight. Once I know who— what—these people are, it will be a long night of travel back to Delta to warn Firehorn of the impending arrival.

I move as quickly as I dare, stopping to listen every twenty paces. When the sounds become a consistent if still distant chatter, I must move farther from the guiding road. A dead scout helps no one. Crouching in the skirt of a wide oak, I try to piece together what I'm hearing.

Moans, pleas. The occasional crack of a whip.

"What do you want me to do, shrink the bloody forest?" The low baritone's very clear and close demand launches my heart into my throat. Someone is coming my way. Likely a guard patrol sweeping the woods.

"I want you to keep the Messenger's schedule," replies a second, nasal voice. "We've neither men nor supplies to bed a hundred heathens for the night. March them to the temple abbey while the Holy Guard still holds patrol duty in Delta."

My mouth dries. So these are the prisoners the roses were expecting, and there are a hundred of them. My back presses hard into the bark and I dare not move a muscle, even as a troop of ants marches across my shin.

"Through the dark?" says Baritone. He and Nasal are no more than ten paces from me now.

Nasal growls. "They are whisperers, aren't they? Have them tune some crystals. If they want to keep their necks in one piece, they'll keep the bloody things bright."

Stars take me. Blood leaves my face, a chill settling deep into my bones. I went out looking for Viva Sylthia terror mongers, and instead I found hired thugs dragging a hundred whisperers to be sacrificed into Bahir's care. Innocents. Like Leaf.

Another wail, this one too high to be an adult's. Bile rises in my throat. A child. A precious, rare child. Little wonder Bahir and the Holy Guard do these harvests by night and in secret—seeing this much suffering up close might turn the minds of even the most devout Delta subjects. Better for the whisperers to remain a faceless evil, easy to blame and hate.

*The promise of a bright future and the love of a goddess gives hope and purpose to those who have nothing left,* Firehorn said. *Desperate people need someone to blame. The suffering of a few to give hope and strength to the many is acceptable.*

My hand shakes. Even if I turn around and race back to Delta now, the king will do nothing.

"Tune crystals? You see a pack full of living stones somewhere?" Baritone demands, the sound finally moving away from me. "We bed them down and keep watch. Pick one and make an example—that will keep them hobbled. Better one destroyed than several stray. How far do you want to sweep? I think rain is coming."

"Half mile, no more," the other replies. The sound of twigs crunching beneath their boots grows fainter until silence reigns again.

Watch and report. Observe. Don't rush. Don't interfere. And for stars' sake, don't risk exposure. That's what Lord Gapral would tell me to do. But I can no more obey that than I could let a stable of horses be burned alive.

My body moves without consulting my common sense, taking me closer to the prisoners' camp with each breath. Moving slyly through the woods is a painfully slow affair, and what would be a twenty-minute hike down a cleared road takes three times as long through untamed wilderness.

An hour. That's what I think I'll need to reach the prisoners.

Except I don't have an hour. The sun is already setting and Baritone was right about the rain, the first drops of which are already pattering the leaves. With the gray skies and no moon tonight, the darkness is coming faster than it should. Another fifteen minutes and the forest will turn pitch black, making it impossible for me to continue without breaking a leg. A light crystal would help, but it would attract the guards like moths. Which leaves me with two options—do nothing or use the road.

My gut churns at the thought of that exposed path. The guards who stride along it. *Speed, stealth, proximity.* I can't have it all. I have to choose. Somewhere in the distance, a lone wolf bays a song, clear and defiant despite the lack of moon and pack. I am a wolf too. Not some girl Trace protects, but a predator. A force against darkness.

With shaking hands, I unstrap Leaf's satchel from my thigh and slip it beneath the gnarled roots of a dense fir. If I'm captured, the love stone might lead someone back to Leaf, and I won't risk that.

My heart races as I slip onto the open road and rush forward, pushing myself as fast as my legs can carry, my knives sliding into my hands. My best—my only—chance now is to beat both the setting sun and the two patrol guards back to the camp. Once there, I'll have the element of surprise to conjure enough chaos for the prisoners to melt into the imminent darkness. It's all about timing now. Timing and luck.

My feet pound the path lightly, the drops of cold rain splattering my nose and cheeks. *Thump, patter patter. Thump, patter patter.* I push myself forward. Faster. Smoother. The prisoners can't be far now, not with a babe's mewing cry sounding so heartbreakingly clear in the setting gloom.

*I'm coming,* I shout to the whisperers in my thoughts. *I'm coming.*

*Thump, patter—*

I don't see the guards until two sets of meaty hands clamp on to my arms, slamming me face first into the ground. Razor-sharp steel presses into the base of my skull, drawing blood.

"Who are you?" Baritone demands.

My breath catches. Between the knife at my neck and my face pressed into the dirt, it is a struggle to form words. "Kal," I pant the word. "Guardsman trainee."

"Aye, I've seen the dimwit at the palace," Nasal confirms.

My heart stutters in surprise and I try to turn my head to get a look at the man, but the blade keeps me still. A boot steps on my right hand, pulling my knife from my grasp, then repeats the process on the other side.

"Are you not a wee bit far from the keep?" Nasal asks.

"Ran . . . away." I swallow, my aching hand tightening around a rock. "My sponsor . . . He's a lash-loving bastard."

"And where were you running to?" Nasal inquires with calm curiosity, as if we were having a normal conversation.

"I was following a stream," I say honestly. "Then found this wide path. Heard voices. Was going there."

Baritone clicks his tongue. "Running away never helps things, you know. Usually it just leaves you dead. Allow me to demonstrate." The knife cuts deeper into my flesh, making a warm, viscous stream run down my neck.

I gasp.

"Wait." This comes from Nasal.

The knife stops and Baritone makes a questioning sound in the back of his throat.

"You are the one who wanted an example to hobble the heathens," says Nasal. "Don't kill him yet, not until they see."

"True," Baritone growls under his breath, and the knife withdraws from the back of my neck.

I seize upon the reprieve and swing the stone I've palmed into Baritone's knee. Rock hits bone, sending a satisfying vibration down my shoulder.

Baritone curses.

I scramble to my knees, only to fall back down as a boot

kicks my ribs and tips me like a bug onto my back. I recognize Nasal now—one of the roses who occasionally passed through the keep. His name is Miles, I think. Not that it matters just now. Leaning over me, Baritone spits into my face before plunging my very own throwing knife hilt-deep into my left thigh.

A heartbeat later, my other blade pierces the right.

I AM NOT BLEEDING FAST ENOUGH.

If they just pulled out one of the knives, I might bleed faster. Might go unconscious. If I'm very fortunate, I might die.

"Bring him closer to the fire," Baritone orders. "I want everyone to see what awaits them should they try to flee tonight."

I scream as they haul me forward, the pain exploding through every ripped muscle fiber. It's been minutes since I was captured. It's been hours. It's been years. Long enough for the dozen guards in charge of the prisoners to have built a fire beneath a dense tree, illuminating the clearing where the captured whisperers are bedding down for the night. Long enough for the first demonstration.

"We've already discussed the consequences of disobedience," Baritone tells the hundred hollow faces staring at me through the smoke. His voice is calm, as if instructing a class of novices, and loud enough to carry over the sobs and retching. "Before I bid you goodnight, I wish to discuss the consequences of running. Some believe ropes and chains are needed to keep a rabid animal at bay. But that is utter folly. All you need is to hobble the beast. This is how it's done. Miles, shatter the boy's legs, please."

The man I've called Nasal unhooks an ax from his belt and stalks slowly toward me.

"Why are you doing this?" I yell at him, fear tearing at my throat. "You are a holy guardsman. You trained beside me, you—" I give up shouting as Miles approaches, struggling instead against the two men holding my arms. They only torque my shoulders until my protests become babbling screams that even I cannot understand. My eyes are wide, my heart ripping through my chest as my breaths fall in short desperate pants.

The last thing I see before the back of Miles's heavy ax strikes my shin is his loose shirt collar shifting open and a Viva Sylthia tattoo flashing in the firelight.

## 24

## VIOLET

*S*tanding before the fireplace in her room, Violet watched the flames consume the last bits of her favorite dress. The cloth crackled and smoked, but the raging storm outside kept Violet's windows closed. She was severing ties with the Dark God, and he had no intention of making it easy for her. She coughed and turned away from the choking fumes until the worst of them passed, then picked up the next bin, this one filled with childhood toys.

She had neither use nor time anymore for the silliness in her hands, not when the great battle was coming and she had so much to do. The Messenger needed her; the whole True Family did. And unlike her brother—a princeling stuck in childhood mischief—Violet had become a reliable soldier.

The time had come to let the world know.

Violet's one regret was how long it had taken her to hear the Goddess's call. Had she been paying better attention, she could have saved her mother. If Violet had embraced the truth earlier, her mother's death wouldn't have been needed to awaken Violet to the truth. Swallowing, Violet pulled up the floorboard and added the wooden box and velvet puppy to the pile.

Her hand felt empty immediately and Violet dipped into her pocket, wrapping her fingers around the yellow memory stone Joshua had entrusted to her. A tool to replace a toy. When the Goddess's victory was assured, the acolyte who'd tuned it would be overjoyed to learn how much good he'd heralded into the world. For the acolyte, for the Messenger, for her mother's soul, Violet would make the stone count.

At first, Violet mistook the insistent pounding on her door for the wind rattling the shutters. The horrid weather was unusual for this time of year, and Violet's initial suspicions of the Dark God's presence behind the change were growing more and more vivid. First Wil, now a brewing storm out of season—something dark was trying to keep Violet from the temple.

Then her brother's voice penetrated the walls. "Vi? Vi, are you all right?"

More banging. "Princess Violet, it's Luca." The guardsman's voice that had once quickened Violet's heart now sounded flat to her ears. "Is all well?"

Violet turned her back to the noise. Joshua and Zalia had warned her to expect the Dark God to interfere. They'd prepared her for this trial as much as they could, and Violet had prepared herself as well, keeping a vigil throughout the night. Her vision was clear now. There was evil in the world, and that was of the Dark God. All that was good was of the Goddess. The Messenger was the embodiment of the Goddess's teachings. If Violet followed the Messenger, the Dark God would be defeated. If Violet counterbalanced her mother's sins, they would reunite in the Goddess's embrace.

"Vi!" Wil called again, shaking the door. "I'm coming in."

Violet threw the first handful of toys into the hungry flames and picked up more. Cathy, a doll she'd slept with when she was small, stared at her with large painted eyes. Violet's mother had made Cathy's clothes by hand, down to the tiny shoes with yellow flowers. Then they'd started stitching little plush animals together.

Thuds echoed through the room as someone struggled to break down her door. Violet's chest tightened as she realized how the Dark God was blinding her brother to the Goddess's truth.

The doorframe collapsed with a crash, admitting Wil and Luca. Both men panted and stared wide-eyed at what remained of Violet's suite.

"What are you doing, Violet?" Wil asked. "Where are the servants?"

Violet sighed. "I sent them away."

"Are you insane?" Wil demanded, while Luca used a bucket of water to douse Violet's flames to a hissing wetness. "You could have burned down the whole palace wing."

A smile touched Violet's lips. She would *not* have burned down the palace, but explaining the Goddess's influence to Wil would take more time than she could spare. One day he'd understand and feel foolish for his worry, but for now . . .

"The Goddess has plans for me, William." Violet squared her shoulders and faced the brother in whose shadow she'd once lived. "And I've heard her call. If you listen, really listen, you will hear it too."

"Stars, Violet," Wil whispered, staring at her. "When did you last sleep? Or eat? You look like—"

Violet stepped away from him.

Wil held up his palms. There was something different about him now, as if he'd grown more in the past week than he had in years. His voice was a gentle caress when he spoke again. "That's Cathy, isn't it?" he said. "I remember you sitting beside Mother for hours, making her dresses and hats. I was so jealous of how happy Mother was, sewing and singing with you."

Violet's hands tightened on the doll. The Dark God cackled.

With a will to rival a mighty army, Violet shoved the darkness away and threw Cathy into the remaining blossom of flame that the Goddess had protected. "You may take anything you wish from my room, William," she told her brother before turning to Luca, surprised to find the enchantment that had once surrounded him gone, revealing a bewildered guard. "Arrange an escort for me to the Temple of Dansil. Now."

Wil blocked what was left of the door. "No."

Violet sighed, but Zalia and Joshua had predicted this very moment and prepared her for it. They'd practiced the words together until Violet could say them without effort or thought. "I claim the protection of the Goddess, as is the right of any woman," she said formally, confidently. "To stand in my way is to raise a sword against the Order. Let. Me. Through."

THE TEMPLE COURTYARD was predictably empty when Violet arrived. Shedding her oilskins and the few belongings she'd brought in the foyer, Violet descended the stairs and strode to the Revelations Room, only to stop in the doorway, staring in bewilderment at the chaos of Children rushing about and huddling in small groups, each talking urgently.

"The weather kept them . . ."

". . . coming in now."

"Well, wake them up. We need all hands!"

"Violet?" Brother Joshua, busy issuing orders to a trio of unfamiliar boys, was the first to notice Violet's appearance.

Dasha, Zalia, and many of the others Violet knew were nowhere in sight. "An unexpected surprise," Joshua said with a frown.

A wave of uncertainty twisted Violet's heart. "Am I not welcome today?" she asked, retreating a step. When Zalia had presented her with a copy of the Revelations Room key last week, she'd assumed no further invitation was needed.

Joshua's face softened. "Of course you are welcome, Violet. Just unexpected."

"Do you wish me to leave?" Violet asked.

Her face must have betrayed her fear, because Joshua strode to her, taking both her hands in his. "Only if you don't wish to stay," he said, looking into her eyes. "It will be hard work today. A soldier's work. Do you think you are ready?"

She nodded quickly. It hurt that he doubted her to begin with, but perhaps this was a test the Goddess was laying before her.

"Very well." Joshua squeezed her hands. "You will work with Zalia and Dasha in Intake Three. We've more patients than teams today, and an extra set of hands will be welcome. Vas will take you."

At the sound of his name, a boy separated from one of the groups and motioned for Violet to follow. Vas was reed-thin, with blotchy red skin and a too-big nose that dominated his face. He chewed his thumbnail as he walked. "Have you been beyond the arch before?"

"I don't even know what the arch is," said Violet.

Vas pointed his chin forward, to where a yellow-orange light beckoned from the end of a descending passage. Walking closer, Violet gasped. An arch of living crystals, pulsating with brilliant colors, stood right in the Order's own temple. A breeze kissed her cheek, the ribbons on her dress ruffling to point toward the arch like little flags. And . . . "Is that music?" she asked Vas, tilting her ear toward the arch.

Vas nodded. "Memory crystals. If they go out of tune, they start memorizing whatever pleases them, random bits of conversations included. It's a pain to keep up, but tuning the arch is part of the treatment program for the acolytes—the patients on the mend."

"How does it help them?" Violet asked, her heart singing with the majesty of the crystals.

"Tuning the arch provides a means for the acolytes to pay their tithe." Vas nudged Violet into a walk. "The Goddess's magic is meant for her Children, not for heretics. The more the acolytes contribute to the Messenger's battle, the cleaner their souls become."

Violet nodded. It made sense. Living crystals, like the memory crystal Joshua had entrusted her with, weren't evil in and of themselves. The question was whether their magic was used in accordance with the Goddess's will, or for selfish, personal gain.

Stopping beside a wooden door, Vas knocked a pattern on the frame. A moment later, Zalia stepped out into the hallway, closing the door behind her. The girl looked grave, her hair tied back with a handkerchief the way a peasant might wear one. Violet's heart quickened.

"Vas?" Zalia asked in confusion. "Why is Violet here?"

"Brother Joshua said to bring her to you," Vas said. "With a hundred acolytes to intake, he said we could use the help."

Zalia's face melted and she took both of Violet's hands in hers. "Of course. Hello, sister."

*Sister.* Yes. A knot loosened in Violet's chest as she squeezed Zalia's hands in return. "What would you have me do?" she whispered.

"It's difficult work, but if Brother Joshua thinks you are

ready, then you must be," Zalia said solemnly. "Today, the Holy Guard brought us one hundred gravely ill patients to cure—whisperers corrupted by the Dark God's taint. Dansil's rural temples are able to gather them, you see, but the temples lack the resources to treat them. So the poor souls have to be moved en masse here." She sighed, rubbing her face. "We expected them yesterday and it's a scramble down here."

That knot in Violet's chest tightened again. For all the talk of curing the whisperers, no one had truly explained to her how this was to be done. She opened her mouth to ask, but altered the question at the last moment. "Won't our harboring whisperers upset the Goddess?"

"Not at all. We do this at the Messenger's command, you see. The Goddess asked us to bring her wayward Children back into the fold. So long as we follow the Goddess's will, she will not punish us." Zalia's hand gripped the door handle, her eyes on Violet. "Brace yourself, sister. The Dark God little likes surrendering his subjects, but we fight for the acolytes' souls, as we must."

The room was freezing. Stone walls, stone floors. A reek of pain and terror. A single chair bolted to the floor. And on that chair . . .

Violet's breath caught, bile stinging her throat.

"Violet, this is Eris," Zalia said, gesturing to a gagged boy who struggled like a trapped animal against the metal shackles cutting into his wrists. The whites of his frightened eyes shone in the green light of the living stones that illuminated the cell. What little he had of clothes were drenched in water, which dripped to the floor and escaped into a drain.

Dasha, who was also in the room, stepped aside.

Eris's gaze found Violet's, the plea in it so potent that her knees weakened.

"Eris has served the Dark God for sixteen years," Zalia

explained as Violet continued staring at the boy. "His family tried hiding him, but the Goddess found Eris and brought him here to be turned from a sinner into an acolyte. It is our duty to let Eris pay the tithe for his sins, so his soul will one day be welcomed by the Goddess and her light."

Violet's heart pounded. Eris was Wil's age. He was terrified and shivering, his breath misting in the cold.

"You must be strong, Violet," Zalia told her. "A soldier."

Yes. A soldier. Violet swallowed. She was a soldier of the Goddess, and she was ready to stand her first trial.

Stepping forward, Dasha squatted in front of Eris, her voice soothing. "You'll be safe from the Dark God soon," she told him, promising that there was nothing to fear, that the Dark God's mark could be erased and the gates of the Goddess's realm opened.

Eris shook his head violently.

Zalia sighed. "We try talking to them first, but it never works. Better to get them started on their tithe and speak again once the Dark God's taint lightens. Fighting the infection is seldom comfortable, but the patient can hardly be expected to recover with corruption eating his flesh."

That too made sense. Violet had heard much the same from medics and surgeons. "Show me?" she asked her sister.

Picking up a small living crystal with swirling tufts of orange magic, Zalia brought it within the boy's reach. "This is a light crystal, Eris," she said firmly. "Tune it, and we will add it to the arch—the Goddess's shrine."

Brilliant. They would use the Dark God's own corruption to light the way for the Children of the Goddess. Courage creeping slowly through her, Violet found her voice and stepped beside her sister. "Each grain of aid you give the Goddess erases a bit of sin from your soul," she explained to Eris. "It will all count in the coming battle."

Instead of succumbing to reason, Eris snarled at her through the gag.

Violet flinched back from the hate flashing in the boy's eyes. He wanted to *hurt* her, his gaze said. He *would* hurt her if not for the chains. The shock ricocheted against Violet's bones, but instead of cowering, she stood up taller.

If Eris was yet unready to see the truth, it fell upon Violet and her sisters to set him on the righteous path.

"Tell me what to do," she asked Zalia.

The girl handed Violet a bucket of water.

Nodding with understanding, Violet gripped the bucket tightly. It was heavy and cold, but that was all right. Eris needed redemption. And since he was not yet ready for reason and kindness, a simpler motive would do for now. It would all still count in his soul's favor at the end.

Saying a quick prayer, Violet looked Eris in the eye as she doused him with the ice-cold liquid. "Tune the crystal, and I shall get you a blanket," she said. "Otherwise . . ." Violet lifted the bucket to show that there was more water still inside.

## 25

## KALI

"Kal. Kal!" The voice calling my name beats against me, demanding to be heard. There is a faint smell of lavender and blood. "Open your eyes."

I do no such thing. Something very bad waits there. A distant part of my mind, one wrapped in dreamlike cotton, informs me that I should feel something about the voice's appearance. That the voice belongs somewhere else. Not here with me. Wherever it is I am.

The voice curses.

My eyes slide open, just barely, but enough to see fading wisps of daylight reflect off silver hair. I try to focus on it, but the world it's attached to swims away in a dizzying sea. The ground beneath me sways and I fall back into its abyss.

THE NEXT TIME I WAKE, it is to fires of scorching agony. I scream until my breath ends and darkness returns.

~

WATER. Drops swatting like flies at my face. I try to pull away from the assault and can't. Can't move at all. My breath quickens, heart beating in concert with the pattering rain. My eyes fly open and I stare at green lit rock. I fill my lungs and—

A hand clamps over my mouth, silver hair flashing before my eyes again. "Stay quiet and still. Understand?" Trace. Of course it would be Trace here. Because whatever happened, it wasn't bad enough on its own.

He keeps his hand tight over my mouth until I nod.

Releasing me, Trace returns to his task of layering branches atop each other to cover the entrance to what must be a cave that we are in. "Several wild boars trampled by an hour ago," he says over his shoulder. "I little wish to attract their attention just now."

The air hangs thick with earthy dampness and a green crystal provides faint but serviceable light. The pouring rain outside drums a rolling beat, but finds its way inside less and less with each branch Trace adds to his barricade. I'm lying flat on my back, the ground beneath me soft dirt covered with a blanket that scratches my bare skin. I'm not wearing anything save for undershorts and my chest wrap—now loosened—though there is something heavy atop me that smells of maleness and leather. A coat, I think. Or a cloak. I can't lift my head to see.

I pull at the straws of memory to get my bearings. I was tracking Viva. I found whisperers being held prisoner. And then . . . A wall of obsidian slams through my mind, ordering my thoughts to go elsewhere. To never, ever come back to what happened then.

Trace places the last of the branches against the cave entrance, blocking water and moonlight both, and strides to my side. Even in the odd light, the dark circles of fatigue are stark beneath his eyes.

"How did you find me?" My mouth is dry, the words raspy.

He holds up a red living stone and the pouch I left in the fir tree. "Leaf gave me her half of the love stone and I followed it. I told Luca my suspicions that you were off doing something stupid—he thinks I'm tracking you down in more civilized parts, but he'll cover for my absence well enough. You are fortunate your captors didn't find the satchel you stashed."

My captors. I swallow. No, they hadn't wanted my things. They'd . . . My memory flashes, my heart quickening its beat. With an effort that feels like it could crush boulders, I lift my wrist to grab at something, anything. My fingers close around cloth—Trace's pant leg. He squats down beside me and touches my shoulder, sending a wave of fire through my muscles. *What is it?* his eyes ask.

"Viva Sylthia," I whisper desperately. "That's who caught me. They were moving whisperers, a hundred of them. I think they work for Bahir. Said something about the Messenger's schedule and at least one of them was a holy guardsman. Like Samuels. The roses . . . They were expecting prisoners, remember? Stars." My breath shakes as I speak. "I don't understand how or why, but Viva Sylthia is in Bahir's employ. Do you hear me? Tell me you hear me."

"Easy." Trace's hand brushes my shoulder again. "I hear you."

I let out a breath.

Trace studies me, his brows knitting together. "Is that why you left Delta? You wanted to rescue a hundred whisperers from Viva Sylthia's clutches by yourself?"

I try to shake my head but it's too heavy to move. "I was searching for Viva agents. I didn't know Viva was trafficking whisperers. Only realized it . . . only put it together at the end."

Trace's eyes flash. "You left the palace alone to seek out terror mongers who'd already tried to kill you once?" His voice rises, nostrils flaring more with each word. "What did you bloody think was going to happen? Did you bloody think at all? You said you work for Firehorn—pray explain how your being dead would help the king."

Considering the state I'm in, Trace's scolding has little of its intended effect. I open my mouth to tell him so, but it's difficult enough to speak without wasting breath. "They didn't kill me." I meant it as a question, but it comes out a statement, defiant.

"If you think that's a credit to your luck or skill, disillusion yourself of that this damn minute. You know how I found you? Hanging from a tree by your wrists, your shoulders dislocated, your—" He cuts off abruptly as blood drains from my face. His voice reins itself in to an even calmness. "It doesn't matter. You are alive. Like you said."

It's too late, though, the attempt at calm. My breath quickens, memories shoving against my consciousness. Knives. Ropes. A throat gone raw and bloody from screaming. A horrific pop of joints. The dull side of a heavy ax . . . I choke on air.

"They wanted an example." The words bubble out, bile rising in my throat. I was supposed to help the whisperers. I became an instrument of fear instead. "They wanted an example. To keep others in line. I . . . I was the example."

"Breathe," Trace whispers. "Try to breathe."

I try. Fail. Try again. My breaths come too quickly for the air to do me much good, but the faster I gulp, the worse it gets.

Trace's hand hesitates above my face, then lowers slowly to my forehead. Fingers calloused from years of training and holding weapons brush hair from my eyes. "It's over," he whispers. The apple of his throat bobs as he swallows, tense muscles sharp against his square chin. The silver-blond hair hanging loose from Trace's bent head tickles my ear. "You are all right now. I won't let them hurt you again. I promise."

I focus on the path of Trace's touch, my flesh tingling at the lethal power caressing my skin. *I won't let them hurt you again.* I grip on to those words. I'm not with Viva anymore. I'm not alone. Trace is here and I am safe. His touch is proof and it feels good.

Too good. Too safe. Lord Gapral's warnings ring in my mind. *The only person who can protect you—who* will *protect you—is you. Forget that and you are dead.*

"It's all right," Trace murmurs. "You're all right."

I jerk my head away from him as if scorched. Swallowing painfully, I force my body to evaluate itself. It's not all right at all. I can't move. I can barely breathe. I'm as far from *right* as it gets this side of death. "Liar."

Trace doesn't deny it. He pulls his hand back and tucks it beneath his knee.

"How bad?" I ask.

He shakes his head.

Cold fear grips my chest. My heart speeds. "How. Bad."

Trace sighs. "Lacerations. Two puncture wounds, one in each thigh. Multiple fractures." His eyes survey my prone form, his voice matter of fact. "I set and splinted the bones in both your legs. Don't ruin my work."

Fractures. Splints on my legs. Trace's words echo and the sleeping memories bang against my mind's shield. Stars. The panicked realization shoots through me like lightning. They broke my *legs*. I can't walk. Not now. Perhaps not ever. Not like I could. Leaf's useless clubbed foot flashes before my eyes.

Trace's hands grip my shoulders, caged strength vibrating

from his body as his worried gaze rakes me. "Look at me. Stay with me."

I blink at the green-lit stone wall of the cave. It's cold and hard. I try to move again and can't. Panic creeps back in ragged breaths and flashing fear. *Something else*, I shout at my mind. *Focus on something else. Anything else.* "You need to go. Tell the king about the whisperers. Find them before they get to Bahir."

Trace raises a brow. "You want me to leave?"

"Yes."

He snorts. "And what is to become of you? Or is dying the point of this brilliant plan?"

"A hundred innocent people—"

"—are already with Bahir. It's been two days since Viva discarded you." Gripping my chin, Trace forces my gaze to meet his. "I've worked too hard keeping you alive. So you are going to stay that way, understand?"

I try to pull away.

Trace holds fast. "Understand?" he demands again.

Strength drains from my limbs. My eyes sting. I hate them for it. And I hate Trace for seeing the glimmer of tears. "They shattered my legs."

"I know."

"If I live—" The strangled words escape my throat, and I read the answer in his eyes before even asking the question. "Even if I live, will I walk?"

Trace looks down.

I nod, my hands gripping the dirt, letting it press beneath my fingernails. A single tear slides from the corner of my right eye, slithering down my cheek.

Trace tightens his jaw, as if determination heals bones. "You'll walk," he whispers.

"Ah." My voice is flat and so lifeless it frightens me. "The power of hope."

"No. There . . . Hope isn't going to suffice. Not with this damage. Healing magic may work, though." He sighs and sits back on his heels, pinching the bridge of his nose as he studies my body. "I've just never tried something this complex before."

"Feel at liberty to start making sense anytime now," I say after a few minutes of silence. "Trace? Trace."

He startles free of his thoughts. "Do you remember anything after I found you?"

I dig through my memories, careful not to stray too deep. "My name being called. A blaze of searing pain. That's it. Probably when you set the bones. Or my shoulders."

"No. That pain was me stopping the worst of the bleeding." His gaze finds mine. "Do you remember what your sister said about the magic in healing crystals? How potent it is, how it penetrates through the crystal's walls and into the body? That pain you felt, that was healing magic."

I've the oddest experience of hearing and understanding each word without grasping the meaning of their combination. The way Trace is talking, it's as if . . .

He nods. "Yes, I'm a whisperer. A trained healer."

I move my mouth, but it takes a moment to make sounds come out. "But we've no healers in Dansil," I say stupidly.

He gives me a hard look. "There are a lot of people in Dansil you think don't exist."

I close my eyes, my mind racing as I try to put the pieces together. "When you asked Leaf about using the healing stone . . . you were really checking to ensure she knew its dangers."

"Yes." Trace sighs, his fingers brushing my forehead again. "Look at me, Kal. What I did earlier, that was rudimentary. To mend the bones properly is . . . It's the difference between painting a fence and a portrait. I can't promise I'll succeed, but I can promise to try if you want me to. It will hurt, though. Very much."

I nod, a small bud of hope blooming in my chest. Of course I want him to try. I set aside my roiling thoughts and questions for later—walking comes first.

Unbuttoning the top of his shirt, Trace removes the thong holding the blue healing crystal and wraps the leather around his hands. The small crystal appears to be in tune, with the magical tufts already woven together in its center. Probably from the previous healing Trace performed on me.

"How . . ." I massage my words, trying not to sound like the coward I suddenly feel. "How will this work exactly?"

"I will press the crystal between my hand and your body." Trace uses his teeth to tighten the last of the knots that secure the stone to his palm. He nudges down the cloak covering my body and probes the space just below my right collarbone, the touch expertly professional. "There is a plexus of energy pathways here, which the magic will enter through. The healing crystal will connect our bodies, letting me wield its magic against your injuries."

"All right," I say, though it's anything but that.

"The magic will flow but I'll stay right here." Trace offers a hint of a smile. "No needles, though. That's something, right?"

I try to nod, but my bravery is failing more with each heartbeat.

"Just keep breathing," Trace tells me as his hand finds my chest again and his eyes take on the glazed look of concentration I've so often seen on Leaf's face. Stinging bees swarm into my blood. I gasp and it's all I can do to keep from pulling away. Trace's face hardens. "Both femurs are intact," he says through clenched teeth. "But the lower legs . . . I think I can work with them." His words are strained.

"Are you . . ." My breath catches as I realize what's happening. "You are feeling what I feel. The wounds. Their pain."

He nods roughly.

"If you feel my sensations, why don't I feel yours?"

"I'm keeping the magic focused inside your body," says Trace. "Brace yourself."

I've no chance to ask what I'm bracing for before a sudden agony, like on oily fire, engulfs my body. The viscous flame pools in the crevices of my shattered right shin and starts to sear the bone. I dig my nails into the ground, my back arching as a whimper I can't bite back escapes my lips.

"I know," Trace whispers, his free hand finding mine. "But this is the only way."

I try to settle, but everything inside me rebels against the pain. Pushes against it. Against the magic melting my bones.

The magic pushes back, worming its way in. I push harder.

Harder still.

And the magic . . . It recoils. Right back into Trace.

# 26

$\mathcal{T}$race's body goes rigid.

Beneath the pulsing pain of my own wounds, I feel another set of legs and arms, another body. The muscles of that other body are tense with fatigue, the heart racing in panic. One of the hands holds something precious and warm, but not warm enough. The temperature of my own hand. Trace jerks the healing crystal away and stares at me, hints of panic and bewilderment shimmering in his gaze. "What the bloody stars did you do?"

With the contact severed, my body is once again just my own. My breaths come in broken pants. "I don't know."

His eyes tighten, a hundred thoughts racing through them, before his face becomes stone once more, and a very displeased stone at that. "I've had just about enough of Kal and Lianna and whatever other masks you wear."

"I'm not lying to you." My chest squeezes tight around my ribs. "Trace, I swear it. I wanted to push the pain away and then . . ."

"And then?" he demands.

And then I felt what he felt. Intruded without his permission. And he thinks I did it on purpose. "I pushed and it worked. It was like jerking a finger away from a fire—it's not something you plan, it just happens. I don't even understand what happened, much less how."

"You pushed the magic?" His brow creases, but at least the anger seems to be melting away.

"I don't know." I swallow. "I'm not a whisperer."

"No," Trace agrees. "You are not. We work through crystals."

I say nothing until the silence claws at me from the inside. "Then what am I?" I whisper finally.

Trace runs his hand through his hair. "I truly don't know. Nothing odd happened the last time I healed you, but you were unconscious then. We'll try it again. Don't fight me this time."

I nod and press the back of my head into the ground while Trace checks the binding on the healing crystal. "Trace." I reach out and touch his hand before he can pull away. "I'm sorry."

Trace looks down at my hand, and just when I'm sure he's about to jerk back, he squeezes my fingers. "The pain ends," he whispers. "It feels like it won't, but it will." He holds my gaze as his other hand, the one holding the crystal, reclaims its spot at my collarbone and that oily fire sears me once more.

I bite back a howl that would wake the whole forest. "You . . . feel that?" I ask.

Trace nods, beads of sweat rising on his temple. "I feel the pain, but I'm aware that it is a phantom, the injury not truly mine." The words are strained and Trace's dark eyes shimmer in the crystal's pale glow. "It makes it easier. That, and being the one in control."

The shackle of flaming agony shifts closer to my knee, and gripping Trace's gaze is all I can do to keep myself together. I wait for him to look away, but he never does.

WITH THE EXCEPTION of a few short breaks, Trace keeps the healing going for hours on end, moving with meticulous care from bone to bone. I am fortunate enough to black out several times, but Trace has no such luxury. By nightfall, the splints are off my legs and I crawl outside the cave to be sick. When I return—slowly, on legs that feel like a newborn foal's—Trace is holding the wall for balance just to remain upright. Through his haze of exhaustion, he gives me a small, triumphant smile.

A sudden overwhelming desire to touch him washes over me. I want to rest my forehead against his shoulder, feel the rise and fall of his chest against my cheek, the familiar rhythm of his breath that I clung to while he healed me. I want to say thank you. To ask why. *Why did you come after me, Trace? Why did you save me? Why did you work through hours of agony for my sake?* No one but Leaf does that. Not for me.

I go to the opposite wall and slide down it. If there is a proper way to go about thanking someone for one's life, Lord Gapral hasn't taught it to me.

Beyond the cave, the thunderstorm rages in full glory.

Trace's smile dissolves and he watches me wearily. I wonder if he is yearning for Raza just now. I would be if I were him. *Stars.* No, I wouldn't. Of course I wouldn't. Because I'd have known better than to get involved with someone in the first place. And they with me.

I search my mind for words. Something appropriate. Something a man might say. "We should eat."

"I'm not hungry."

"You have to be hungry." Mostly because it's the only

appropriate activity I can think of. My clothes, the ones Trace removed while I was unconscious, are little more than blood-soaked rags. I put them outside to let the rain wash off some of the gore and scoot to our small stack of provisions. A handful of dried meat strips, a canteen, the thin blanket I was lying on, and the cloak wrapped around me. We only have one. My hesitation is ludicrous, considering that his hands have been on my body all day. But it's different now. I procrastinate another moment, then surrender to practicality and settle beside him. "Where did you learn to heal?" I ask, pushing food into his hand.

Trace takes the meat. Chews. Swallows. Shuts his eyes for a moment of respite. "Monastery of Qilar, like everyone else. You can see why healing is an unpopular field of study."

"Is Leaf right about it being dangerous?"

Trace nods. "The training itself breaks most before they learn even minor skills."

"It didn't break you," I say quietly.

Trace closes his eyes, leaning his head back against the stone. "Only because there was nothing left to break," he says, so softly and distantly that I'm certain he meant to keep the thought to himself.

I let him believe he has.

After a moment, Trace takes hold of the hem of his shirt and pulls it over his head. "You need something to wear," he says, holding it out to me.

I open my mouth to protest, but he is right. Besides my underclothes, the only thing I have for covering is Trace's cloak. Trace turns his head while I pull the thick cotton tunic over my head, letting it fall down to my thighs like a dress. Thus clothed, I return to my slot beside him, maneuvering the cloak to cover both our bodies against the cold. Leaf's heat crystal lost its tune hours ago, and Trace can barely sit up, much less attempt to tune it again.

I shiver, hugging my knees and listening to the staccato of falling rain. It was raining when I first decided to go to that prisoner camp too. The cool drops landed on my nose, the *thump, patter patter* a prelude to what would come next. And then—

A bolt of lightning slices the air, silhouetting our wall of tree branches, before thunder cracks. My heart leaps. *The crack of branches snapping beneath my captors' boots is deafening in the evening rain. Prisoners' silent, horrified eyes watch me. My blood—*

"Frightened of lightning?" says Trace.

I gasp, focusing my eyes on him. My mouth is dry, my breath quick and ragged. I swallow. "No." I clear my throat to get my damn lungs under control. My teeth chatter. "Just startled. And very cold."

Trace reaches out a muscled arm, hesitates a moment, and then, with a decisive swoop, gathers me against his body. Settling me between his legs, Trace wraps his arms around me, pressing my back against his chest. The smell of him—the lingering lavender soap and the stronger musk of sweat, leather, and steel—fills my nose and lungs. The heat from Trace's chest seeps through the single layer of fabric between us, warming my shivering muscles. I let myself melt into him and feel Trace's slow breath caress my ear.

Stars, it feels good. Blissfully, sinfully good. Like a cocoon of strength and warmth and concern wrapped around my soul.

I bite my lip. It is cold and Trace is practical. And with Raza. I would be a fool to forget that. Ignoring the feel of Trace's arms, I focus my attention on the steady rhythm of his breathing, letting my own match his. "Why did you come after me?" I whisper into the cold.

Trace's arms tighten around me, pulling me closer. "I was afraid something had happened." His voice is soft. "That you were hurt. I couldn't not go. Not when it was my fault you left."

"It wasn't your fault at all," I mutter, resting my cheek against Trace's bicep until my eyes finally drift closed.

Only to pop open a second later, quick as a child's toy. My heart thunders.

"What is it?" Trace asks.

"Nothing." I rub my face. It is nothing. Just my body adjusting. "The storm is keeping me up."

"It's not the storm," Trace says tiredly. "Trust me."

I ignore him.

"Suit yourself," says Trace. Within minutes, the stillness of his body informs me that at least one of us is smart enough to sleep when he can.

I watch the darkness. Lightning sears the sky again. I brace myself for the coming thunder, but jump all the same when it comes. Trace startles awake.

*"Sorry." I scrub my face. "The noise just . . ."*

"Sounded like a bone breaking?" Trace offers, ignoring my shaking head. "Or the crack of a whip?"

"Stop it."

*He brings his lips close to my ear. "Or that ringing in your ears when—"*

"Stop it!" I press the heels of my hands into my eyes, the obsidian wall blocking my memories shuddering precariously. My face heats, my racing heart ferrying a sudden burst of energy through my limbs. "It was a loud sound, no more, no less. I'm tired and I want a little leeway to bloody shudder at a sudden noise."

"Is that all?" Trace's voice has a growl to it, which vibrates his chest.

"What do you want to hear?"

"Start with the truth and we'll go from there."

"What truth?" My head pounds, words rising in my throat and demanding escape. A torn abscess spilling puss. "That I was stupid and reckless and overconfident? That I got caught and endangered people and failed to rescue a soul? That you had to come save my sorry hide? It's all true and I know it, and I'm sorry. All right? I'm sorry." The thin tremor running its course through my body grows violent. "I'm sorry."

Trace says nothing.

I breathe deeply, ordering my body to quit its relentless shaking. When the order fails, I try digging my fingernails into my palms instead. Then stealing my breath altogether. Nothing works. But Trace never lets go of his hold.

"I was sixteen when Viva captured an infantry company that I'd recklessly led into Sylthia," he says after a stretch of silence. I shift in his arms to see his face and brace myself for the coming deserved scolding. But Trace isn't looking at me. Or at anything. His unfocused gaze stares only into the past, and his words are soft. "I'd never been in true combat before. I chafed for glory and I'd disobeyed orders to go into the zone in the first place.

"Viva thought I had information they needed, and that I'd give it to them if they hurt me. They were right." The apple of Trace's neck bobs as he swallows, and the muscles anchoring his cheekbones tighten with tension that I long to brush my fingers across. Trace exhales. "It didn't take them long. I told them everything, even when I knew my information would kill people. And it did. People died. More died getting me out, and I think they were glad to give their lives just to stop the damage I was doing." He shakes his head, his gaze refocusing. "I did everything, anything, just to stop the pain. But even when that stopped, the fear didn't. Not even when I got out." His voice grounds, reclaiming its usual hard timbre. "Which is to say that I know a thing or two about arrogance. And about flinching at sounds."

Not the response I expected. Or deserve.

I wait for shock to ripple through me, but it never comes. I've always known *something* happened to Trace, and in the wake of the last two days, I can believe many things. That day early on, when I told him off for trying to whip Kal into telling on Wil, Trace asked for Kal's age. And when I said sixteen, Trace went silent and abruptly ended our training session. I understand now. Truths that would have once shattered my whole view of the guardsman are now just other strands woven into the rope of confessions and secrets that ties us together. And in my gut, I know that he knew as much before speaking.

So instead of gasping or staring at him with wide, shocked eyes, I simply nod. "When does it stop?"

"I'll let you know when I find out."

My hand rises to rest against Trace's face, my thumb rubbing small circles over the coiled muscles of his jaw. "Deal." The skin beneath my fingertips is rough with stubble. "I hope you know soon."

"As do I." Trace shifts me again, once more nestling my back into his bare chest, and adjusts the cloak that's slipped down from our shoulders.

"You know, if Raza saw us right now, she might get the wrong idea," I say. I mean the words as a jest but it sounds flat even to me. I beg the stars to keep Trace from hearing my heart pounding.

Trace sighs. "It's more complicated than you think."

"That's impressive, because I think it's plenty complicated already." I pause. "You really love her, don't you?"

"Yes." Trace answers with no hesitation. Just as before.

My chest tightens. "And she loves you."

"Yes."

I turn my face up toward him. "So why not leave with her? What is there for you in Dansil but a guardsman's post?"

Trace shakes his head and shuts his eyes. "It's more that there is little good I can do in Everett. As I said, it's complicated. You'll have to sleep at some point. Try to do it at night."

## 2 7

*I* wake with Trace's arm still around me, my head nestled in the hollow of his muscled shoulder and —*stars take me*—I've somehow shifted from sitting on the ground to being *on* his lap in my sleep, Trace's muscled thighs hard beneath my rear. Flushing furiously, I pull away from him and use the wall to help me stand. My body roars in protest, but holds. Trace's shirt falls down to my mid-thighs, the chilly air brushing my bare legs. I wrap my arms around myself, the previous evening pulling my insides in different directions.

Trace saved me. Healed me. Held me.

Trace is in love with Raza. Trace shared his clothes and body heat to keep us both alive.

I am a girl who enjoyed a man's arms.

I am a scout who should know better than to indulge in such folly, an idiot who left herself unguarded as recklessly as she did days ago when pursuing the prisoners. This last one hits deep, and I force my body to straighten into Kal's masculine posture. "I'll check my clothes," I say by way of morning greeting. The sooner Trace is back in his shirt, the sooner the hard planes of his chest will stop distracting me.

Trace weighs me with his eyes—those of a practical and practiced healer—and sets about assembling his pack with brutal efficiency. "Keep the shirt until your things dry. It's too cold to be walking in wet clothes if it can be helped."

With the crawling pace I'll be forcing us to set, it will take two days or more to return, and the displeased angle of Trace's jaw says he's just come to a similar calculation. Stars, Leaf must be climbing the walls with worry.

*Leaf.*

"Did my sister ask you to have your lover take her to Everett?" I ask, breaking down the barricade Trace built to cover the cave. One of the branches makes a likely candidate for a walking stick and I grab it with more force than necessary.

"No, she didn't." Trace puts on his pack. "But Raza will take you both." The last part he says matter-of-factly, as if rendering a decision.

I lift a brow. "I never said I wanted to go."

Trace shrugs one shoulder and motions for me to precede him out of our sheltering cave. The sun is bright outside and the forest rustles its song. Droplets of rain hang heavily off the leaves and pine boughs, and the wet, earthy smell fills my nostrils. In the distance, a hint of a rainbow arches over the sky. Having wrung out my clothes, I tie them to the walking stick and take a moment to orient myself before starting back toward the palace. My boots, still wet, sink slightly into the moist dirt.

Walking. I'm *walking*.

My chest prickles as Trace catches up to me, his strides long and confident. Since I am still wearing his shirt, Trace has his cloak strapped to his bare chest, making him look a bit feral. "What do you think you are doing, exactly?" he asks after matching my steps for a few minutes.

"Hiking to the palace." I cock a brow. "Is there some other place we are expected?"

"No, but you can't honestly expect to continue at the palace," Trace says. "You said it yourself, that one of the Viva terror mongers recognized Kal. I imagine he will not let him—you—live long on the palace grounds."

I stumble but manage to keep my balance. "I'll work something out."

"I didn't come find you just to let you rush back into danger," Trace snaps, then draws a deep breath as if battling for patience. His hands rise to pull his hair back and tie it into a knot. "You'll be safer in Everett as Lady Lianna. Hence, you will go there."

I cut my eyes to him. "Did I do something to suggest I would let you make decisions for me?" I ask in a too-even tone that had better send alarm bells ringing in Trace's head. "Or are you bored and trying to provoke a fight?"

Trace stops in front of me and turns, cutting off my path. "Which part of *not safe* confuses you?" Trace says. "You've discovered Viva Sylthia's association with Bahir and the Order of the Goddess—that alone puts a death threat on your head the moment Kal steps onto palace grounds. Your sister is a whisperer. Delta is too dangerous for you both."

"*Lady Lianna*—"

"—was already a target of an assassination attempt." Trace throws up his hands. "In case you've forgotten that."

Bahir. A memory flashes behind my eyes and I sway despite standing still. Trace's hand shoots out to steady me but my thoughts race too quickly to pay him any mind. "Viva Sylthia targeted Lady Lianna. And if Bahir and Viva Sylthia are in bed together, then Bahir is likely behind that foiled assault."

Trace frowns but apparently concedes to following this line of thought for the time being. "Go on."

"What does Bahir have against Lianna, though?" I continue. "The only meaningful interaction they had was at dinner, when I touched his ring. There was a burning pain when I touched it . . . and Bahir felt it too. I saw it in his eyes."

Trace stiffens suddenly, a muscle along the edge of his jaw rising beneath the skin.

I cross my arms. "You just realized something. What are you not telling me, Trace?"

"Nothing." A lie.

I wait.

Trace lifts his chin. "If I tell you, will you promise to go to Everett?"

"Of course not." I shake myself and walk around him, my heart pounding with growing fire. I've enough problems without Trace keeping secrets from me. Not that he actually owes me answers. Stars, Trace owes me nothing—I'm the one who is indebted to him. And the sooner I can discharge that debt, the better.

"Kali."

My name, my true name, rides Trace's voice into the center of my chest. I know I should tell him never to use it, but I can't. So I do the next best thing—feign deafness and keep walking.

"Bahir is a mage," Trace says into my back. "Someone who manipulates magic directly. And he is the only mage on the whole bloody continent."

*I freeze. "How—"*

"It doesn't matter how I know. I do. The point is, I think your reaction to Bahir's ring was a reaction to his magic. Just as you reacted to the healing crystal's magic. This makes you a threat to his secret."

A puzzle piece clicks into place. "Which is why he had Viva Sylthia target Lianna," I say.

"Yes." Trace catches up to me, his voice dropping. "So if you won't go to Everett for your safety, then go to discover what your relationship to magic is. Find out whether you pose more danger to Bahir than comes from just knowing his secret."

## VIOLET

*B*ehind the heavy curtain of King Firehorn's study, Violet's heart fluttered like a butterfly. The air hung heavy with heat and dust and the familiar staleness of aged velvet. Violet took a steadying breath and pressed herself into the deep windowsill. She was getting a bit large for her nook now, but perhaps that was all right. The Goddess had been preparing her for this moment for a long time, teaching her how to hide and listen. How to put her invisibility and unimportance to good use.

The men on the other side of the curtain resumed speaking on the heels of silence. And it was the Goddess's own hand, Violet was certain, that guided her to take out the memory crystal *now*. Reaching into her pocket with a trembling hand, Violet pulled out the precious pouch Brother Joshua had entrusted her with and peeled back the cloth to expose the crystal in time for Firehorn's first words.

"What would it take?" The ghost of surrender in the king's

voice chilled Violet's bones. "For you to stay, for the war to end?"

A pause. Long, pregnant, and devastating.

"Sylthia," Envoy Jajack said steadily. "All of it, including the few acres that Everett did not conquer in the original assault. Dansil will surrender all claims to the territory and its resources, stop any attempt to regain the lands, and officially announce that Sylthia is forever a province of Everett."

*"That isn't a negotiation,"* Firehorn barked. *"That's—"*

"It's a price," the envoy said coolly. "Reparations for allowing Viva Sylthia terror mongers to thrive under your reign, to kill Prince Rune and assault Princess Raza in the midst of a ceasefire."

"Stars. Do you realize what you are asking, Jajack?"

Jajack's voice softened. "Political statements aside, this is far from a bad offer, Firehorn. With the rise of the Order of the Goddess in Dansil, your people use so few living crystals that, frankly, purchasing what you need would be cheaper and safer than mining it yourselves in Sylthia. The black powder used in the mines kills the workers as often as not. Dansil needs fresh blood; it needs its soldiers and miners home, working fields and raising families. You've not the people to spare to fight for a slab of land that Dansil has no use for."

Violet's stomach tightened at Jajack's honeyed words. How conveniently the man failed to mention the Dark God guiding Everett's hand in expanding his domain. And the punishment Dansil would endure for allowing evil to thrive.

Firehorn drew a sharp breath. "Bastard," he spat. "Sylthia is *our* land, Jajack. You invaded."

"Sylthia *was* your land until we conquered it twenty years ago." Jajack's unapologetic voice is firm but not altogether unkind. "Now it is ours."

"Then let us split it," said Firehorn.

"No."

Violet's small hand around the memory stone became slippery with sweat. On the other side of the curtain, a *tap tap tap* of pacing footsteps, then a creak of wood taking weight. A familiar sound. Violet's birth father settling into his favorite, aged chair.

"What you must decide, Firehorn," Envoy Jajack continued, "is how much more pain you are willing to inflict on Dansil to continue to deny reality."

Firehorn's answer, when it finally came, was barely a whisper. "Viva Sylthia wants Sylthia returned to Dansil. If I announce that I've given up the struggle for the territory altogether, Viva will raze my cities."

"It's that bad?" asked Jajack.

"Yes."

A slow release of breath. "In that case, I can commit to a peacekeeping force from Everett. Soldiers who would come under your command and protect Dansil from unrest. We can have them in place before the announcement."

*No,* Violet wanted to shout. *You know nothing of what you say. Sylthia and its crystals belong to the Goddess.*

But Firehorn did not know he was negotiating with the Dark God himself. So instead of running from the room, the king chuckled without humor. "And what assurance do I have that these peacekeepers, once allowed into the heart of Dansil, will not decide to put an Everett flag on my palace?"

"You have my word," said Jajack. "And the fact that capturing Dansil, with its Drought and terror mongers, its Order of the Goddess tramps and shattered economy, would be the height of folly for Everett. We want Sylthia, as we always have, for its living crystals. The rest of Dansil is yours."

"I need more than your word."

"Very well. Princess Raza will remain in Dansil as your

ward for however long an Everett peacekeeping force remains inside your borders. Solid collateral, is it not?"

"It is," Firehorn agreed.

"The offer expires as soon as I walk from these doors. What say you?"

Silence. One heartbeat. Two. Ten. Hope bubbled in Violet's dry throat.

And then shattered into a million shards that pierced her soul.

"Write your dispatch to Everett," said Firehorn. "We will announce peace the moment your soldiers arrive."

Violet didn't remember the next hours. How long her birth father remained in his study after the Dark God's disciple departed. How much longer she remained behind the velvet curtain, tears silently sliding down her face. How she made it back to the temple. She just knew that it all happened. And that there was a reason for it.

She knelt on the plush rug before the Messenger, trying to keep her eyes piously on the ground as Brother Joshua had instructed. It was hard. A large crystal, like a miniature Eye of the Goddess, hung suspended from the ceiling and bathed the room in ethereal light. Violet wanted to look at it, but she wanted to touch the bishop even more, for in doing so, she would touch the Goddess herself.

"Welcome, Child." Bahir's voice was deep and fatherly. "Brother Joshua and I were just grieving for two young acolytes who fled our temple early this morning, lured by the Dark God to their damnation. The joy of your visit is most timely."

Despite having sat beside the bishop at many formal dinners, it was only now that Violet really heard him. Because she was ready.

Bahir took Violet's hands. His were rougher than Violet

had expected, with callouses that spoke of labor, not luxury. But they were also warm and strong, with love flowing through them right into Violet's blood. "You followed Brother Joshua's instructions?" Bahir asked.

Violet swallowed. If her birth father ever learned what she'd done . . . Violet shook her head violently, clearing the Dark God's veil. "Yes. I hid in the king's study and triggered the memory stone when Envoy Jajack came in."

"Give it to me." Bahir held out his palm, letting Violet lay the stone upon it. With a murmured prayer, Bahir closed his hand around the stone. It flickered once, then sprang to life, and the damning words imprinted in the crystal's magic filled the room.

Violet only realized she was shaking when the Messenger placed a calming hand on her shoulder. "You did well, Child," Bahir said softly. "You did very well."

Violet swallowed. "What shall we do now?"

The Messenger smiled warmly at her. Rising, he placed his palm against the miniature sun, the metal of his ring clanging melodically. He closed his eyes, breathing deeply. When he opened them again, he extended his palm flat, a sword made of pure light hovering above it. "Now, we shall save Dansil."

## KALI

*B*ahir is a mage. I am some odd magic-interference aberration. Trace is a whisperer. My mind spins. I am not going to Everett, of course, but I need to think. To absorb it all. So I'm quiet as Trace and I make our way toward the palace, and the man lets me have my silence. I stay off anything that resembles a trail, stalking in a quiet rhythm through the rustling forest. While a chance encounter with another segment of Viva Sylthia is unlikely, the risk is not worth the small convenience a path would offer. Plus, I like picking my way through the forest, the damp leaves and pine needles shifting obediently away from my touch.

Whether Trace consenting to my taking the lead shows a respect for my skills or resignation to the simple fact that we can move only as quickly as my quivering legs allow, I don't know.

By the time we come upon a burbling creek around midday, my thighs burn, threatening to cramp with each step. Even focusing on the squeaky chatter of finches and a woodpecker's rapid beat isn't helping. We've walked for four hours and it feels like four days. But I walked.

"Do you need to rest?" Trace asks.

"No."

"I do." He surveys me from head to toe, and I am suddenly very aware that I still wear only his shirt, which swishes over my thighs. Trace faces the creek again, turning a bit too quickly. "And we should wash up."

"Yes," I agree just as quickly as he turned. I'm little looking forward to dunking in freezing water, but the slide of Trace's concerned gaze left me too torn between wanting to slug the concern from him and burrow myself into his chest, like I did last night. "Clean is good."

Laying my walking stick on the creek's sloping lip, I untie my still-soiled bundle of scouting clothes. Returning to the palace grounds wearing only Trace's shirt would be as bad as walking in covered in blood. Laundry thus in hand, I wade in, letting the freezing water rush around my ankles. Stars take me. My toes curl and I cringe, failing to bite back a short, undignified yelp.

Trace chuckles behind me.

Without turning, I give him a vulgar gesture and dunk Kal's tunic and pants into the stream. I'm still leaning over when a pair of muscled legs appears beside me. My gaze crawls up Trace's toned calves and corded thighs, over his undershorts and the scars crisscrossing his torso. Some a match to my own. Others . . . I jerk my eyes away as Trace catches me watching.

"I'm . . ." I stumble, a *sorry* lingering on the tip of my tongue. Sorry for what? For looking at him? He walked up to me, so what was I supposed to do? My mouth dries, the icy water suddenly not frigid enough. "What should I do with your shirt?"

Trace's hand reaches forward and my breath catches as he fingers the material. "I'd prefer to keep it dry. We'll need dry things if the temperature drops quickly."

"Right. I'll take it off before going deeper." Clearing my throat, I wring out Kal's freshly rinsed outfit, watching swirls of red float about my ankles before dissolving into the creek. The problem isn't the shirt; it's the logistics. Would it be more awkward to insist that Trace turn around, despite him already having seen me in my smallclothes, or to disrobe without any such instruction? Certainly, he has little concern over standing beside me in his own undershorts.

The real problem is that none of this should be an issue to begin with. I've changed before male scouts at the estate without a second's hesitation. Stars, if it were Luca here in place of Trace, I'd have removed the shirt long ago. No one sane goes bathing fully dressed. And I already did that.

"Are you all right?" Trace cups my elbow, and I realize I've been staring at nothing.

My heart thumps against my ribs, the chill of the water clashing with my flaming skin. Trace's grip is strong and familiar, his hair living silver in the small breeze. The *drip drip drip* of my scouting outfit, clenched in my free hand, is the only sound between us. *Trace is in love with Raza. Trace wants you gone from Dansil altogether. Trace is not for you.* "Yes. Of course," I say quickly, and just to prove my indifference, I grip the hem of the shirt with both hands and—

"What are you doing?" Trace asks, a note of alarm in his low voice.

"Taking off my shirt. Your shirt. Your shirt that is on me." Stars take me. I shake off his touch before my hot skin sets Trace, the creek, and the whole bloody forest on fire. "I'm a scout. Scouts aren't raised to have much modesty." There. An

225

explanation. I'm one of the men, and it would behoove both Trace and me to remember that.

"Yes, well." Trace coughs and turns his back to me. "I'm not a scout. So . . . just tell me when you are through."

Right. I take a few steps toward an overhanging branch where I can hang my scouting outfit, and I'm spreading them to dry when Trace's soft voice hits my back. "You are a great deal more than a scout."

I swallow and feign deafness. When I turn again, Trace is submerging himself in the freezing creek. He surfaces with a snarl, like a disgruntled lion, the water lapping his waist and running from his silver hair down the grooves of his spine.

"Hurry up and wash," he calls without turning.

"You could wait on the shore, you know," I call back, pulling off his shirt.

Trace makes a sound in the back of his throat. "I prefer this," he says tightly and takes a step deeper into the freezing water.


HALF AN HOUR LATER, we are hiking again, our damp clothing sticking to shivering muscles despite a reasonably strong sun. I've returned Trace's shirt to him, letting the theoretically warm day dry the scouting outfit I wear. "Perhaps cleanliness is overrated," I mutter, earning a lopsided grin from Trace.

The orange light of the Eye of the Goddess penetrates through the forest foliage, casting its tint along my skin and coming closer with each step. We'll be at the palace by tomorrow, and there isn't much more time to put off the discussion of what to do once we arrive, especially if I'm to leave room for arguing. The last time we touched the ground of my work, it ended with Trace insisting I run off to Everett. And we didn't even broach the more delicate topic of why in stars' name a whisperer is working under Bahir's nose.

"I need to brief King Firehorn as soon as we return," I say, moving aside a branch that scrapes my cheek. "Tell him about Bahir's control of Viva Sylthia."

"You want to stride through the palace in bloodstained rags?" Trace cocks a brow. "Your notion of discretion is awe inspiring."

"No," I say evenly, "I want to return to the keep in bloodstained rags, take the passage from there to Lianna's suite, and attend the king as his beloved niece. If you can escort Lady Lianna to Firehorn's study, you can tell him about the bishop being a mage while we are there."

"No." Trace's voice is quiet but not weak. "I will not be doing that."

"Escorting Lianna?"

"Discussing what I know of Bahir with Firehorn," he says bluntly.

"Why the bloody hells not?" I draw a breath, forcing my voice to casualness despite the growing unease in my gut. That Trace might be keeping secrets that eclipse even mine—and I've been trusting him with my life. "Speaking of Bahir, you never told me how you know he is a mage."

Trace's whole body tenses. I can feel it. I can smell it too, the sharp tang of a predator deciding whether to fight or flee.

"I do not wish to say." His voice is tart. "I ask that you accept this fact on trust."

"First Raza, then whispering, then insight into Bahir. I'm asking for an explanation, Trace."

"Like the detailed explanation you've given me for all your secrets?" Trace lengthens his stride, making me struggle to keep up. "I'm asking for your trust."

"You've also asked that I commit treason by running away

to Everett and then that I trust Princess Raza not to throw me into the dungeons for questioning. Because taking care of a lover's female friend is what princesses do." I stop walking, stop playing catchup. After a few steps, Trace realizes I'm no longer beside him and returns.

I plant my walking stick in the soft earth, working the wood in deep. Having something to do helps. My heart pounds. I don't want to say my next words. But I must. "Why do you wish to keep vital information from the king you are guarding? And if you've been paying enough attention to Bahir to know him a mage, how did you not suspect foul play before today? How did you meet Raza?" The unease in my gut grows to a painful throb as I speak, trying to put together the many small pieces of Trace that still don't combine quite right. There is certainly more to Trace than I know, but how big a threat might lurk in the shadow of Trace's mystery? Dread turns my stomach. I've let Trace—my feelings for him —cloud my judgment. And my judgment and Leaf are all I have in this world. I continue with more force. "Why did a whisperer and a true healer seek a position in the king's guard? I'm a scout, not a mindless courtier, Trace. I need answers. And I need them before I see the king."

Trace's face darkens. He rocks his weight back onto his heels, his arms crossing his chest while his cloak whips around him in the rising wind. "You think you are a scout? Your scouting career ended when you barreled into a nest of Viva Sylthia scum and got yourself all but dead. I promised to save your legs, not your job." My heart pounds, each of Trace's words slicing into me like blades. He takes a step closer, looming over me. His dark eyes flash and the heat of his skin rakes my neck. "I don't owe you answers. I'm not *suggesting* you go to Everett—I am telling you that you are going. I will pass a message to King Firehorn for you, because you are not walking into the palace either."

I back away a step, my nails digging into the fleshy heels of my hands. I wait for my mind to conjure words, but nothing comes. How in the stars' name did I get myself here, thinking Trace a friend? I shake myself, trying to dislodge the delusions pricking at my skin and eyes. Stupid. Stupid to trust Trace. To let his words touch me deeper than a mark's comments. "That's enough." The cold steadiness of my voice takes me by surprise as my training finally regains its hold. I was an idiot. Am an idiot. I need to get away. Now. Need to work alone and figure things out for myself. "We are done, Trace. Keep your edicts to yourself and save your breath."

I go to step around him, the cold clinging to my skin.

Trace blocks my path with a taut arm, his lips flattened into a line. "See reason. You don't know what awaits you should you stay in Delta."

"No." I force my way past Trace's arm, resisting the urge to run, my mind roaring at being blocked. Trapped. Held. Hobbled.

Trace follows. Steps in front of me. His hands clench tightly around my upper arms, his eyes intense as blazing suns.

*Bring him closer to the fire. I want everyone to see what awaits them should they try to flee tonight.* Baritone's voice brings a sour rush of bile into my throat. The sickly fire, the rain, the prisoners' gaunt faces push against my mind. My heart stops, a sharp ping sounding through my mind as the obsidian wall loosens.

Fingers dig into my flesh. "Yes. You owe me your life," Trace hisses. "And I'm calling in the debt."

## 3 0

The obsidian wall collapses. Icy shock smashes through me. Then fear. The rustling and chirping of the forest is suddenly a deafening hum. My face tingles, my arms and damn weak legs readying to sprint. I flick my wrists, seeking knives that are not there.

Trace's eyes widen. "Kali. No. I didn't mean—"

I don't wait to hear what he meant. I yank my walking stick out of the ground and run.

Twigs crack beneath my stumbling feet, branches reaching out to snag my face and clothing. Small, distant cuts and rips that I don't feel. Faster. I need to go faster and I can't. Pain that's not of the flesh sears my chest. My boots thump the soft earth, kicking up bits of mud. I don't even know where the hells I think I'm running.

*And where were you running to?* Nasal whispers into my ear. My mind rings with cold panic.

"Kali." Trace's voice sounds close behind me. Closer.

I press on. Fast. Hard. Futile.

"Listen to me." Trace grabs my shoulder and spins me toward him.

My balance wavers. I twist against Trace's hold, but it's too strong, too hard. My legs buckle beneath me, protesting my demands.

Trace's hand tightens. "Kali. Stop. I'm not going to hurt you."

Yes, he will. He did. He already did. *All you need is to hobble the beast.*

Trace gives me a small shake, his fingers digging into my flesh. "Listen, damn you."

I pull again, realizing I'm truly trapped. My breath quickens. The man holding me is bigger, stronger, and healthier. He's captured me. Restrained me. He thinks my life is his. To give. To take. To shatter. The edges of my vision darken, panic thundering through me. Boiling blood rushes to my hands and legs and heart. My hands tighten on my staff.

The man releases his hold and backs away, his palms suddenly in the air.

My body follows, my staff aimed at his heart. A din fills my ears, a furious harmony of rushing blood and screaming prisoners. My wrists flex. No ropes, no shackles. Not this time.

The man speaks.

I can't hear the words. I don't care about the words. My nostrils flare. My life is mine and I will fight for it. By stars, I *will* fight for it. With each and every breath. I advance my staff.

The bastard drops his hands to his sides. "I won't fight you."

Lip curling, I punch him in the face.

He staggers, touching his hand to his bleeding cheekbone. "Are you mad?" he barks, eyes flashing like a storm. I swing again.

This time, he grabs my arm. The world spins, the trees circling around me like spilled paint. I struggle against my binds. Not again. Not this time. Not ever. I step into his body and twist, my back pressing into his chest as I throw my weight under his. With a pop of my hip, I launch the man into the air.

He rolls through the fall, coming up in a crouch. His leg sweeps my ankles and it's my turn to tumble into the dirt. He follows, landing atop me, his thighs straddling my chest.

I bump him forward, forcing his arms to brace the ground for balance. The moment they do, I trap his left hand and leg, and bridge to that side. The shift of balance and momentum rolls us sideways until it's me straddling his chest. Cocking my fist, I swing it at his jaw.

He bucks against me, as I did, and my blow only grazes his mandible. The storm in his eyes explodes, and in the next moment, I'm flying off him.

I land hard on my back.

Burying his fists in my tunic, the man hauls me to my feet and slams my back into a tree. The force rattles my ribs, the rough bark taking skin.

"Is this what you want? A fight?" he demands, his face close to mine. "Because I'm going to win. Every time."

I laugh without humor and drive my knee into the meat of his thigh.

He grunts but holds his place. Pulling me back from the tree trunk, he goes for another solid slam.

My body hits the wood so hard that my head bounces, my scalp catching on a jagged edge of bark. The world blinks. I touch the back of my head.

The man flinches, blood draining from his face as he marks the slash of red on my hand.

I slam my knee into him. Again. *Again.* He shudders but takes the blows.

I growl. "You won't win every time," I yell into his face. I'm right. I have to be right, because the alternative is a nightmare of snaps and slices and binds. "Not every time." Tears pour down my cheeks in warm, wet rows.

"No, not every time," he whispers in agreement. His arms reach for me through the storm of my assault and gather me against his chest.

I strike him again and again and again until I can't hit anymore because his mouth is on mine and an explosion of fire and need singes my every nerve.

## 31

My eyes sink closed. The pressure of Trace's mouth engulfs my world. His lips are smooth and warm. Hot. Trace's damp hair, smelling of the creek's freshness, falls across the groove of my exposed neck. I grip his arms, clawing my fingers into his flesh, dragging him closer.

Trace growls against me, his hand cupping the back of my head. His tongue claims my mouth and my core vibrates in answer. I can't breathe. Can't think. I want.

Trace jerks back. His eyes are wide, his fingers pressing against his mouth. "I . . . I'm sorry," he says hoarsely.

I groan in frustration and pull him back down, feeling the noise he makes in the back of his throat all the way down to my ankles. He presses me into the tree with his whole body, running a hand up my side under my damp shirt, leaving a trail of heat from my waist to my ribcage.

This time, we both push away. He takes two steps back, just out of my reach. I swallow hard, the air suddenly cold and empty. We both breathe heavily, watching each other. Trace breaks the silence. "Stars. I didn't mean to do that."

My mouth opens. I shut it. The world spins and it's an effort of will to keep my hands from grabbing on to his arms once more. "No. Of course not. We . . . I didn't mean it either. Attacking you." My voice sounds wrong. Everything I'm saying sounds wrong. I am a better liar than this. I grab my walking stick. Feel its rough bark. "Let's just return to the palace, all right? I . . . I won't press you for secrets. Or reveal them. Your decisions are your own. As are mine."

Trace nods but avoids my gaze, staying several paces away from me as we reclaim our way back in uncomfortable silence.

WE SAY little to each other for the rest of the afternoon. Too much has been said already. In the evening, we trap a rabbit for dinner and kindle a small fire to cook it over. There is curiously little that two people experienced in setting up camp must say to work in harmony. Eventually, however, we run out of chores, and the quiet stretches from practical to pregnant.

"I didn't mean what I said," Trace says finally. He rubs his palm over the side of his face, where a bruise is blossoming in earnest, and adjusts the log he sits on for a more comfortable fit. I have my own sitting log. And my own bed of gathered pine brush to sleep on. Trace clears his throat. "About being owed anything. I was frustrated. The words slipped past better reason."

I add a slab of firewood to the flames and watch them lap it up hungrily, changing colors in their bliss. I don't disbelieve Trace exactly. I just know it's not really Kali he sees sitting beside him, but the woman he thinks I *should* be. I choose my words carefully, as if handling eggs. "I'm sorry about your face." Truth. I regret his bruises. I don't regret taking the swing.

Trace braces his forearms against his knees. "You didn't know who you were fighting."

I tense. "Someone who was trying to take my life. The specifics seemed of little importance." Truth. Rising, I stack our remaining firewood into a neat pile. It keeps my hands busy.

"And now?"

"The specifics still seem of little importance."

Trace makes a sound of disagreement.

I throw up my hands and turn to him. "It doesn't matter. It was just a fight, Trace." I pick up a branch and start stripping it of its leaves. "And just a kiss. I imagine it wasn't your first—of either. Don't make an epic battle from a few glancing blows. Would you even bring the bloody thing up again if I were Luca?"

He crosses his arms. "What we did wouldn't have happened with Luca. Either part."

No, it wouldn't have. I rather doubt Luca would have started that fight at all, much less ended it entangled in Trace's lips. "I'm not going to Everett. If that's where this conversation is heading, save your breath."

"I'm just asking that you listen. The decision is yours."

Fine. I raise my brows expectantly.

"It was five years ago that Viva captured me. When I escaped, I knew that my death would serve my family better than news of my capture and questioning. So I ran."

I drop the stripped branch back on the pile and put up a hand. "Trace. Drop it. I'm not running away or doing anything stupider than usual. I'm—"

"Shut up and listen. This isn't about you." His voice is hard and shadows play along the angle of his jaw. A trick of the fire. When I look into his eyes, though, there is no steel there. Just resolve and fear in equal measure. I shut up as he asked and wait for him to break the silence. He draws a breath and stares into the flames. "For the first two years, I ricocheted from one master to another, the harsher the better. Trying to get tougher, stronger, faster. Then I went to the Monastery of Qilar, in part to train, in part to test myself, and in part to pay penance for my weakness."

I start to nod but halt myself, lest I interfere with his words.

"Meanwhile, Bahir's power continued to grow. We'd suspected he could manipulate magic for years, but the trail of blind devotion and self-righteous hate that he sowed in his wake took even pessimists by surprise. It was time to return to the duties I was born to fulfill, even if I had to fulfill them from a different role."

"Wait," I frown. "Born?"

"Yes, *born*," Trace snaps. "I needed to learn where the true threat to my kingdom and my people lay. And how to stop it."

The implication of Trace's words brushes my hackles, shifting and turning as it tries to arrange itself in my mind. "So you joined Firehorn's Royal Guard?" I say.

"So I joined Firehorn's guard," Trace echoes in unapologetic agreement. "To keep an eye on the Dansil king and the magic-wielding Bahir, who was ensnaring Delta in an ever-tightening noose."

My breath catches, as though a draft horse struck my chest. "Princess Raza isn't your lover, is she?" I'm only half-surprised at my words. Of all the things to ask just now, this is by far the stupidest.

"No," Trace agrees, and an owl hoots her assent as well. "Raza is my sister."

Stars. *Prince Rune.* I knew as much many moments ago, but hearing the confirmation . . . I stand. Pace. Stop. Sit back down. Feed more wood to the fire that I'm bloody sharing with Everett's long-dead crown prince. Except he isn't dead. He's a spy. "That night outside the Wandering Dog—I was right when I said your hatred of Wil was personal, wasn't I?" I say finally.

Trace shrugs. "I know the damage an heir's recklessness can do firsthand."

"And the prisoners . . ." I sort through my memories, examining my conversations with Trace anew. "Since you—your kingdom—has been watching Bahir, did you know he uses Viva Sylthia to collect whisperers? When I said the Holy Guard was expecting prisoners, did that mean something to you?"

"I did not know about Bahir's connection with Viva Sylthia, no. Did not even suspect it until you mentioned Samuels—and even then, I had little reason to think you were correct." He stretches, cracking his back. "But yes, I did know that Bahir's guards round up whisperers for forced labor. I've helped several escape to Everett over the years—it was the best I could do."

My memories of watching Trace disappear into the forest at night take on a new light. I thought he'd been trying to find his lover. But now . . . Trace is Prince Rune. Of course he's been doing *something* at the palace these past years besides protecting the king of Dansil. I idly wonder whether, like me, he was supposed to have not interfered.

Right. I blow out a long breath and brace my forearms on my knees. "All right, Trace. Rune. Why did you just tell me all this?"

"Because we need to stop Bahir before he strangles Dansil and starts in on Everett. Because there is something about you that threatens him. You may be the key to peace." Trace swallows and I know there is something he's not saying, though what he does utter is potent enough. "I've tried asking and intimidating and demanding. And now . . . now I'm begging you. Showing you what I'm willing to risk for your trust and for your consent to go to Everett."

My chest tightens, but I'm back on familiar footing now. I'm a tool, like I've always been. Except now I'm a tool with enough potential for Trace, for *Prince Rune*, to find it useful. I summon my own stony expression and still my face. "Thank you. That was . . . helpful. I will think on your request and give you an answer once I report my own—and only my own—findings to my king. You must agree that's fair, as one spy to another."

"*Kali*—"

"Kalianna. My name is Kalianna." I move away from the fire and curl onto my sleeping pallet of sweet pine. "Let us get some rest while we can."

THE FOLLOWING DAY, Trace and I finally near the edge of the North Wood, where the forest opens to the palace's back courtyard.

"Wait." I hold out a hand to stop Trace's advance. The familiar smell of sap mixing with the spices of the palace's latest deliveries tickles my nose in welcome. I close my eyes to draw a deep breath and feel my muscles tighten instead. Something feels wrong. It's too loud. Not shouting or banging or anything in particular—just an increased volume of the regular, everyday din that I'm used to hearing from this spot.

"I don't hear anything unusual," Trace says when I share the observation.

"You are not the scout who's spent days sitting here." Finding a wide-branched tree—one of Kal's favorites from his days of watching the palace traffic—I swing myself up to survey the palace grounds. The now-familiar sights splay out before me, from the royal stables on the castle's eastern side to the keep on its southwestern side. The rich colors, the flowers that house those bloody wasps, the scurrying servants, strolling courtiers, patrolling guards—all is as it was. But there is something else too.

"There are too many roses around," I tell Trace as I scurry back down to the ground, my forehead tight. "They are everywhere—an extra two hundred men, at least. Like there were after the Viva Sylthia attack."

Trace's brows pull together. "Another attack while we were gone?"

I shake my head. "The Royal Guard's numbers are standard for this time of day. Just more roses. A lot more."

Trace raps his knuckles against the tree trunk. "All right, then we adjust. You stay here, I go fetch Lady Lianna's clothes, and then you enter in her persona. There is no reason to risk the roses catching sight of Kal just to get you into your rooms."

"Nooo," I drawl, a small smile touching my lips and growing as Trace rolls his eyes to the stars. "On the contrary. Let the bastards catch a glimpse of risen-from-the-dead Kal in the keep. It will send the lot into a tailspin that may tell us something. Kick up dust."

Trace curses.

My grin widens. "Chin up, Prince. They can't kill Kal right then and there in the middle of the keep, and we won't linger long." Adjusting my clothes, I widen my stance to fall into Kal's male stride, claiming more space. "I wasn't making a suggestion," I tell Trace over my shoulder as I start toward the keep.

Despite my swiveling neck and rising pulse, the roses we

pass on our way to the barracks are preoccupied and apparently unaware of Kal's recently attempted murder. We are ten paces from my door—with me contemplating walking up to a random holy guardsman and starting a conversation, just to stir up some action—when someone finally approaches.

"Where in stars' name did you two disappear to?" Luca demands of Trace and me, a mix of fatigue and frustration weighing down his words.

*"Kal had family matters,"* Trace says dismissively. *"I ran into him—"*

"Tell me later." Grabbing Trace, Luca manhandles him into the closest of our rooms, which happens to be mine. Ignoring my torn, bloodstained clothes, Luca wheels on Trace. "The Holy Guard has been searching the whole bloody palace for you since yesterday. They are trying to arrest you."

"Arrest him for what?" I ask.

"Last night, two young girls—both runaway whisperers—killed a rose," says Luca. "When caught, they claimed to be working with Trace."

## 32

Days ago, I would have thought the accusation absurd. Now I can only curse the damn timing. Not that there is ever a convenient time to be exposed.

"Am I on the Royal Guard arrest list as well?" Trace asks after a pause, his voice as even as if discussing new mess-hall bannocks. "Or only the roses'?"

Luca groans. "I was really hoping to hear you curse and proclaim your innocence just now."

"Anyone who believes I ordered those girls to commit murder would unlikely be swayed by my insistence to the contrary," says Trace. "Are you supposed to be arresting me?"

"Stars, but you are a pain." Luca sighs with resignation. "No, Wil is holding up the roses' request for a reciprocal warrant. He wants to talk to you first."

I clear my throat. "Is this why the palace grounds are bleeding holy guardsmen?" I ask. "Two hundred of them are all looking for Trace? They are not doing a very good job of it, considering none challenged us on the way here."

"Let us not stop to offer critique," Luca tells me, his face tight. "And yes, that is why they are here. The numbers are all about politics—a demonstration of Bahir's outrage and all that."

"Or they are not truly looking for Trace," I say, though neither man pays me much mind.

"You said Wil needs to see me," Trace tells Luca, his shoulders tense despite an even voice. "Then take me to him."

"Us," I say, my glare daring him to object. After years of ignorance about Bahir's allegiance, Firehorn can wait another hour while I see what other trouble is brewing.

Trace's jaw tightens. "Us," he finally agrees but waves a hand over my tattered clothing. "Though the shorter part of *us* might wish to change and arm himself as befitting a guardsman before attending the crown prince."

"Trace," Luca studies the floor, his voice quiet, "the prince waits with Questioner Calvin in the dungeon hold." He focuses on straightening his own clothes as the words and their meaning percolate. After a moment, Luca turns on his heels, nodding to no one in particular. "I've something to attend to before meeting you there."

The words Luca didn't say aloud squeeze the air from my lungs. *If you need to disappear, this is your chance.* Never mind that Luca would be flogged within an inch of his life for it.

Lord Gapral warned me about the dangers of friendship.

Trace's hand snaps around Luca's wrist. "Escort me first, if you don't mind."

Dread and relief flooding me in equal measure, I quickly turn away to pull on a fresh tunic and breeches, letting Trace subtly nudge Luca out of the tiny room. Another few moments to strap Leaf's pouch to one thigh and a sword to my waist, and I'm as ready as I'm getting. My forearm is bare and too light without my vambrace of throwing knives, but there's little to be done on that front. Even with the knives missing, the change of clothes feels unexpectedly soothing, like a bandage topping a wound.

When I step outside, Trace gives a small, understanding nod.

Hooded cloaks covering our faces, Trace, Luca, and I walk purposefully toward the dungeon. Around us, red-coated holy guardsmen scurry about like cockroaches. Spotting Sergeant Samuels across the courtyard, my hands tighten into fists.

Luca shoots me a dark look, then slows as we approach the dungeon doors. "Trace . . . you can still—"

Reaching past Luca, Trace opens the door to the moldy gloom and starts down the steps. Lanterns in hand, Luca and I follow the echo of Trace's boots against the stone. My chest squeezes at the thought of what each of these motions costs Trace. And if he is discovered as an Everett spy . . .

"It will work out," Luca tells me quietly, having read my tension if not my thoughts. "That one always lands on his feet."

*No, he doesn't.* Except I've neither the heart nor the right to tell Luca exactly how much worse this all is than he thinks.

We are halfway down the staircase, bracing for the inevitable stench, when Calvin blocks our path.

"Hoods off," he orders with a deathly quiet that allows no disobedience. Holding up a lantern, he inspects each of us, moving from one set of eyes to the next, until coming to a halt before Trace.

"Allow me to make something perfectly clear," the questioner tells him. "I have two young girls in a place in which they have no business being. If I so much as smell an intention to intimidate them into anything, your day will go from bad to worse very rapidly. Prince William or no Prince William. Do you understand me, guardsman?"

*"It's a misunderstanding, Calvin,"* I hear myself say. *"There is—"*

Trace silences me with a hand. Raising his chin, he stares at the questioner and, after a moment of heavy silence, bows with his hand over his sword. With a jerk of his head, Calvin leads us the rest of the way down and into the dusty meeting room.

Wil stands with two girls of twelve or thirteen years. One petite and agile with coal-black hair and an angled face, the other plump and ungainly. Both frightened. The girls shy away from us. If they've seen Trace before, they give no sign of it now.

Wil, his hair and clothes equally disheveled, steps forward. "I think I like it better when it's you pulling me out of trouble," he tells Trace.

Trace bows his head, the short nod carrying more weight than a glamorous display. "I understand that I'm wanted for murder."

"You are not wanted for anything," Wil snaps, though his voice's rising inflection takes some of the power from the words. "Not by the Crown, at least. The Holy Guard has made a claim based on Alexa and Jasmine's words." He points to the girls. "They are—were—runaway Order of the Goddess acolytes. A rose caught them in the North Wood and attempted to take them back to the temple. Jasmine hit him on the back of the head with a rock, which ended the pursuit more permanently than intended. The guard's partner found the body and, shortly after, Alexa and Jasmine themselves. Who gave the Holy Guard Trace's name."

"An accident, then," I say. "Not murder."

Luca and Trace exchange glances. "The specifics will little matter to the Holy Guard," says Trace. "And King Firehorn may be pressured to agree to the charges to appease the Order.

I wager it is the escape more than the guard's death that upsets Bahir."

The girls shrink back, pressing against each other, and Calvin shifts his weight to subtly impose himself between Trace and his accusers.

"It's all right," Trace tells them. "You are whisperers?"

Hesitant nods. Trace turns to Wil. "Bahir's men round up whisperers and force them to labor in the Order's fortress. Kidnapping, enlisting, buying—whatever it takes. 'Acolyte' is the bishop's term for slave. I help escapees get to safety."

I glare at Trace, whose meddling in Dansil's affairs—and putting himself in danger of several executions—appears vaster than even I imagined, the matter of this being the pot calling the kettle black notwithstanding. *Being an Everett prince in Dansil court isn't enough? You needed to subvert the Order of the Goddess while you were at it?*

His eyes flick to me. *What did you expect me to do?*

"Slaves?" Wil shakes his head, his long lashes cutting the air with a sharp arc. "Surely you exaggerate."

Trace snorts. "What exactly did you think happened to all the whisperers turned over to the Order for 'salvation'?"

Calvin rubs his top lip. "How do you go about the rescues?" he asks mildly.

Trace draws a breath and faces the questioner. "A meeting point in the woods. I check it routinely for runaways, but I've been away for several days."

Because of me. Trace is a hair's breadth from being uncovered and it's all because of me.

Alexa's throat bobs. "We went to the woods. And we waited a long time. But we were unsure of what Master Trace looked like, and when we heard someone coming . . . By the time we realized we should have stayed hidden, it was too late." Her voice drops to a whisper. "We didn't want to go back to the Order."

Calvin studies the floor, as if regretting his own question. "And where do you take the escaped slaves, guardsman?"

My stomach clenches, because deep in my bones, I know the answer. *Lie*, I beg Trace with my mind. *Make something up. Say there is a town somewhere. A small town at Dansil's outskirts, far away from Delta.*

Trace's spine straightens. "Everett," he says firmly. "I arrange for their passage to Everett."

Cold silence fills the room. Luca's eyes widen as he stares at Trace, as if waiting for the punchline of a jest.

Wil steps back. "That's . . . Stars. You made secret arrangements with Dansil's enemy at a time of war? That's treason."

Trace turns to face Calvin, each movement slow and measured. "I imagine you have other questions for me, sir. Where would you like me?"

I freeze. *No.*

"I think we're comfortable here for now," Calvin says, crossing the room to his steeping pot. "Especially after the fine work the ladies did cleaning it up. Tea?"

"Your Highness!" The door to the room crashes open, halting Calvin's hand short of the first porcelain cup. Trace, Luca, and I all reach for our swords before a young guardsman trainee's explosive appearance registers in our minds. The boy surveys the room frantically, stopping only when he finds Wil. "Thank the stars. I heard you were here," the boy manages, his chest heaving with ragged breaths. "We're under attack. The Holy Guard has taken the palace."

"A coup." My face snaps to Trace. Of course the hundreds of holy guardsmen roaming the palace weren't really seeking him—they needed an excuse to fill the palace grounds. And that day after the Viva attack when I noted how very diligent the roses were—they weren't looking for Viva agents. They were scouting. The bastards.

Trace nods as if he's read the deductions in my eyes and they match his own. "We need to get the prince out," Trace says curtly, replacing the teacup in Calvin's hand with a lantern and herding everyone toward the door. "Is there another way out of here besides the main door?"

"This is a prison," says Calvin, gathering a pair of stray cloaks. "The only other way out is with the Goddess."

"Then we run," Trace says. Gathering Wil, Calvin, and the girls between us, Trace, Luca, and I rush up the stairs, leaving the trainee to continue passing the word. My pulse beats hard, my mind still numbly stumbling over the news, waiting for someone to laugh and call us all sorts of idiots for believing the jest. Instead, the tap of our boots on stone echoes against cold walls, and the clash of blades and screams grows louder as we approach the sun.

The bright light of the outside hits me just as a blade does, and I parry before I can even see the rose whose steel tried to take my life. The man backs up a step, then widens his eyes as Wil spills out from the dungeon entrance. The rose opens his mouth to scream, but Trace cuts him down before any sound emerges. Ripping the cloak off himself, Trace shoves it into Wil's arms, and the prince obediently conceals himself while we take quick stock of the battlefield.

At the west end of the palace compound, the dungeons are somewhat insulated from the chaos of the main courtyard, a hundred paces to our left. There, bodies litter the grass and bleed rudely over the bright flowers. Some guards still face off, their swords glinting cruelly in the sunlight. But most of the screams and sounds of combat are coming from within the palace itself.

*Leaf.* My mind is suddenly blank except for one purpose. I adjust the grip on my blade, readying myself for battle. Leaf is in the palace, a lamb for the Order's slaughter. *I'm coming for you.* It's all I can do to keep myself from bolting there blindly, soldiers and swords be damned.

"North Wood," Trace shouts, a commander on a battlefield. "Shelter there." He makes a hooking motion with his bloody blade, ordering us to turn right and circle back to the rear of the palace.

Luca pushes Calvin and the girls along the ordered path, but Wil and I remain rooted in place. I know I need to leave, to grab Wil and run. But leaving Leaf here, even temporarily, cracks open my soul. It little matters that I'm coming back for her the moment I ensure the future king's safety—it still hurts.

*I'm coming, Leaf.* I send the thought as hard as I can with my mind, hoping she hears it. *Hold fast a few more minutes, and I'll be back.*

Trace grabs the prince's arm. "You want to live? You do what I say," he shouts into the boy's face, twisting him toward the path. "Follow Luca. Now."

The prince stumbles and stops, his voice flat and distant. "My father. I don't need to live—the king does."

Trace opens his mouth to reply but I speak instead, the words too horrid to be my own. "You are the king now, Wil," I whisper, pushing him forward before he can turn to see what I just saw.

King Firehorn's severed head being hoisted up the flagpole.

With one more glance at the palace—at my sister—I grab the new king's hand and I run.

End of *Tracing Shadows* (Scout Book 1). The adventure concludes in *Unraveling Darkness* (Scout Book 2)

REVIEWS ARE AN AUTHOR'S LIFEBLOOD. If you enjoyed the story, please consider saying a few words about this book on Amazon.

Reviews are an author's lifeblood. Please consider saying a few words about this book on Amazon.

# ABOUT THE AUTHOR

Alex Lidell is the Amazon Breakout Novel Awards finalist author of THE CADET OF TILDOR (Penguin, 2013). She is an avid horseback rider, a (bad) hockey player, and an ice-cream addict. Born in Russia, Alex learned English in elementary school, where a thoughtful librarian placed a copy of Tamora Pierce's ALANNA in Alex's hands. In addition to becoming the first English book Alex read for fun, ALANNA started Alex's life long love for fantasy books. Alex lives in Washington, DC. Join Alex's newsletter for news, bonus content and sneak peeks: www.subscribepage.com/TIDES Find out more on Alex's website: www.alexlidell.com

SIGN UP FOR NEWS AND RELEASE NOTIFICATIONS

*Connect with Alex!*
www.alexlidell.com
alex@alexlidell.com

www.ingramcontent.com/pod-product-compliance
Lightning Source LLC
Chambersburg PA
CBHW031232120726
47905CB00002B/569